His mission should be clear— determine her identity and find out if she was tangled up in anything illegal.

She didn't fit the picture of a felon. Damp hair framed her face. A soapy clean fragrance filled the air between them. His eyes trailed down the two enticing legs that spanned the break between shirttail and floor.

There were dozens of reasons he should keep an emotional wall between them.

But right now he didn't want a wall between them. Hell, he didn't want that T-shirt between the two of them and couldn't ignore the inappropriate thought pounding in his brain.

The only thought firing every cell in his brain.

He wanted her. Bad.

Dear Reader,

Make way for spring—and room on your shelf for six must-reads from Silhouette Intimate Moments! Justine Davis bursts onto the scene with another page-turner from her miniseries REDSTONE, INCORPORATED. In *Second-Chance Hero*, a struggling single mother finds herself in danger, having to confront past demons and the man who haunts her waking dreams. Gifted storyteller Ingrid Weaver delights us with *The Angel and the Outlaw*, which begins her miniseries PAYBACK. Here, a rifle-wielding heroine does more than seek revenge—she dazzles a hot-blooded hero into joining her on her mission. Don't miss it!

Can the enemy's daughter seduce a sexy and hardened soldier? Find out in Cindy Dees's latest CHARLIE SQUAD romance, *Her Secret Agent Man*. In Frances Housden's *Stranded with a Stranger*, part of her INTERNATIONAL AFFAIRS miniseries, a determined heroine investigates her sister's murder by tackling Mount Everest and its brutal challenges. Will her charismatic guide be the key to solving this gripping mystery?

You'll get swept away by Margaret Carter's *Embracing Darkness*, about a heart-stopping vampire whose torment is falling for a woman he can't have. Will these two forbidden lovers overcome the limits of mortality—not to mention a cold-blooded killer's treachery—to be together? Newcomer Dianna Love Snell pulls no punches in *Worth Every Risk*, which features a DEA agent who discovers a beautiful stowaway on his plane. She could be trouble…or the woman he's been waiting for.

I'm thrilled to bring you six suspenseful and soul-stirring romances from these talented authors. After you enjoy this month's lineup, be sure to return for another month of unforgettable characters that face life's extraordinary odds. Only in Silhouette Intimate Moments!

Happy reading,

Patience Smith
Associate Senior Editor

Please address questions and book requests to:
Silhouette Reader Service
U.S.: 3010 Walden Ave., P.O. Box 1325, Buffalo, NY 14269
Canadian: P.O. Box 609, Fort Erie, Ont. L2A 5X3

Worth Every Risk
DIANNA LOVE SNELL

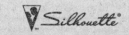

Silhouette®

INTIMATE MOMENTS™

Published by Silhouette Books

America's Publisher of Contemporary Romance

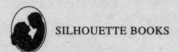 SILHOUETTE BOOKS

ISBN 0-373-27426-2

WORTH EVERY RISK

Copyright © 2005 by Dianna Love Snell

DIANNA LOVE SNELL

always liked to do things big. Dianna started out hand painting larger-than-life murals and outdoor advertising over 100 feet in the air throughout the Southeast. When technology advanced, she moved into creating spectacular marketing projects that light up the sky across the country from Boston to Dallas, and unusual designs for Olympic venues in Atlanta and Salt Lake City. Dangling high above ground must have gone to her head, because she began creating stories while she worked and decided to put her thoughts onto paper. Winning the Golden Heart and Daphne du Maurier Awards convinced her she was on the right track. Now, her books feature larger-than-life characters who conquer insurmountable odds to save themselves and the people they love. When not writing action-packed suspense stories, she rides her motorcycle in search of new locations to use as settings in future books. She lives in the Atlanta, Georgia, area with her motorcycle-instructor husband and a tank of unruly saltwater fish named after television characters. Please visit her Web site at www.diannalovesnell.com to contact her by e-mail and learn more about Dianna, or send snail mail to 1029 Peachtree Parkway North, Suite 335, Peachtree City, GA 30269.

To my dear friend and first critique partner, Mae Nunn.
To good friends—Sharon Yanish and her pilot husband, Ron,
who critiqued and helped with research (any mistakes
are my own), Donna Browning who cheered me on,
Haywood Smith for her incredible brainstorming
and Rita Herron who assured me this book
would be published.

To Terri Love, Manuella Robinson, Jane O'Hern,
Walt and Cindy Lumpkin for encouragement
and reading first drafts.

Last and most important, this book is dedicated
to the one person who supports everything I do…
my best friend, my champion and the love of my life, Karl.

Chapter 1

Lightning crackled nearby. Close, but not close enough.

"Come on, God, *please*." Angel Farentino whispered the desperate prayer for the hundredth time since midnight. But lights still burned through the opulent compound, her prison for the last seven days.

Wind whistled across the beveled panes outside the French doors.

"I should have asked for a hurricane instead of a thunderstorm," she muttered under her breath. She nervously rolled a golf ball–shaped compass in her hand. Would Mason Lorde snap her fingers like twigs if he caught her with his solid gold desk toy?

No chance he would let her off easy. She'd learned that lesson the hard way.

Just like everything else in her life.

Mason Lorde, her dream employer. Angel chuckled, a humorless sound. Mason had turned into her worst nightmare.

But what young woman with her past wouldn't have jumped at the chance for a job with a highly reputed firm? Assisting the warehouse manager for Lorde's revered import company beat cleaning commodes any day.

She'd thought.

Brilliant light flashed across the heavens, highlighting the brass bed on her right. A silk duvet covered the lump she'd built with pillows. The sleeping effigy would gain her an extra minute.

Angel consulted her black sports watch.

In sixteen minutes Kenner would begin his 2:00 a.m. round. On the dot.

Unlike the rest of the security, the new knuckle-dragging commander in charge of Mason's thirty-room mansion lacked any sense of tolerance. Kenner had replaced poor Jeff who'd overseen the property for the past ten years.

She could still hear Jeff screaming that bit of information as he pleaded for his life.

Another glance at her timepiece: Fifteen minutes, thirty-three seconds.

Angel fidgeted with the compass, desperate to turn the knob and flee, but patience was her only ally. Kenner certainly wasn't. Who could fault him for his inflexible attitude? He had no intention of repeating Jeff's mistake. His predecessor had smoked one too many cigarettes a week ago while she'd scurried down hallways in a fevered attempt to flee.

No, Kenner followed instructions explicitly. Like when Mason had ordered everyone to witness Jeff's punishment. Kenner had brought her outside and clamped hands the size of catcher's mitts on each of her arms, scooting her up to the show performed for her benefit.

Poor Jeff.

Not a word had been uttered in the deep woods of North Carolina in Jeff's defense as he cried and begged. No one in nearby Raleigh would ever believe what went on inside the private compound belonging to one of the city's most prominent businessmen.

Just over six feet tall, with thick golden hair and a champion's physique, Mason, the Nordic Antichrist, had calmly raised his repulsive .357 Magnum handgun to Jeff's head and pulled the trigger. A deafening explosion. So much blood.

She'd have hit the ground when her knees buckled if Kenner hadn't held her upright. And the smell. Who could forget the god-awful coppery stench? Her stomach roiled again.

Angel clenched her fists, squeezed her eyes shut. The horror still seared her brain with gruesome images of death. Only a week had passed since her failed escape attempt. But the brutal image of the hole in his forehead and Jeff's eyes locked open in panic would stay with her for as long as she lived.

Along with the responsibility for his death.

And all because of a job she thought was a godsend at first. What had she done so wrong in her life to end up working with a criminal again?

Twelve minutes, forty-two seconds until room check.

Jagged sparks flashed across the eerie sky, nearer, but still too far away. Her heart pounded against her breastbone.

Please, God, make it happen.

Thunder rumbled through the black heavens, longer than it had during the two power outages this past week, a common occurrence at the estate remedied temporarily by generators. She'd timed the last one. Should God deem to knock out the main electrical feed once more, she'd have nine minutes until three thousand volts surged back through the chain-link fence.

Three thousand volts or face Mason when he returned tomorrow morning—not much of a choice.

She was leaving whether the power went out or not.

If Mason caught her running this time, her penance wouldn't be light. She'd used her second chance and still nursed wounds from the aftermath. Her foiled escape had ended badly once his goons made quick work of recapturing her. Angel realized too late she'd mistaken Mason's charm and attention as sincere interest, not the obsession of a twisted man.

Her first clue came when the smooth businessman who'd flattered her with well-bred manners used his manicured hand to backhand her into a wall. Mason explained it as step one in teaching her compliance and submission.

He'd wasted his time.

Thunder barreled across the sky, directly overhead, rattling the delicate glass panels in front of her.

Ten minutes, eighteen seconds left.

Her restless fingers worried the cold silver band Mason had locked on her wrist. The slime actually smiled when he assured her the tracking device was for her own protection. He promised to return by the time she healed.

Cuts and bruises weren't major concerns, but living to see her twenty-sixth birthday was questionable.

The guards had all breathed a sigh of relief.

Only a crazy person would try to escape again.

"We'll see who's crazy," she whispered, "you son of a—"

Lightning exploded in a clap of thunder, so close her arm hairs stood on end.

The entire compound fell dark.

Angel hit the self-timer on her watch and dropped the compass down the front of her Lycra bra top covered by a butter-yellow T-shirt. Mason's choice of colors, not hers. Combined with the matching shorts, she'd stand out like a beacon when the first light popped back on.

She pushed the French doors open and rushed into a cooling August rain that battered the private balcony. A worn navy blue cap blocked her eyes from the downpour and hid the shoulder-length auburn hair she'd fastened in a ponytail.

There was no going back. Guards would enter the empty bedroom by the time lights flicked on.

Feeling blindly in the dark for the rail enclosing the balcony, she gripped the ledge, eased over and locked her legs around the center column. Her arms strained to hold her body's dead weight. Tremors shook through her at the fear of falling twenty feet. Slick, wet marble offered no traction to slow her descent.

She slid down the soaked surface, slick as a greased fireman's pole. Friction burned both her hands and exposed legs in seconds. Tears, mixed with rain, poured down her face from the searing pain.

She lost her grip.

Anticipating the impact, her muscles tensed. She plummeted through a black vortex. Sharp points stabbed into her shoulders and hips when she landed, but no excruciating pain from a broken bone. A boxwood hedge had spared her.

Like an upside-down turtle on a bed of nails, she lay still, panting. The insides of her outstretched legs burned and wet bullets of rain pelted her face. She kicked both feet, rolled and dropped into a crouch to listen.

No one was coming—yet.

Through the darkness, she counted memorized steps across the lawn. Lightning crackled and fingered through the dark sky. When grass changed to concrete, she sidestepped around the Olympic pool. Raindrops slapped the chlorinated water.

Her feet met grass again. She picked up the pace then bumped into a stone arbor strangled in vines. The scent of jasmine registered before she tripped on a thick stem and went down hard, scraping her palms.

She gulped a deep breath, listening. No boots splashed across the wet ground anywhere near her.

Angel jumped up and lunged into the blackness.

Heel to toe, heel to toe. Don't smack the ground.

Finally, the big elm came into view during a quick flash of lightning. She stepped around the tree, sucking in short gasps of air, safe for the moment in a deadly game of hide-and-seek.

Her hand shook violently as she pressed the button to illuminate the watch face.

Four minutes and twelve seconds. Time to see if God thought she deserved one more break.

Her ruse of a docile nature had paid off so far. The perimeter guards' overconfidence had bred complacency when their boss was away.

But what if someone started the generators too soon?

She sprinted eight big steps forward and stopped. Drenched to the bone, trembling from fear, not cold, she reached out to touch the ten-foot-tall security fence. Survival instincts stayed her hand at the last second, but she still had to touch it.

No tingle.

Thank you, God.

The current normally surging through the steel mesh could toss a grown man like a discarded rag doll.

Kenner's roar of anger from the balcony reached her. He'd found her empty bed.

She clenched a handhold and began her ascent.

Freedom came closer with every move. She hauled herself over the top. Her hand slipped. Soft flesh tore on the twisted chain link. She bit down hard to swallow a cry of pain. Her foot caught a toehold, and she scrambled down the other side.

Leaping away from the fence, she froze. Lights blazed on across the compound.

Wet chain link sizzled with renewed power.

Angel fought raw nerves pushing her to tear through the woods like a madwoman. Instead, she backed away, her feet on autopilot. Thick underbrush clawed her calf, shooting a stab of pain up her leg. Still, she plunged ahead. Sheets of rain blasted through breaks in the trees. Thunder boomed overhead.

How far could they track her?

Would lightning interfere with the signal from her bracelet? She'd never know.

A jagged branch snagged the edge of her thin nylon shorts and ripped a searing gash across her thigh. Adrenaline spikes forced her strained lungs to struggle for more oxygen. She caught quick glimpses of her surroundings during brilliant electrical displays.

At an opening in the brush, she sucked in air and stumbled to a stop. Angel reached between her breasts and snatched out the gold paperweight then flipped it to the compass embedded in the top.

The small airfield should be dead ahead.

Distant barking broke through the deluge. She gripped the compass, tension racking through her. Could a dog pick up her scent in a storm? Angel leaped into a sprint, pushed on with one thought—surely someone at the airfield would help.

Her fingers trailed over the band around her waist, an added weight that slowed her down. But leaving the eight rare coins wrapped within the plastic sleeve was not an option.

She swore she'd never go to jail again. Her one and only conviction had not been her fault. The police hadn't believed her story then.

They'd laugh in her face this time—right before they handcuffed her.

Jail was no longer her worst fear. The fact that she'd taken her employer's newly acquired Saint-Gauden's Double Eagle gold coins had sealed her death warrant.

But the rare pieces didn't belong to Mason, either. Possession doesn't count if it's stolen property.

And those eight coins were her only hope for vindication.

The FBI should be thrilled to have the priceless collection returned and be handed the scoop on Mason's crime ring. Happy enough to hear her side once she could prove her alibi during the theft. None of that would happen until she was safe.

As if someone had thrown a switch, the downpour fizzled into a steady shower. Angel burst through a break in the trees, slowed while her eyes adjusted, then moved forward steadily.

She stumbled down a slight drop into a ditch, climbed up and touched pavement.

The runway.

Thank goodness there'd been no fence around this airport. She scrambled to stand, then drew a quaking breath. Her body vibrated with excitement until the bays of pursuit dogs closing in on her pierced the night.

A fence might have had merits.

An open hangar glowed brightly a quarter of a mile away. With no time to celebrate, she sprinted toward the illuminated area.

Her thigh throbbed from the deep gash trickling blood. She ignored the ache and crept to the edge of the building. A tall, lanky man in mechanic's coveralls loaded boxes into a small twin-prop cargo plane.

When the worker finished, he walked across the spotless floor toward a brightly lit office.

She could just make out two men standing inside. The mechanic pushed the door open and announced the airplane was ready to go.

The pilot would take off soon and, when he did, she'd be right there with him.

One more gift from God.

Zane Jackson peered through the small window on the office door into the pristine hangar. Hack's man loaded the last box into his Cessna 404 Titan. Zane moved over to the pot of strong coffee always ready for pilots and filled his thermos.

"I have to make this run," Zane casually answered Hack before shifting around to face the terminal manager.

"You cain't be serious 'bout flying in this mess." Hack laid a dog-eared queen of spades down, completing another game of solitaire.

Oh, yeah, dead serious, for more reasons than just keep-

ing my cover intact. Regardless, this was a rare opportunity Zane wouldn't pass up.

Genetically engineered white mice packed in six cases had to arrive alive and on time. Zane didn't plan to blow the first chance he'd had for business with High Vision Laboratories, target of his DEA—Drug Enforcement Agency—special task force.

"H-o-o-wee. Nobody needs to fly in a front like this one." Hack shifted his bulk. "Didn't you hear about that fellow down in Jacksonville? He told his wife he *had* to fly in that bad squall come off the ocean. Said he'd lose his contract with Shoreline Delivery if he didn't. They used a bag to pick up parts of him scattered across Alabama."

Zane shrugged. Life was a gamble. He didn't have much choice anyhow.

Everyone vied for High Vision's business. He'd finally gotten a shot with the group suspected as a principal connection in a drug-smuggling ring. If he didn't meet the delivery deadline, somebody else would the next time.

His orders were uncomplicated. Fly every shipment High Vision would give his bogus charter business, making him privy to their activities. The task force had an agent inside the High Vision operation who alerted his unit to *questionable* shipments. Zane's job was to be in the right place on a moment's notice. In the meantime, he'd cart lab mice or anything else High Vision requested.

"Don't you see?" Hack continued. "That pilot didn't keep the contract anyways. He should of just stayed home and lost it."

Bad weather upped the potential for a problem, but compared to Zane's past experiences, making Charleston tonight would only warrant a little more attention than usual.

He'd flown his share of dangerous missions. On the last one, he'd barely walked away. In the Navy, he'd been a revered fighter pilot instead of a field agent who worked with the scum of the earth.

But that was three years ago and this was today.

Hack's police scanner crackled with a short conversation in law-enforcement code.

"A slow night for the boys in blue," Hack declared.

"What happened now?" Zane asked with feigned confusion over the cryptic announcements. He knew exactly what had transpired.

"Got a couple hotheads having at it in a beer joint down the road."

Hack's man loading the Titan shoved the door open and said to Zane, "All fueled and loaded, ready to go. You got to feed those critters if you're late?"

"Beats me. Vision doesn't make allowances for late."

With a nod, the worker pulled the door closed and strolled across the hangar toward the maintenance shop.

Rain drummed against the metal roof.

"H-o-o-wee. Listen to it come down out there. You hang around and we'll have a couple hands of poker."

Zane ignored Hack. A movement in the hangar caught his attention.

He couldn't believe his eyes.

Had a woman just slipped into his airplane? She must be nuts.

And where in the hell had she come from?

Zane snatched up the thermos. "Thanks for the coffee." He left before Hack could offer additional tales of aeronautic suicide. The last thing he needed tonight was trouble, even if it came in a long-legged package.

An odd sound outside carried with the swirling wind. Misting rain drifted through the haze of light beyond the hangar.

He stopped to listen.

Dogs bayed in the distance. Bobbing lights flashed near the woods at the far side of the runway. It didn't take a detective to figure out they were hunting something—or someone.

His stowaway was sadly mistaken if she thought he'd help a fugitive.

Zane paused.

A fugitive on the run from the law would be all over Hack's police scanner, but the only alert sent out in the last thirty minutes had been the barroom brawl.

Concern tapped along his spine. He stuck his head inside the Titan and scanned the secured cargo. Hundreds of tiny toenails scratched frantically against the aerated crates. A faint putrid smell accompanied the chattering racket.

In the shadows, he spotted a bruised leg. Blood trickled from deep scratches. When his vision adjusted, two enormous, terrified whiskey-dark eyes came into focus.

Who was she and why were they after her?

And if the police weren't the ones chasing her, who had turned dogs loose to track her?

Amplified barks and howls echoed louder across the airfield. The leg disappeared and the two eyes ducked away. A memory of his younger sister found, battered and bleeding, in the wrong place at the wrong time, crossed Zane's mind.

No one had lifted a finger to help her. Three years of buried guilt came roaring to the surface. He'd cursed the spineless men who had turned a deaf ear to his sister's screams.

He'd cursed himself worse for not being there to save her.

Zane climbed inside, slammed the cargo door then tossed the thermos into a bag on the floor. He jumped into the left seat, cranked the engines and jerked on his headset.

As he pulled onto the runway, he passed two black Land Rovers screaming into the terminal, sliding to a stop on the taxiway. Out jumped five men in dark suits with bodies the size of refrigerators.

Static crackled in his ear. He keyed the radio to activate the automatic runway lights then spoke into the microphone. "N 9095 Papa preparing for takeoff."

Two trackers with dogs appeared in his headlights, farther

down the runway. The ensemble raced toward him. Both men struggled to keep up with hounds charging against their leashes and howling.

Zane gunned the engine, taxied straight ahead.

Hack's excited voice burst from his headset. "Zane, come on back. Got some men here want to see you."

What if the brutes were in law enforcement? He'd have to hand her over. No woman was worth blowing his cover.

A hundred yards ahead, dogs scattered in different directions and men dived away from the churning props.

He clicked on his mike. "Are they feds?"

"No. Private security, but they really want to talk to you. Says there's big money in it for you."

Zane continued to flip levers. "What type of security?"

He swung around the far end, barely slowing. A squeak sounded in the rear, but he couldn't decide if it had four legs or two.

Two sets of high beams shot around the opposite end of the runway thirty-five hundred feet away to face him. He had a bad feeling those headlights belonged to the two sport utilities full of muscle.

Damn. He eased the throttles forward.

What kind of trouble was this woman in?

To keep an eye on his cargo, he'd installed a rearview mirror. He shot a quick look at the cargo hold. A pair of wide eyes stared back, more panicked than before.

He understood that look.

She was running for her life.

After a long silence, Hack finally answered his question. "Private security like…Big Joe Levetti."

Hair stood up across Zane's neck. Hack always joked that Big Joe worked for Goons-R-Us. No way would he turn that haunted, frightened woman over to a bunch of hired guns.

Zane barked one last message into the radio. "You're breaking up. I've got clearance from center. I'm gone."

As the aircraft picked up speed, the four headlights grew larger. Zane gripped the controls tighter. Playing chicken in a loaded Titan on a rainy night wasn't covered in his pilot manual.

Buffeted by the wind, the plane rocked and careened closer to the Land Rovers, the distance between them shortening with every second. He'd never get this weight up before reaching the vehicles. When he backed off on the controls the craft wobbled from side to side.

He'd never be able to stop in time, either.

Seconds until impact, he rammed the controls hard with everything he had. Each pair of headlights peeled off in opposite directions.

He shot the space between them and felt the lumbering craft catch air.

"Yes!" Zane laughed out loud and exhaled a deep breath at the same time. He hadn't felt an adrenaline kick this strong since running missions during the Gulf War.

On the radar, a gap through the weather had opened up to the west. Not a trouble-free route, but one that offered potential. He radioed Air Traffic Control for permission to alter his flight plan.

The radar changed in a heartbeat. A line of heavy squalls blocked his path to Charleston.

Hell, he couldn't go back. Just have to circumvent the bad stuff in a wider arc and exchange additional fuel use for landing alive.

Once he received clearance, Zane maneuvered the plane up to the new altitude where the skies were friendlier. He placed the Titan on autopilot, whipped off his headset and unbuckled. In another fifteen minutes things would get dicey. Might as well take a break while he had the chance.

He poured two paper cups of coffee, hit the dome-light switch and twisted around.

"Welcome to Fleeing Felons Express, otherwise known as Black Jack Airlines, where the coffee is black and there's no going back."

Chapter 2

Between the Titan's engine rumble and the mice digging to China, Zane didn't think his stowaway heard him. A small voice in his brain needled him. *Well, superpilot, did you stop to consider if she was a mental escapee—with a gun or a knife?*

No. Gut instincts had saved him too many times to question them now. This woman needed help.

"Want some coffee?" he asked a little louder and swung his legs over to the side of his seat. Should he go get her?

No answer.

"Sorry, that's the only refreshment on this flight." He watched as large curious eyes moved into the light.

"Coffee is good." Her cautious voice barely rose over the noisy cargo.

"I've got it on autopilot, but I'd rather not leave the cockpit. If you'll come up here with me, I promise not to bite," Zane offered.

A dirty yellow running shoe appeared first, followed by an

endless leg, from behind the crates. When the second limb slid out, he had to admit, cuts and all, she had a stellar pair. She slowly unfolded a body that appeared stiff and pained, based on her grimace.

Man, she had to be at least five-ten. Thin, athletic women had never appealed to him. His taste ran along the lines of dangerous soft curves with an accommodating disposition.

Passenger seats had been removed for maximum shipping capacity in the Titan. Stooped over, she traversed the twelve feet of cargo space, reaching out for support along the way. Her muted yellow T-shirt, still soaked through, clung suggestively to her chest.

Okay, she had curves after all, and in the right places, but they weren't in a Ft. Lauderdale bar about to exchange addresses. Unfortunately, a bad bunch of men were chasing her. Now that he'd plunged into the foray by sweeping their prize out of reach, they'd also be after him.

Women couldn't stay out of trouble. He knew firsthand.

She raised her head until the cap bill no longer hid her face. Two of the prettiest doe-shaped amber eyes adorned with thick cinnamon lashes gazed back tentatively. She chewed on her lip. He could understand her nervousness.

Rather than expect her to climb into the copilot seat until she had a chance to settle down, he reached over to knock several rags off a box behind the passenger seat for her to sit upon. That's when he got a close look at her cut and bruised legs.

"What in the hell happened?" he said louder than he'd intended.

She backed up a step, arm wrapped protectively around her waist. Fingers trembled, a ruby ring on the middle one.

Damn. She was frightened enough without him adding to her worries. He was definitely torqued, but not at her. Those goons deserved a few bruises of their own.

"Sorry, didn't mean to yell. Please have a seat."

A bulge around her middle didn't belong to the slender

build. What in the world was that? Before he could ask, a call over the radio beckoned him.

When the pilot twisted around and spoke into his mike, Angel eased down onto the crate. She brushed a loose hair behind her ear with a shaky hand.

Not exactly a textbook escape, but she had no complaints—now that they were airborne. For a minute, that had been in doubt. Much as she'd love to enjoy her success at thwarting Mason's men, common sense kept dousing the flame of celebration.

Who was this guy?

He knew she'd hidden on his plane, but still took off with men chasing them. That departure had been anything but standard. And he'd actually laughed after barely missing those two sport utilities.

Had she stowed away with Indiana Jones or a lunatic?

"What's your name?" His deep voice interrupted her thoughts.

She gazed up into the warm cocoa eyes of her savior. Big guy, probably a couple inches over six feet. He had the upper torso of a jock—a football linebacker if she had to guess by his size.

He didn't *look* crazy. Rich black hair curled over the collar of what had to be an extra-large leather flight jacket, adding to his rogue appearance. Maybe Indy does exist.

"I'm Angel."

His eyebrows furrowed in question, then he held up his index finger in the universal sign to wait a minute. He donned a pair of earphones, handing her a second set she slipped on.

"Now we can talk while I monitor the radio," he explained.

She nodded her understanding and repeated, "I'm Angel."

"Zane Black, at your service." His firm lips widened in a devilish grin.

She lost the fight to remain neutral and smiled back.

When his gaze traveled down the length of her damp T-shirt, she wrapped a protective arm around the band of coins hidden beneath the shirt, expecting the inevitable questions.

But they never came.

Instead, he dug out a towel from a duffel bag behind his seat. "Here, why don't you dry off. If you're cold, I have a blanket in the back."

His consideration made her pause until she remembered her manners.

"Thanks. I'm not cold, just a little tired." Exhaustion had replaced her adrenaline rush. Only frayed nerves kept her from keeling over. "I'd love some coffee."

His hand brushed hers when she took the thick paper cup, catching her off guard with the tingle she felt. She shifted on the seat and his smile morphed to a frown when he glanced down at her legs.

"We need to clean you up."

"I'm fine, really," she protested mildly. "It's just a few scratches." Minor injuries compared to what Mason would do if he caught her.

Her words didn't seem to faze him.

From a first-aid kit mounted on the wall next to his seat, he removed assorted medical supplies then reached for her leg. His hand hesitated in midair, obviously waiting for her permission.

Long seconds passed as they locked stares. She realized how foolish she must look, but lowering her guard and trusting a man had put her in this position.

He patiently waited. Understanding filled his eyes. His apparent comprehension of her reluctance to easily comply caused her to admit the obvious. Surely this man wouldn't hurt her after risking his life to save her.

Angel raised one leg for him to clean. The antiseptic cloth stung, but embarrassment was worse. She hated for even a stranger to see what Mason had done.

The airplane skimmed along through inky darkness as he

gently tended her raw cuts. Her pulse jumped the moment his long, tender fingers wrapped around her ankle, lifting it to apply a salve. A sizzling sensation slid through her body. Her system was on overload.

Zane Black filled the cockpit. His shoulders stretched beyond each side of the worn leather pilot seat. He leaned forward as he lowered her leg from his lap. She inhaled musky male mixed with a scent of citric cologne. The sexy combination overrode her rattled nerves to ignite a purely feminine response—the last thing she'd expected.

Life had been strange to this point, but not this strange. To be flying in a twilight zone, miles above the earth, through fathomless skies with a man who radiated both danger and compassion boggled her mind. Added to that, a maniac was chasing her. Then there was the fortune in rare coins wrapped around her waist that would either vindicate or convict her.

But being saved by a dark warrior who could turn a nun's head topped everything.

And he hadn't hit her with fifty questions. Those would come. For now, this Zane guy seemed content to repair his damaged cargo.

At his gentle pull, her leg moved up and across his lap. She didn't resist, didn't want to. After seven days of pure torture, Angel couldn't muster the energy to raise the wall of cool disinterest she normally offered men. One of his hands drifted absently across her calf, carefully angling it as he dabbed at cuts with a cloth in his other hand.

A warm tremor stirred in the pit of her stomach. Her breathing quickened at the intimate contact.

There couldn't be a worse time for her to be attracted to a man, so why was she? Having had few positive experiences with men, she came up with one explanation based on the mock survival training she attended monthly.

Complete strangers would bond almost immediately when thrown into life-and-death situations during extreme exercises.

It made sense. Mix fear of dying and adrenaline with one mouthwatering white-knight hunk for instant attraction.

That explained her lack of a love life.

"Let me see your arms," Zane said.

She jerked at his voice.

"Sorry, didn't mean to startle you."

"No, I'm sorry. Just a little jumpy I guess." She extended her free arm and held her breath as he inspected the scratched limb. When he paid no attention to the plain silver band locked to her wrist, she relaxed. Most men would ignore it as a piece of jewelry. One she'd like to remove.

Asking for a hacksaw right now might throw a kink into how well things were going. If he knew she wore a tracking device, he might jump to the conclusion she was a criminal and bring in the law. That would be a problem.

Never again would she blatantly trust anyone, especially not the law.

Imprisoned for a week with Mason and his flying monkeys reminded her just how vulnerable a woman could be, no matter what kind of physical condition she maintained. After Mason's brutality, this pilot's consideration was a balm to her ragged emotions. She hadn't felt the sting of tears in years, but his sensitive touch had her eyes burning.

"Speaking of being jumpy, and given the send-off we just got—want to tell me what's going on?" His concerned voice flowed over her like a hot shower on a winter morning, but the question snapped her back to reality.

He'd waited longer to ask than she'd expected and he deserved an answer. But telling this guy anything would be foolhardy.

Still, she despised lying. Lies had cost her a future she'd trained years to earn as an elite runner. Her life had changed irrevocably seven years ago.

As always, she'd adapted.

Now was another story. She stood to spend the rest of her

life in a federal prison for getting involved with Mason Lorde. Surviving this time might be beyond her abilities.

Men and lies went hand in hand. She'd never see this pilot again. The less he knew, the better off they both would be.

"Angel, maybe—"

"Have you ever had a relationship go bad?" she asked.

"A few that were difficult, but not quite that bad." Zane's raised eyebrow suggested his skepticism.

"Let's just say it's kind of complicated. I won't burden you." *You wouldn't believe me anyhow.*

"Burden me. I have nowhere to go for a while."

Just my luck to be rescued by Dr. Phil. Damn. "I wanted out of an arrangement. He didn't see it my way." Angel sent the cavalier answer with a shrug of one shoulder.

Rain pattered against the outer covering of the fuselage, and the cargo chattered during the silent pause. The pilot's eyes hardened. He probably assumed she meant a personal relationship. She should be so lucky to have a normal woman's problems. To clear up Zane's confusion would involve details she could never share.

After several seconds, he held out his hand to her. "Let's check your other arm."

She hesitated to move the arm shielding the coin bulge around her middle. "It's fine, really. Thank you." He definitely wouldn't understand if he saw the coins.

His eyes flickered, but he said nothing.

"Where are we headed?" she asked in an effort to change the subject.

"Charleston is my last stop before heading home."

Her head snapped up. *Oh, no.* Mason had a division in Charleston.

"We're going to land at the international airport?" She hated the distress in her voice. For a few minutes, she'd enjoyed a reprieve from life in her lofty hideaway.

"No. There's a small airfield nearby where I'm making a

delivery to a client. I've got plenty of time if the storm doesn't force me to circle very far out."

"Is this your plane?"

"Yes. I have a charter company," he answered.

"What's it called?" She reached for any subject that steered the conversation away from her.

"Black Jack Airlines."

"That's right. You told me that. What do you do?" Seemed like a cargo pilot wouldn't have to work in the middle of the night, flying through storms. Good thing he did, though.

"I handle special cargo that normally can't be transported by most commercial carriers. We're based in Ft. Lauderdale at Sunshine Airfield. Those ventilated boxes contain lab mice my client needs right away."

She gulped coffee to cover a shudder. Ugh, she hated rats. The slight smell and frantic scratching emanating from the boxes suddenly made sense.

"Sounds like an expensive way to ship rodents."

"These are special rodents." He turned toward the control panel, searching for something amid the mass of lights and gauges.

"They do tricks?" She couldn't resist teasing him if for no other reason than to get the sexy pilot to look at her again.

She got her wish.

He answered her grin with a devastating smile. A purred sigh escaped from her lips before a dose of common sense tamped down on her burgeoning attraction.

Hadn't she been just as taken when she first met Mason? Too late, she'd found out what kind of animal hid behind the million-dollar smile and impeccable manners. Only a fool would flirt with a man who'd helped her escape without even knowing why. Would she ever learn?

Annoyed at her naiveté showing again, she frowned.

Confusion crossed his face. "What's wrong?"

"Nothing, uh, I just wondered how long the airplane would

fly by itself." *Yeah, right.* Well, she *had* thought about it a few minutes ago. To support her claim, she glanced at the controls.

"We're fine until I take it off autopilot." He put away the first-aid kit and moved back into the left seat.

Limitless black heavens changed from a constant patter of rain to a loud drumming over the entire craft.

"Quick. Jump into the copilot's seat," he ordered.

She leaped up on stiff legs and scooted into the cool leather seat.

He secured her harness then took control of the airplane. She didn't move a muscle while the plane dipped and bucked against the turbulent atmosphere.

Zane calmly discussed weather with Air Traffic Control. Vicious wind and rain pummeled the outer shell. When the fuselage shuddered hard several times, she questioned her choice of nights to escape.

Temperature inside the plane had cooled. The damp clothes chilled her to the bone, but she refused to complain and distract Zane. Warm air began to migrate through her space. When another dry towel fell in her lap, she wrapped it around her shoulders and cut her eyes left. He maneuvered the buffeted aircraft with amazing dexterity.

In the midst of a storm, he must have noticed the goose bumps on her arm. Where had this man been when she'd been in the market for a nice guy?

The airplane dropped hard in a downdraft. Her stomach lurched. Just when she thought her heart might come through her throat from sheer terror, he glanced over long enough to wink and smile.

That little reassurance was all she needed.

Air Traffic Control cleared them to enter Charleston airspace an hour later. The aircraft began to drop steadily. Nothing in the inky darkness beneath them resembled an airport.

He pressed his mic but didn't talk. Down below, out of nowhere, two straight lines of white lights beamed up from a tiny spot on the ground. Would the landing be as wild as the takeoff?

The aircraft lights danced across the runway ahead of them. She gripped the harness straps and held her breath, but the touchdown was surprisingly smooth.

A light mist drizzled against the windshield as he slowed the plane.

She scanned the airport. Halogen lights glowed over the flat terrain.

This facility appeared larger than the one they'd departed near Raleigh. Three imposing hangars stood along the terminal.

As he finished his radio confirmation, Zane taxied to a parking spot near the main hangar. With the engines silent, noise from the aerated crates echoed through the cabin. He flipped off his headset.

"Why don't you stay put until I locate my client," he suggested. "He's probably holed up waiting somewhere dry."

"Sure." There had to be tools on board. She'd disable or remove the armband once he was gone. Surely Mason's men couldn't track her this far away, but no point in taking chances.

Zane left the steps in place when he exited through the door.

Angel waited until he'd walked around to the opposite side of the airplane and headed toward the terminal before she unbuckled her harness. One more glance then she hurried to the rear of the cargo hold.

Searching blindly in the darkness with her fingers for a bag or storage bin, she smacked into a rectangular box mounted against the wall. She felt the top, recognized the latch and popped it open. Fingers quickly explored. She identified a screwdriver, pliers and a file kind of thing, but grinned in relief when her fingers caught on two sharp points—tin snips.

Another divine gift.

Voices carried across the still airport. She rushed forward. Through the rain-streaked window next to the pilot's seat, she spied Zane speaking with a man wearing khaki pants and a windbreaker. She dropped down and quickly cut through the bracelet, then crimped it several times to destroy the tracking components.

Another peek outside ended her moment of relief.

A black Land Rover bearing the signature gold triangle of Lorde Industries parked next to the far hangar sent chills of dread down her spine. Mason's men had tracked her after all. She checked to see if Zane had noticed them, but he stood talking with his back to the vehicle.

Life never got any easier. Her pulse throbbed in her throat. If they caught her with the coins, she had no bargaining power and no way out of this mess. In addition to that, Zane Black would be a mere inconvenience in their way.

She rummaged through the flight bag behind Zane's seat, hating to rifle through his things. Locating a flashlight eased her guilt.

Most of the containers in the cargo hold were consigned to High Vision Laboratories. She ran the beam close over the labeled boxes, looking for one not slated for Charleston.

A soft package three feet square and a foot thick covered in brown paper lay in the very back. The company label adhered on the upper-left corner displayed the printed quote "Best custom boat curtain east of the Mississippi." She made a mental note that it was addressed to the security office at Gulf Winds Marina in Ft. Lauderdale, Florida, slip eighteen.

Not as close as she'd like, but a safe distance from Mason's home turf. And if she didn't reach the Gulf Winds Marina by the time the coins arrived, it would only be because she was dead.

Making the coins a nonissue at that point.

First she'd find someone to corroborate her alibi for the day the coins were stolen then she'd go to the FBI and gamble. Recognizing a heisted painting recently plastered on the news she found hidden in Mason's warehouse had shocked her. Innocently bringing it to the attention of her sainted employer had put her life in jeopardy.

If she convinced the FBI one of the ten wealthiest men in the country ran a crime ring, then she'd agree to testify against Mason—once they committed to placing her in a witness protection program.

Why not? She had no family and no life at this point.

Angel carefully pried the wrapping tape away from the paper and ran her hand deep into the package that held heavy canvas material with seams and pockets. Groping blindly along the edge of the material, she snagged a hemmed pocket wide enough to slip three fingers inside. With a quick jerk of the plastic sleeve of coins under her T-shirt, the clear tape holding the ends together broke.

Feeding the narrow sleeve of coins into the canvas pocket was tedious, like pushing a rope. Once she'd pressed the tape on the large package back in place, Angel scurried forward and wiped down everything she'd touched before replacing the tin snips.

Based on one solitary fingerprint, she'd been convicted of a crime she didn't commit. Never again. Her prison cellmate had chided her over the fastidious habit of wiping everything she touched, but Angel ignored the jibes. After a year in jail, the habit was as ingrained as taking her next breath.

She rushed to the window for a quick check of Zane's position. He was striding back to the airplane. She searched the area beyond him.

The man in khakis Zane had spoken to was nowhere in sight. Neither was the black sport utility.

Time to make a run for it. Now.

Angel tiptoed down the steps, cringing when one creaked. Her legs were pumping before her feet touched pavement. She ran through the shadows, along the front of several small planes secured with ropes to the ramp.

The rain had ceased. Her heart raced at every noise her sneakers made as she moved between the planes. She stooped beside a sleek white aircraft with a blue stripe along its fuselage. It glowed in the ambient lights.

Through the stillness, the sound of Zane's shoes scrunched against the steps to his airplane, no more than a hundred feet away.

Stopping to listen was a mistake.

A nearby scrape on the pavement raised the hair on Angel's neck. She made a half pivot away from the bright plane. A thick arm clamped down around her chest and jerked her back against a wide chest.

"No!" She choked the word out before a hairy-knuckled hand cut off her next breath. Kicking frantically, she fought to break loose. The stench of nicotine on his fingers gave Vic away. He ran Mason's Charleston division.

He dragged her backward.

Angel dug in her heels to slow him down. Muscles contracted in her chest. She couldn't breathe. He got her to the nose of the plane, but no farther.

Vic made a gurgling sound, then his hands jerked away. She spun around.

He struggled in a headlock of Zane's powerful forearms.

"You know this guy?" Zane barked.

"He jumped me."

A strangled noise wheezed out of Vic. Zane wrenched a little tighter. "Go call the police."

"No!"

"No?"

Angel silently pleaded for him to understand. "Thanks for the ride. I'm sorry."

She turned and ran.

Chapter 3

"Who are you?" Zane loosened his grip enough to let the mugger speak. His captive reeked of cigarette stench and heavy aftershave.

"Take your hands off of me, you fool." The stocky goon, a head shorter, appeared neither threatened nor concerned.

Not the reaction Zane expected when he had the clear advantage. He ground his teeth in frustration. If he arrested this guy his cover would be blown, but turning the scumbag loose wasn't a desirable alternative.

"You've got maybe ten seconds to let me go," the stubby captive warned, sounding annoyed and impatient, not the least intimidated.

Amused by the guy's show of bravado, Zane started to ask, "Or what, Shorty?" when he heard the distinctive "click" of a gun hammer cocked next to his ear.

"Turn him loose."

Zane dropped his arms.

Smoothing back his short black hair, the cocky mugger jerked away from Zane. He spun around and straightened his indigo silk suit with a look of pure hatred on his dark Mediterranean face. He threw a short chin jerk as some signal to his gun-toting partner.

"Turn around," the partner demanded. A cold gun barrel kissed Zane's cheek, once, twice.

Zane shifted with slow, deliberate movements to face the owner of the 9mm Smith & Wesson pointed at his head. A faint light cast by the distant halogens outlined stern features on the mahogany-skinned gunman. He stood inch for inch as tall as Zane and outweighed him by twenty muscled pounds. The mountainous body filled out a dark, tailored suit no CEO would refuse to hang in his closet.

High-priced hired guns. Was Angel some mob leader's private toy?

"Where'd she go?" Shorty asked, evidently the one in charge.

Zane affected his best rendition of a confused look accompanied with a good-old-boy repertoire.

"Hey, man, I don't even know the broad. I take off with some maniac driving down the runway, get up to ten thousand feet and the crazy woman climbs out of the cargo hold. Says some guy doesn't want to let her go. Must be a hell of a lover's quarrel. She belong to one of you?"

The two best-dressed henchmen in Charleston exchanged unreadable looks.

"I don't fly passenger charter," Zane continued. "Said she'd pay me to drop her off here for a little vacation, but she didn't flash any cash. You got an address where I can send a bill? Got to make this month's lease payment."

"Hey, Zane, you ready to unload?" a voice called out from the direction of the Titan. The High Vision client. Damn. Now what was he going to do?

Shorty and his sidekick tensed.

Zane had to keep his client out of this. "Hey, man, taking a leak. Be there in a minute."

"No problem," came the reply.

The gunman didn't move, but Shorty stepped up close. Evil, coffee-bean eyes shot contempt above his ugly smirk. He flipped a switchblade open, the sharp tip nicking the underside of Zane's chin.

Zane clenched his jaw to keep from snarling.

"Listen closely," Shorty warned. "You mention this little event to anyone and we'll be back to see you. And if you *ever* touch me again, I'll cut off your hands." He snapped the knife shut, threw a "let's go" head jerk at his towering sidekick and stalked off toward a black SUV thirty yards away.

Walking sideways, the big guy kept his gun leveled on Zane until he reached the driver's door.

Zane squinted to make out the emblem on the door, but the vehicle was parked just out of visual light range. Gravel crunched as the driver backed up a fast hundred yards, spun around and tore out of the terminal.

He let out a pent-up breath. Close encounters with lethal weapons still played through his nightmares, years after he'd been rescued from enemy territory in the desert—the longest thirty-four hours of his life.

Just who in the hell was Angel and why were those men chasing her? Professional security all right, but not the garden variety found in the local Yellow Pages. No wonder she'd panicked. But where had she gone?

A bowl of blackness surrounded the airport. He scanned the direction she'd run as if expecting her to be waiting within sight. Had she made it to the road and flagged a vehicle?

She could be a stone's throw from him or traveling sixty miles an hour in an over-the-road transport truck right now.

One look at those legs would bring any eighteen-wheeler to a screeching halt.

Reality intruded on his bizarre evening. He had a delivery to complete and an informant to meet.

An hour later, Zane checked the Titan, disappointed to find it empty. His analytical mind flipped through what little he knew. The two goons had found her quickly, which suggested they were local. They couldn't have made the trip by car. Hack didn't have his flight plan. That could only mean one of two things: either the goons had a contact where his flight plan was filed or Angel was tagged with a tracking device.

If she was, they'd find her again. This time she might not have someone willing to save her. He mentally kicked himself for worrying. The woman had shared only her first name, she was tangled up in something questionable and thugs with guns wanted her. He should forget the whole incident, just deal with his already loaded plate.

If only it were that easy.

Terrified eyes and a battered body kept flashing through his mind, reminding him he'd failed to save another woman.

A hint of dawn lightened the skies enough to see clouds moving off to the east. Zane checked his watch. It had been a hell of a start to Wednesday morning. Most people were on their way to work. His day was just ending.

Standing on the ground, Zane was eye level with the bottom of the copilot's seat. He leaned close to see what was under the corner of the seat support.

A silver wristband. He used a small pocketknife to move the band out from under the seat. It had been cut in half and crimped in several spots. Had to be a tracking device. His stowaway had spent her time wisely while he'd met with the High Vision representative. Zane dropped the band on the copilot seat and climbed into the cockpit. When his vision skated over the cup holder, he smiled.

It wouldn't be a completely fruitless trip after all.

He plucked a small plastic bag from a pocket next to his seat. Lifting Angel's paper coffee cup by the edge with his fingernails, he slipped the cup and silver band into the bag. By late afternoon his buddy in the lab should know her name and background. Hopefully she wasn't running for the wrong reasons.

He'd hate to see the doe-eyed woman go to jail.

Bright sunlight slashed between tall pine trees along Interstate 95. Angel squinted against the strobe effect. She draped a forearm over the worn leather door handle and tapped a quiet rhythm with her fingers. Quiet or not, no one would hear it above the diesel-engine groan.

"Sure you're not running away from home?"

She swung her gaze left at the question from the truck driver. Sixty, if he was a day, Pete had offered her a ride in Charleston even though she knew he hadn't bought her story of hitching her way cross-country. She hadn't lied, just withheld what she considered too much information. Lies were more than a pet peeve to her. They were unforgivable.

"No, I'm not a teenager," she assured the talkative old guy. He bounced from subject to subject, with occasional pockets of silence, before straying back to her. She preferred his over-the-road stories to questions she'd be hard-pressed to answer truthfully.

She couldn't risk sharing information with anyone.

"Don't look much older than my granddaughter who just graduated from high school," he prodded.

"I'm twenty-five. Little old to be running away from home." Angel smiled just to let him know she wasn't insulted.

He scratched his white beard that matched the thin hair on his head. Denim overalls shrouded his lanky body. Shifting gears smoothly with wrinkled fingers, he maneuvered the big rig with ease, content with his own thoughts.

A good man, one of few she'd ever met…like Zane Black.

Guilt still punched her over abandoning the pilot.

Where was her white knight now? Black hair, eyes the color of dark tea, and large as a bear, Zane might have championed her, but he was no fairy-tale knight. There'd been a dangerous glint in his eyes when he held Mason's man in a headlock. Zane handled himself well, as if he'd been in tight spots before.

For a brief flash in time, he'd sent her heart tripping. Angel rolled her eyes. Timing was everything. Hers had pretty much stunk since the day she fell from the womb.

Besides being ruggedly handsome, he seemed to be decent and honest, but she'd never have the chance to find out for sure. And even if she did, no decent and honest man would want a woman with her past.

"You gonna be hot in that long-sleeved shirt," Pete said.

Angel glanced down at the white cotton blouse. Comfort hadn't been a consideration when she'd selected a change of clothes at a salvage store. After the old guy had been kind enough to buy her breakfast, he'd dropped her at an aging strip mall while he unloaded a shipment nearby.

"I'll be fine. I prefer sleeves." Angel smoothed her hands over the jeans that also hid dark bruises and cuts. Her butter-colored running shorts and equally bright T-shirt were stuffed inside a linen shoulder bag along with the baseball cap.

Unfortunately, she had to choose between spending on another pair of shoes and something to cover her hair. The yellow sneakers remained, but her hair was twisted up under a floppy hat. Sunshades covered half her face. Angel could pass for an incognito celebrity on a tight budget.

"What happened to that pretty ring you had on?"

"I had to take it off," she said, noncommittal.

"Yeah, have to take mine off sometimes. Been married forty-eight years and my wife knows it don't mean nothing. But I can't wear it when I'm driving. It bothers me."

Angel unconsciously rubbed the middle finger on her right hand. The ring had bothered Angel as well…when she handed it over to the owner of a pawnshop near the salvage store. She'd worn the ruby heirloom ring since the age of twelve, when her dying mother had passed the cherished possession to her only child. Other than sentimental, the jewelry had little value, but enough for pocket cash—all she had to survive on.

She swallowed the lump of remorse in her throat.

Changing clothes and surviving until she could clear her name was priority number one. Mason's gold compass would have brought more at a pawnshop, *if* she hadn't lost the stupid desk toy. Even if she still had the coins she'd hidden in the boat canvas package, she couldn't sell them without connections.

Wouldn't sell them. To do so would jeopardize her only chance at staying out of prison.

If she hadn't recognized the small painting hidden within a shipping crate as the stolen art flashed across television screen and newspapers for a week, she'd still be working for the animal. What a fool she'd been, racing to Mason with evidence of illegal activity in his warehouse—certain he'd thank her for it.

Mason had just chuckled. "Welcome to the *family,* Angel. I hired you *because* of your record, not in spite of it. You're just the person I want on my team. You'll need some training, but I'll handle that myself."

Refusing to join his band of merry thieves hadn't gone over well, to say the least.

"Be a better person" had been her motto. She always believed she could overcome the trouble dealt her, but right now being a better person had her running for her life.

The engine chugged down when Pete slowed to exit the interstate.

"Thanks for going out of your way." Angel picked up the cloth bag she'd wheedled out of the pawnshop owner.

"Shoot, this ain't out of the way. I'll just run on down A1A a bit and cut back to the interstate." He handled the big truck better than most people drove a car, slowly working his way through busy streets until he found a spot to pull over.

"Pete, I really appreciate everything."

"Just be careful…and, uh, here." He dug a card out of his pocket. "You need some help, give me a call. Okay?"

She hesitated then smiled. "Thanks." Angel accepted the card, gathered her bag and climbed down from the truck. She waved as he left. At the first garbage can, she shredded the card into pieces. If Mason found the card on her, Pete would be in danger.

Angel jogged away at a subtle pace. Damp within minutes from the thick humidity, she passed through the Gulf Winds Marina entrance a half mile down the road. No one paid her any attention. Floridians definitely had an easygoing attitude.

Small white signs above each dock listed the slip numbers. The second one read: 11–20.

Twelve hours after thumbing a ride with a trucker, she'd found the dock for slip eighteen. Hopefully, the package hiding her coins had arrived.

For the benefit of anyone watching, Angel strolled casually down the weathered planks. Most of the slips held twenty-thirty-foot long boats backed up to the covered dock. A copper-tanned young man dressed only in a pair of faded cutoffs scrubbed a boat named *Wet Dream*, moored in slip seventeen.

A snow-white center console fishing boat, outfitted with impressive tackle, floated silently in slip nineteen.

Two seagulls paddled through the middle of slip eighteen. No boat.

Now what? She turned to the guy laboring on *Wet Dream*. "Excuse me," she called out.

He dropped the scrub brush and ambled to the rear of the boat. "Yes, ma'am."

"Do you know who owns the boat that stays in slip eighteen?"

"No, ma'am."

She waited for him to offer more than a charming smile, but he didn't seem inclined to elaborate. This was a little too laid-back.

"Do you know the name of the boat that parks here?"

"Can't say." He scratched his head covered in sun-bleached shaggy hair. "Slip's been empty for three months. Heard someone rented it, but the boat hasn't shown up yet."

The package had been addressed to the security office for the marina, which now made sense. The boat hadn't arrived.

"The security office was closed when I passed it. Have any idea when it will be open?"

"Yes, ma'am. Soon as I finish cleaning this boat, I'll be back up there."

Going through the tiny office shouldn't take long.

He grinned with apparent satisfaction over having given her the right answer.

Angel smiled, happy to find an advantage in being female for a change. "You'll save me some time. My company sent a package of boat curtains marked for slip eighteen in error. I have to make sure it arrives at the correct boat. Would you mind if I checked to see if you received that package?" She held her breath, waiting on him to ask the obvious questions, starting with identification, what boat it was intended for and on and on. She had no idea what she'd say next, but somehow she'd gain access to that office.

The mocha-skinned guy didn't ask her the first question, just shook his head and said, "I'll save you a lot of time. We haven't had a delivery all week."

Damn. Where was that package?

A possibility popped into her mind.

"Do you know where Sunshine Airfield is?" she asked.

He smiled. "Yes, ma'am."

"What do you mean there are no prints on the cup *or* the band? Even I touched the cup at one point," Zane barked into the cell phone as he jockeyed through A1A traffic along the beach. He'd tossed and turned during the few hours of sleep he'd managed.

Long, bruised and bleeding legs had haunted his dreams.

"Sorry, Zane, I've been all over this thing. It's clean as my mother's kitchen floor," Ben Stevens said.

"Damn," Zane swore. She had to leave a print somewhere. "I'm going back to check again. I'll swing by as soon as I get something."

"Sooner the better or I might not be here."

"Haven't you had that baby yet?" Zane asked.

They'd met in grade school and grown up together in Texas, staying in touch over the years. Having been hired after college by the DEA, Ben encouraged Zane to join the task force and use the skills he learned in the military. Besides being a whiz in the lab, he was Zane's best friend.

"She's overdue." Ben's weary voice attested to the strain of waiting to be a father for the first time. "We're scheduled to induce on Tuesday, if she doesn't go into labor before that. Made her doctor swear I could reach him over Labor Day weekend. Hey, man, if I'm not here the lab will have someone on call."

"If you aren't there, I'll wait. This is for something I'm doing on the side."

"Oh, I see." After a pause, Ben asked, "What you up to?"

"I'll tell you about it when I stop by." Zane wasn't ready to discuss this yet, not even with Ben.

"Get me a print as soon as you can. I'll try to turn it around quick."

"Thanks, Ben. See you later." With a couple hours of daylight left, Zane headed for Sunshine Airfield.

The cup and band had obviously been wiped clean.

Not a good sign for a person with nothing to hide.

Who was she hiding from? He'd run a check on all police activity in the Raleigh area from the night before. Nothing significant had shown up, leading him to believe someone chased her for personal reasons.

Removing her fingerprints stumped Zane. Angel didn't

know he was in law enforcement and she hadn't stolen from him. So he couldn't assume she'd done it with criminal intent.

Someone wanted her back bad enough to band her with a tracking device and send a team of trained thugs after her. Why? And the guy played rough.

Zane clenched his fists. No woman should be mistreated. After seeing the brutal marks on Angel's body, he couldn't blame her for covering her tracks so well. He should have pushed for more information, a last name.

He wheeled into Sunshine Airfield. As he drew near the whitewashed, concrete-block office building, a leather-faced elderly man stepped from the door.

Zane slowed the truck to a stop and rolled down the window. "*Hola*, Salvador," he said, smiling at the old guy.

Salvador's sole purpose in life these days was to make coffee in the airfield office and offer a game of checkers to anyone willing to be beaten by the wily opponent. Long since retired from managing the terminal, he was unwilling to abandon the airport entirely.

"*Buenos días,* Señor Black."

For the next few minutes, Zane chatted amiably in Spanish with Salvador about airport activities. Zane kept his language skills sharp though he used them sparingly. Sometimes it served his needs to hide them as much as it did to use them. It was amazing what someone would say when they thought you couldn't understand their language, particularly a criminal.

With a nod goodbye, Zane moved on to the last building. The overhead door to his hangar stood wide open, allowing access to anyone, but he was unconcerned. His mechanic was bent over the Titan, working neck deep on the scheduled service required before he could fly again.

As he strolled by, the mechanic lifted a finger off his flashlight in acknowledgment, obviously too busy to visit. Zane headed to the storage room to get another stack of rags to replace the ones he'd used cleaning up yesterday. He reached for the door, but stayed his hand at a sound on the other side. Had a cat or raccoon gotten in? A cat wasn't a problem, but he wanted no part of a cornered raccoon.

Rotating the handle slowly, he eased the door ajar and peered inside. Instead of a wild-animal sighting, a fine-looking derriere, covered by a pair of faded jeans, faced him.

Bent over at the waist, the denim-clad owner inspected a large package on the floor.

Zane's gaze skimmed down to the yellow running shoes. It couldn't be.

Chapter 4

Where is that blasted package? Angel leaned down to read the label on another odd-shaped box, grumbling to herself over the haphazard room. Assorted shipping containers and mechanical parts covered every inch of the disorganized storage area from cluttered floor space to packed shelves.

None were addressed to the Gulf Winds Marina.

She lifted her hands to her hips as she straightened up. Iron fingers locked around both of her wrists, snatching them behind her.

"Oh, oh…no." She wrenched around to see who held her immobile and came face-to-face with the pilot who'd saved her. Staring up into his narrowed gaze, every coherent thought fled her mind.

"Nice to see you again, Angel." Rich brown eyes walked up and down her. "The Annie Hall look is different." His warm demeanor from the day before now flashed stormy dark. A good match for his irritated tone.

She dropped her head down and her shoulders slumped from relief. He didn't sound happy to see her again, but at least he didn't want to kill her.

Twisting around for a second glance, Angel realized she might be wrong. They hadn't parted on the best of circumstances. Getting back into his good graces as quickly as possible was her first mission.

"Hi. How are you?" She lifted her eyebrows, hopefully.

"How *am* I? As in, was the flight back smooth? Or as in, how did I get away from your buddy?"

"I'm sorry," she whispered. What had Vic done after she'd left? Mason's men never traveled alone. Had they ganged up on Zane and hurt him? "Did you have a problem with that guy?"

"Problem?" Sarcasm laced through his voice. "Nooo, not unless you consider having his sidekick shove a gun in my face a problem."

"Oh, God. What happened?"

Zane shrugged. "I told them I didn't know who you were and that I thought you'd had a falling-out with your boyfriend. Once you were gone, they lost interest and let me go."

Luck had never been her strong suit, running from bad to worse. She'd spent a large portion of her funds on clothes. In the past thirty hours, she'd had one meal and a few hours of sleep. Now she couldn't find the damn package hiding the coins. If Zane—the sole person who knew where the package had gone—handed her over to the police, she was sunk.

Yeah, this qualified as bad to worse. Time for some major sucking up.

"I'm sorry," she started. "I didn't mean to involve you in my problems. I had no idea where I was going and didn't know those guys would show up in Charleston. I was too afraid to think clearly." She was babbling. *Shut up and change the subject.* "I never thanked you for getting me out of Raleigh."

Angel took a breath. "Thank you."

His face softened. The muscle in his jaw no longer

twitched, but his eye had a tic. Zane might not kill her, but calling the authorities was still a high possibility. Between smoothing things over with this guy and figuring out what happened to the package—without specifically asking where it was—she had her hands full.

How did a simple plan to hide the coins get so screwed up?

She wrenched against his steel grasp. "Would you let go, please?" she implored sweetly. "You're hurting my wrists."

His fingers loosened immediately and she freed one hand. He kept the other hand, massaging it with his thumb.

"Sorry. I didn't realize how tight I had you." He didn't stop until both wrists had been given equal attention, confusing her completely.

Zane Black went from annoyed to caring within a heartbeat. Like the heartbeats rapidly thumping in her chest from his warm touch. He'd touched her with the intent to soothe more in two days than any male had in the past seven years. Except for her one failed relationship as a teen, contact with men had not been by choice. Her limited experience amounted to being handcuffed and physically abused.

Gentle had rarely entered the equation.

Merely standing next to Zane Black catalyzed a physical response. She'd definitely never had a man excite her just by rubbing her wrists.

Chocolate cake had raised her pulse more than any male who'd shown an interest in the past.

"Angel, why don't you tell me what's going on before someone gets hurt, mainly you?"

Her heart did a small trip at his genuine concern. His intense stare roamed over her face as if searching for a window into her thoughts.

What could she say that he'd believe? Even if he did accept her story as true, he'd want to call in the police. That would drive a nail in her coffin. Once the authorities pulled up her record, they'd lock her away forever. Against a prominent businessman like Mason, her word was less than dirt.

She had one shot at beating this problem and to remain free. It didn't include local law enforcement.

Or sexy pilots.

Besides, if Mason captured her, there would be a price to pay. Telling Zane anything would put him at risk as well.

"I can take care of myself. You're better off not being involved," she said.

His black eyebrows furrowed in suspicion. "Why?"

"Even if you knew, you couldn't help me."

Chiseled lips twisted in a frown as if he worked to figure out a puzzle. "Look, if this guy chasing you is an obsessive male, there are laws that will protect you."

"The police won't take my side."

That made him pause. She tried to read his thoughts, but his expression shuttered.

"Why? If you've broken the law, turning yourself in would be better than being caught by this jerk," Zane pressed.

She bristled at his insinuation that she was guilty of anything. Had he found the coins? No, she didn't think so. If he had, he'd probably be calling the police right now. Still, he was beginning to remind her of the detective who'd railroaded her into jail seven years ago.

"Angel, how much trouble are you in?"

Just like an arrogant man to make assumptions with no inbetween. Either she was a hunted girlfriend or a criminal.

Lack of rest and little food, combined with the missing coins, fueled her already testy mood. A wise woman would calm down and sweet-talk Zane, but she was sick to death of men either lying to her or assuming she'd committed a crime.

"Fine! I admit I broke the law when I stowed away on your airplane. Are you going to have me arrested?" She shoved hands defiantly to her hips.

"Angel, I'm just trying to help you. Don't blow up at me."

"Blow up? Look, it's my problem not yours. Why don't you leave it at that?"

"Because I *can* help you," Zane told her in a tone that suggested she wasn't paying attention.

"You're a pilot, a very good one, but not what I need right now. Just stay out of this." She wouldn't have raised her voice, but had to shout to be heard over his.

Zane retorted, "If you weren't so stubborn—"

"Excuse me, *señor.*"

She and Zane bumped as they swung around to face the open door. Just inside the doorway stood a handsome Latin man of average height, wearing a smart fawn-colored suit with an eggshell silk shirt open at the collar. A smile quirked up on his face when he spoke to Zane.

"Buenos días, Señor Black. I'm here for my shipment."

"Mr. Suarez, good to see you. We were just going over the inventory log."

Angel lifted an eyebrow at the fabrication, but held her peace.

Zane swung his hands out wide, palms up. "Only one box came through customs."

Mr. Suarez's smile fell. "But why? We discussed this before you left." His language switched into a rapid litany of angry Spanish.

Angel had learned street Spanish as a child in New York then found she excelled at the language when she took the course in high school. It turned into an easy credit. Competing for an athletic scholarship had been more difficult. But she'd won a full ride to an exceptional university…then lost it before the first semester, detained in a jail cell.

She stood silently while Mr. Suarez ranted that this was the third time Zane had failed to deliver, Zane was inept and Suarez was ready to sever ties with Black Jack Airlines altogether.

She glanced up at Zane's placid face. The face of a man who didn't understand a word Suarez said.

A person didn't have to be fluent in Spanish to realize Suarez was very angry. She elbowed Zane, who flashed her an innocent look of *what?*

His customer fell silent, evidently waiting for an explanation. She nudged Zane again. This time he must have taken the hint.

"What can I say? The box wasn't there so I didn't pick it up." Zane shrugged.

That's it? He might be a crack pilot, but Zane sorely lacked people skills. Since he had helped her, the least she could do was return the favor.

Angel offered his client a smile, then responded in Spanish.

"Mr. Suarez, please forgive my friend. He is an exceptional pilot but a little rough around the edges. Unfortunately, basic business skills were not required to get a pilot's license."

Had Zane just kicked her? She narrowed her eyes at him. Had he understood her?

His eyes widened.

Suarez's lips twitched, but he gave no indication his temper had completely cooled. She continued appeasing him in his language.

"You are very understanding with Mr. Jackson's shortcomings and we really appreciate your patience. If you'll give him a chance to correct the problem, he'll check into this matter and get back to you once he has answers on your other package."

She finished with, *"Please accept our sincere apology. You and your business both mean a great deal to Black Jack Airlines."*

Suarez returned her smile with a sensational one. The man oozed European aristocratic elegance. He lifted her hand and kissed the back.

A sigh escaped her lips. No woman was immune to that kind of flattery.

"Señorita, you are as wonderful to do business with as you are to gaze upon," Suarez said, then cut his eyes at Zane and

spoke in English. "I suggest you keep this woman if you wish to continue delivering for my company."

Zane handed Suarez a small box then put his arm around Angel's shoulders, shifting her back to the point where Suarez was forced to let go of her hand.

"I was just telling Angel what a good team we make," Zane said. "She generally pops in and out when she wants, but we're hammering out a plan that will work for both of us. Umph."

She'd elbowed him one more time in the ribs for outright lying.

Grinning, Suarez said goodbye as he left with the package under his arm.

She jerked away from Zane. "Don't you care about keeping that client?"

"He's not going anywhere," he dismissed casually. "Only a few groups operate the way we do and none of them fly out of south Florida."

"I wouldn't be so sure. He said he was thinking about dropping your service." She waited to see how Mr. Arrogant liked hearing that little tidbit.

He didn't say anything at first. Crossing his arms, Zane shifted his feet apart and cocked his head to the left, studying her. His stance didn't intimidate her, but she worried about what was going on under all that thick black hair until he finally spoke.

"Where did you learn to speak Spanish?"

"I took a couple years of it in high school and tutored English to the Puerto Rican children in my neighborhood." She cocked her head up at him. "You should consider a few classes."

"You're right, but not about classes. I do need to make a better effort to appease Suarez since he does a significant amount of business with me. You should stick around and translate for me."

Bad idea. "No." Angel shook her head. "I can't do that."

"Why? Where are you going?" he prodded.

Nowhere until she found the coins.

Before she could answer, he asked, "Where are you staying?"

"I don't have a place yet, but I'm not planning on hanging around long."

He leaned toward her and asked, "By the way, just what were you looking for in here?"

Oops. "What would I be looking for in here?" she asked, all innocent.

"That's what I want to know."

Not a good time to inquire about the package of canvas. The truth would only open a bottomless pit of questions. She dug for a good answer, something in a gray area, but close to the truth.

"When I came in, the mechanic said I could wait for you."

Well done, not really a lie.

"You thought he meant *here* instead of the office?"

Angel tried for a surprised look. "*Ohhh,* you have an office. That would have been a better choice." She shrugged.

He rolled his eyes and shook his head. "I'll tell you what. This contract with Suarez is only for a short time. I'll give you a place to live in exchange for translating."

She hadn't planned to hang around any longer than it took to locate the coins. However, figuring out how to eat, sleep and find transportation on less than a hundred dollars would be a challenge. Even though the transmitter was gone, hiding from Mason for any length of time without a chunk of money was impossible. His resources were practically unlimited.

And Zane was the only common denominator for locating the coins.

Rocking back on his heels, as if he had all day to wait for her answer, he unfolded his arms and slid his hands into the pockets of faded jeans that fit his lower torso like a glove. The snug powder-gray T-shirt hugged his broad chest. Her eyes traveled lower to a worn brown leather belt just above…

Embarrassed, her eyes shot up to his in time to catch the twinkle in his eye confirming he'd caught her roaming vision. Spending a lot of time around this man might not be advisable.

"You still owe me for the ride," he pointed out.

She rolled her eyes. He *would* use his ace. Besides, she had no other option.

"Okay," she huffed. "But I'm not promising how long I'll stay."

"Fair enough." Zane checked his watch. "It's almost four. Let's go."

"Go where?"

"Home."

She hadn't even considered where he'd offered for a place to stay. "You mean *your* home?" she clarified.

"Don't worry. I have a foldout and you should know by now you're safe with me."

He wouldn't harm her, but was she safe from her own errant thoughts?

No place was a haven until she found those gold coins. The strain of the last two days began to settle in. She felt light-headed. Not a time to be picky when she desperately needed at least one good night's sleep.

"Okay…thanks." Angel picked up the linen shoulder bag she'd dropped near the door and followed him to a massive Dodge pickup.

That figures. The man wouldn't fit in anything smaller.

Flashy mag wheels gripped black-outlined raised-letter tires. The four-wheel-drive machine was coated in Saturday-night-lipstick red, accessorized in chrome jewelry.

No wonder men referred to their vehicles as feminine counterparts.

Zane opened the passenger door. The new-car leather aroma floating through the cab engulfed her as she stepped up to the high seat. What a great smell. She'd never owned a car, much less a new one. She peddled a bike everywhere she went. Her triathlon training paid off. Her insides kinked at that thought.

In two months the Tamarind International Triathlon would be held in Colorado where elite competition from all corners of the world would gather. Last year, it had been held in Greece.

She'd trained for the past sixteen months straight to prove to the world and herself that she was an athlete, not a criminal. Every waking minute not spent working, she'd trained. Her times slowly improved until she was in shape to be a contender, or would be if she hadn't been a conscientious employee.

She might not be alive in two months and, besides, she'd probably never compete again anyhow. They probably frown on that in the witness protection program.

Zane climbed in and cranked the engine. A wide console separated them, suiting her just fine. Calm dove-gray covered the interior, contradicting the screaming exterior. She did a visual sweep, hoping to find a brown paper package with Gulf Winds Marina labeled as the destination.

No such luck. Several ropes were piled across the narrow back seat of the extended cab. A large bundle of half-inch-thick rope lay in the rear floorboard. What in the world does he use that for? she wondered, then switched mental gears to more important concerns.

How soon would Zane fly out again? If she didn't find the package stashed in his hangar, she'd return to the marina in case the boat curtains had been floating around in transit and had finally arrived.

Watching Angel climb into his truck, Zane was amazed she could still stand upright. Pale blue shadowed the delicate skin under her eyes, indicating she'd slept little, if any, since he last saw her. She must have had some funds for the secondhand clothes and transportation to Florida.

His suspicions flared at everything she'd done, from wiping her fingerprints down, to showing up in his hangar. He should turn her over to the police to let them determine if she needed protection or incarceration. But her fear was palpable. After three years with the special task force, he'd learned not everyone who avoided the law was a criminal. Judging this situation without all the facts could get someone seriously injured, or killed.

Also, if he turned Angel over to the local authorities, he wouldn't be able to help her without exposing his identity. Before he did that, Zane had to know from whom she fled, who had abused her.

Frustration at the situation welled up inside him. She refused to fit neatly into one of two categories—guilty or innocent. Someone had definitely held her against her will. Everything pointed to an illegal situation at the heart of this mess. That's where the contradiction was rooted.

Nothing about her fit his gut impression of a criminal.

What about wiping her fingerprints away? Okay, there was that.

And what had she been looking for in his storage room? When she'd spun around with that sweet but worried "Hi. How are you?" his emotions had roller-coasted from annoyed to relieved. Zane had spent a long night awake every hour, wondering if she'd managed to remain free and unhurt.

Why wouldn't she let him help her deal with whoever threatened her? If she knew his occupation, she'd realize just how much he *could* help her. But sharing what he did for a living was out of the question.

Or his real name, since Angel knew him as Zane Black. The only people who knew him as Zane Jackson outside of work were his sister and her roommate, but he'd know who Angel was before that became an issue. The agency had a second apartment in his undercover name as one barrier between him and anyone who snooped around on him. That would only delay someone determined to find him—like the thugs he'd met in Charleston—not stop them.

Zane scrubbed a hand over his face. His misgivings climbed to the point of questioning the logic of bringing her into his home, until he caught her in his peripheral vision.

She rode quietly, staring straight ahead. Her squared shoulders boasted of confidence, but the stiff carriage was belied by her death grip on the linen bag.

After one glance, he went from guarded to protective.

Turning up alone in Ft. Lauderdale could only mean she was on her own with nowhere else to go, on the run from an abusive beast. Zane's stomach twisted. But what would it cost him to help her out?

He sent another cursory glimpse her way.

Angel chewed on her lower lip. One hand relaxed, slipped from the bag in her lap. The ring was missing from her finger. Had she traded the ring for clothes or a few bucks?

Her fingers fidgeted against her jeans, trembled.

No one would get their hands on Angel until he had his answers. No one.

Zane had more than a few questions, but dealing with cagey informants in pressured circumstances had taught him patience. The best way to draw information from a reluctant individual was with slow, calculated conversation. Right now, Angel was both exhausted and jumpy.

Good thing Suarez had come by. The dressed-up-Latin-pretty-boy-pain-in-the-butt's visit had worked in Zane's favor. Pretending not to understand Spanish since the first time he and Suarez met was intentional, even though nothing had come of the ruse…until today. Leverage Zane would exploit to keep Angel near, safe, while he figured out what was going on with her.

Having her close tonight would pay off in one more way.

He'd lift her print and drop it at the lab first thing in the morning.

Then it would be decision time. Bring in the authorities to help her…or arrest her.

Chapter 5

Zane parked in front of the two-year-old sandstone-construction apartment building where he hung his hat. Good thing he'd picked the place up and restocked the refrigerator. He hadn't cleaned with a guest in mind, just made it habitable after being gone for most of two weeks.

He circled the cab and opened the passenger door. Angel jumped out then stuck close to his side. With every step, she glanced around, eyes furtive, as if she expected someone to leap from behind the towering oleander bushes that surrounded his first-floor garden apartment.

During the short drive home, she'd gradually slumped in her seat, stamina waning. She'd get a good night's rest if he had to stand guard over her the whole time.

Zane unlocked the ultramarine-blue front door and stood aside to allow Angel to enter first. Chilly air, hinting of lemon furniture polish, greeted them.

Hazy sunlight filtered through the patio doors into the expansive living room. She ambled past the hunter-green leather sofa and matching overstuffed chair then stopped in front of the sliding glass doors. The linen bag slipped from her fingers to land next to her sneakers. She faced the spectacular vista beyond his patio.

Stone walkways separated tiered layers of immaculate flowering gardens along a boardwalk to the pristine sandy beach. Curling emerald waves from the Atlantic Ocean crashed against the shore.

The sparkling serenity was lost on Zane. He couldn't focus past the foreground. Several loose strands of roan hair dangled below the floppy hat. The white cotton shirt slid over her sleek back and disappeared into a taut pair of jeans covering two succulent cheeks.

"What a beautiful view," she sighed.

Honey, you have no idea. "One of the best I've ever seen," he mumbled. He'd love to pull the hat off and finish the vision.

She looked over her shoulder at him. "What?"

Bright sunlight in the background haloed around her. Highlights danced across the curves of her body, tantalizing the image his mind was determined to create.

Oh yeah, he wanted to take the hat off.

In his fantasy, it would land on top of a pair of jeans and a white cotton shirt already tossed on the bedroom floor.

"What did you say?" she asked.

He snapped back to reality, wiping his hand over his mouth, sure he'd been drooling. This was not the time to stray into dangerous testosterone territory.

"Nothing, make yourself at home."

She didn't move a muscle. "Have you lived here long?"

"Do you mean in this apartment or Ft. Lauderdale?" he asked while walking into the kitchen. "How about something to drink?"

"Water, please," she called out. "How long have you lived in Ft. Lauderdale?"

He handed her a chilled bottle of water on his way to open the glass doors to the patio.

"Three years." Heat blanketed him as he stepped onto the teal and cream ceramic tile. With the crook of his finger, Zane motioned Angel to follow then pulled out a black wrought-iron chair with a burgundy-cushioned seat.

"Have a seat."

Just as Angel set her water on the mosaic table surface, the doorbell chimed.

"Sit tight. I'll be right back," Zane said, strolling away.

Angel popped up, ready to leave if she recognized his guest. She had a clear view of Zane, but not the other person.

He opened the door and stepped back. A tall young woman entered. Thick black curls covered the girl's head like a soft furry cap. On anyone else but the dark-haired beauty, the hairstyle would have come off as goofy. But on her, the dark silky hair and creamy complexion was a striking combination.

She wrapped two delicate arms around Zane's neck and planted a kiss on his cheek.

Why that bothered Angel, she had no idea. Maybe because she'd never been considered delicate. Zane's visitor might match her in height, but that graceful curvaceous body had probably never spent forty-eight hours living through a torturous survival weekend or running a marathon.

Instead of gloating over her accomplishments in the woods and on a track, standing near a perfect specimen of femininity left Angel feeling severely inadequate.

Zane's smile flattened out into a straight-line frown and Angel's mood improved.

Okay, so that might be a bit uncharitable on her part. She could live with the guilt.

Angel moved a step closer to catch what was going on.

The twenty-something woman prancing around Zane in an

ankle-length bright peach dress and straw sandals laced up her calf could be a cover model.

Angel inched close enough to hear the woman say, "Sugar, I'm fine, really. You missed me, didn't you?"

"I always miss you," he answered with a half smile.

Beginning to seriously dislike the beautiful visitor for no apparent reason, Angel stepped all the way around the table. The young woman wrapped an arm around Zane's waist, hugging herself to him.

"I came by three times this week looking for you," the dark-eyed female said. "You're harder to catch than a shadow. Thanks for my surprise. I found the birdhouses when I came in this morning." Her sultry voice carried just enough sincerity to validate Angel's suspicions. The woman was more to Zane than just a friend.

He gathered the beauty close in an affectionate embrace.

Angel imagined those strong arms wrapped around her body.

She frowned. What was wrong with her? This guy has a life and at least one girlfriend. It shouldn't matter to her what he did. Besides, she'd be long gone once the coins surfaced.

Then why did seeing the two of them together grate on her nerves?

"Who's that?"

Angel snapped to attention at the girl's question.

Zane swung around with an armful of female and strolled back to the patio. "Trish, meet Angel, a friend of mine. Angel, this is my sister, Trish."

His sister? Ohhh. "Nice to meet you." Angel stuck her hand out.

Trish gave her an up-and-down once-over then leaned forward a little unsteadily to take her hand. "Angel, huh? Interesting name. Nice to meet you, too."

Trish turned to Zane. "Didn't realize you had company, but I'm glad you've given up celibacy. At least that rules out your being a priest." She chuckled at some personal joke.

"Trish." His single word sounded full of warning. Something else shrouded his gaze...disappointment? Guilt?

"Okay, okay. No games today." She turned back to Angel, "Be nice to him. He's all I've got." Trish pecked her brother's cheek. "Gotta go. Heidi's waiting. See you later, sugar." With that she pranced out the door, reminiscent of a child on her way to play.

Angel started to call her back to correct Trish's misconception of the situation, but the familiar smell of alcohol coming from the woman had hijacked her thoughts. It was cocktail hour for some people.

Propped against the railing, she studied Zane as he returned after seeing his sister out. Shoulders drooping, he seemed to carry the weight of the world on his shoulders. Why? Zane obviously cared about his sister.

Angel shook off the desire to help. An afternoon wind fanned nearby palm trees, rattling the stiff-leaved branches. Zane leaned against the outer wall a few feet away in a relaxed pose, hands shoved into the front pockets of his jeans.

"Sorry. I wasn't expecting her," he said.

"I enjoyed meeting her. She looks like you around the eyes and mouth. How close are you in age?"

"Trish is twenty-three. I'm thirteen years older."

"Why the big gap?" she inquired.

"She was a mistake."

Angel took immediate offense at what she considered a cruel description.

"That's mean."

"Whoa." Zane threw a hand up as a stop sign. "I love my baby sister like my next breath. *I* don't think she's a mistake. I meant she was an oops, unplanned."

"Oh. Where does she work?"

"Trish has a small gift shop near Las Olas Boulevard, an older area of Ft. Lauderdale that's been revitalized," he said.

"How long has she had the shop?"

"About three months. She needed to get out from under stressful jobs. Trish is a social butterfly. Loves visiting."

"What type of jobs did she have before?"

He paused then answered a little defensively, "She's worked in several fields. Not everyone finds their calling right off the bat."

Where was that coming from?

"Trish is excited about her shop," he continued. "I try to bring home unusual items for her when I travel."

"Nice to have a business where she can come and go whenever she wants." Angel smiled, hoping to cure whatever sore spot she'd rubbed unintentionally.

A longer pause, then Zane said, "You ask a lot of questions about someone you just met."

Well, that was stupid. Now she'd ticked him off. How had they gotten off on Trish and so badly? "I'm sorry. I was just curious about her. She seems very sweet."

Zane's anger flared and dissipated with the same speed. "No, I'm sorry. Didn't mean to snap at you. I'm a little sensitive when it comes to Trish. Her life hasn't been easy." He stared off into the distance. "My parents gave me every opportunity, but by the time Trish *accidentally* came along, they were tired of child rearing—what little they'd been interested in to begin with. I took off and she got the leftovers."

"Hard knocks in life make you a stronger person. From the sound of it, your sister is probably pretty tough. What do you mean by leftovers?" Seeing a family side of Zane piqued Angel's interest to know more about the man who'd opened his home to her, a stranger. "You said you took off. Where'd you go?"

Even as Zane sheathed his face in a calm expression, pain filled his eyes. "I went into the navy when she turned eight. My father was a partner in an oil refinery. Sold his part around forty-five, retired a very wealthy man and a happy one, until Trish showed up, unexpected. My parents pawned her off on friends and relatives so they could 'enjoy their life.' Like they knew they'd die in a car crash before reaching fifty."

"Zane, I'm so sorry."

"Thanks, but I'm more sorry for Trish."

"She took it hard? Does she—"

"Enough about Trish." He cut her off and moved forward in the same breath. "Now that we've cleared up her history, what's yours?"

Zane consumed her personal space. Anyone else would have backed away in fear. Why she didn't was pause to wonder, but she wasn't afraid of him.

Angel lived her life in tiny moments and didn't want this one to end.

Mere inches separated his face from hers.

The air sucked from the room, her lungs, with him so close. A tornado churned behind the brown eyes drilling a hole into her soul. Balmy ocean air ruffled the leaves of nearby hydrangea bushes and clouds diffused the late-afternoon sun.

His aftershave swirled around her, blending with the salt air to draw her closer. She wanted to erase the stern line of his wonderful mouth. She was close enough to…what?

Angel threw a hand up between them to push herself back.

He moved forward, cutting off any escape.

"Talk to me, Angel. You said I couldn't help. What can someone else do that I can't?" His deep voice hypnotized her.

"Nothing," she whispered. Fatigue allowed her hormones to answer. She couldn't think clearly. His large warm hands stroked slowly up her arms. He leaned forward an inch, their faces only a whisper apart.

She softened her lips in anticipation.

"The truth, Angel, just tell me the truth so I can help you. What kind of trouble are you in?"

That broke the spell.

She jerked out of his grasp, barely reining in her temper. Tell *him* the truth? Why? He'd already pegged her as a criminal.

"The truth is I hope a shower comes with this apartment, because I'd love one right now."

He shifted his jaw. Firm lips compressed into a disgruntled line.

Too bad if he's exasperated. She needed some space, both from him and from life right now.

"You still have the yellow shorts and T-shirt?" Zane asked, resignation in his voice.

"Yes…but I need to wash them."

"Tell you what." He backed up a step, drew a deep breath and continued on the exhale, his words measured and patient. "Give me those, take off what you have on now and drop them outside of the bathroom over there." He pointed down the hall. "Take your time. Soak in the whirlpool if you want while I toss everything in the washer. There's a dispenser with soap and shampoo. Linens are in the tall cabinet. The bottom drawer of the middle cabinet has new toothbrushes, disposable things and assorted female necessities you're welcome to use."

Another woman's things? Was he nuts? What if his girlfriend just showed up during the night?

"I don't know about using someone else's—"

"My sister put that drawer together for when she spends the night here. There's a hair dryer, and whatever, in there. She hates to be alone and, as you witnessed, she shows up whenever."

Sister. Okay. Why did she feel so relieved? Because her stupid hormones were kicking in again.

Digging out her clothes from the linen bag, Angel felt a little strange about handing the bundle to him. When was the last time anyone *had* washed her clothes? She'd done the laundry for herself and her parents at home from the time she was ten years old.

Regardless, she slipped inside the bathroom, peeled off her garments and deposited them outside the door. Every conceivable luxury installed in the luscious bath was decorated in black marble with copper flecks and adorned with copper hardware.

Zane definitely enjoyed the spoils of being a private pilot. His company must do well in spite of poor business sense.

She ran the whirlpool full of scorching water and squirted some bath foam she found in Trish's stash. After sinking tentatively into the hot water, she soaked to the point of wrinkling. No reason to rush if he was washing her clothes, since that would take an hour. The heat permeated deep into her sore body, banishing any thought of hurrying. Nothing matched a hot bath. She leaned back, closed her eyes.

Angel jerked upright, surprised she'd dozed off. She stepped out of the deep tub, over to the beveled-glass shower, washed her hair and rinsed off the suds.

At the wall-to-wall mirror above the vanity, Angel took stock of her unclothed appearance.

Dark half moons hung under her amber eyes. Her body had thinned some from lack of eating and sleeping over the past week. A few yellowish fist-size bruises speckled her back, but an especially ugly one marred her side near where several cuts were starting to heal.

The single redeeming factor was that the battle scars still belonged to a living body.

She brushed the tangles from her hair, disgruntled as the parts that had dried began to curl halfheartedly. She couldn't have curly or straight hair. No, hers was just limp. She'd love to cut it if for no other reason than how cute Trish had looked in short hair, but changed her mind.

Cut it now and she'd have few options if it became necessary to change her appearance again. For the time being she'd stuff her hair under her hat.

No disguise would keep Mason at bay for long. Every hour that went by decreased her chances of remaining free. Locating the coins didn't solve her problems. She had to find a safe place to stay to give her time to track down a respected person who would go to bat for her. Someone had to have seen her running trails the day the coins were stolen. If it came down to just her word, Mason would go free and she'd go to prison.

But the first order of business was to get her hands on the priceless coins again.

The rare Saint Gauden's Double Eagle gold coins had been stolen from the Bolen Gallery in Boston a few weeks ago. Everyone knew that. The news stations still carried sound bites on the theft. She needed the exact time the coins were taken. Armed with that specific information, she'd find someone who remembered a lone female runner on the trails—a person above reproach who would swear under oath that Angel had an ironclad alibi. But how? Run an ad for witnesses?

Deal with one problem at a time.

Find the coins first, verify the alibi next, then cut a deal with the FBI. Until the first two happened, any contact with the law would ensure her a prison sentence. And, if she pulled it off, she'd have Mason's arrogance to thank. Confident no one could get in or out of his armed compound, he never locked a door. He'd displayed the priceless coins along with other stolen art in his office next to the bedroom where she'd been held.

The coins served her well in two ways. They were a recently documented theft with Mason's fingerprints—she'd seen him handle the packages—and nothing else had been as portable.

After wiping down everything she'd touched in Zane's bathroom, Angel stuck her head out the door. "I'm done. Are my clothes dry?"

Silence.

"Hel-loooo. I'm through showering."

Still no answer.

She wrapped a thick towel around her, but it only reached midthigh and barely covered her breasts. Holding the front of the towel with both hands, she tiptoed out to search for the laundry room, which she eventually found next to the kitchen.

Her clean clothes sat folded on top of the dryer.

* * *

Zane heard Angel call out as he finished talking to Ben. Nothing definitive on the High Vision shipment yet. By the time he hung up and checked on Angel, the bathroom was vacant.

He rushed through the kitchen on his way to the laundry room, halting at the knee-to-shoulder café doors separating the rooms.

The body of last night's dreams, barely covered with a towel, came into view.

Good thing the swinging doors separated them or she'd have seen just how much he appreciated what the terry cloth didn't cover.

Angel turned around, wide-eyed, like an animal crossing the highway, frozen by approaching headlights. He should have been merciful enough to return to his bedroom, but the jolt of finding the bathroom empty hadn't passed. He'd been sure she'd grabbed her clothes and left.

"Find everything okay?" he asked in a hoarse voice.

Damp strands of auburn hair licked her shoulders. One wisp clung to her cheek. Drops of water trickled down her slender neck to the slight crevice created by two soft mounds of ivory breast.

Man oh man, following that trickle with his tongue would be heaven.

"I have to get dressed." She held the wad of clothes close to her chest.

The desperation in her voice got through to him. She didn't need some guy leering at her after all she'd been through. And he didn't even know everything she'd been through.

"Sorry, I heard you call, but I was on the phone. I'll wait in the front room," Zane offered and backed out while the sound of her scampering from the kitchen to the bathroom swooshed behind him. By the time the door closed, his response to her half-clothed body was at rock-hard attention. If she dressed slowly enough, he'd be at ease by the time she got back.

Where had his renowned control gone? He'd never been so…so…turned on, dammit. This was ridiculous. He'd had his fair share of knockout women. Angel wasn't even a knockout, he argued to himself. To begin with, she was too thin.

Okay, she was actually trim and well toned. But her eyes were too big for her face. Big, round, soft eyes like a doe flushed in the woods, and then her lashes would lower to half-mast when her guard was down or she smiled.

Oh man, she had a heart-stopping smile and legs…good Lord, what a set.

Zane groaned. He started to get hard again and she wasn't even in the room.

He had the discipline of a goat.

Shaking his head, he wandered into the kitchen. Maybe another bottle of cold water would help—poured over him.

If that didn't do the trick, then remembering that he hadn't ruled out the possibility she was a criminal should douse any flames of desire.

By the time Angel returned, he'd cloaked his emotions under a veil of polite indifference.

She eyed him warily when she stepped into the room.

It dawned on him she hadn't given him any underwear.

Don't go there.

Accustomed to women with elaborate makeup and chic hairstyles, he found her undecorated appearance and combed hair refreshingly attractive. He particularly liked the soft, barely there curls showing up as her hair air dried.

He gritted his teeth. Polite indifference, remember?

Got it.

Back to wearing the cotton shirt and jeans, she rolled up the sleeves at her wrists. "Thanks for letting me use your bath. I feel much better." A loud growl from her stomach cut her off.

"Sounds like you're ready for dinner." He wondered when she'd last eaten. "Give me a minute to freshen up and we'll grab a bite," He wanted to check the bathroom before they went anywhere.

Zane closed the door to the bathroom then squatted to view the counter and faucets. Every inch had been wiped clean. He lifted the water bottle she'd tossed into the trash basket, but knew when he felt the damp label he'd find no fingerprints there, either.

She was good.

No problem. He had the perfect place to eat. The owner would supply him with her entire set of tableware if he asked.

In the living room, Angel stood planted in the middle of the room gazing out the glass doors. Was she so uncomfortable around the strange environment that she wouldn't sit down on the leather furniture?

Or was she so careful not to leave a print?

"Ready?" he asked.

Wariness shadowed her eyes when she turned to answer. "Can't we just order a pizza?"

"I know a great little Italian restaurant, really a hole in the wall. Only locals go there. They make the best pizza, but you should try their lasagna."

She slumped, obviously tired. Once he fed her a good meal, she'd probably sleep like the dead.

Angel cut her eyes around to the glass doors. Purple twilight shrouded the beach under a setting sun. The cover of dark must have been a key to her decision.

"Okay. If it's not too expensive," she mumbled.

"I'll buy dinner. Consider it a bonus for pacifying Suarez today."

"Just a minute." She retrieved her hat and bag, twisted her hair up and shoved the hat on. "I'm ready."

Hat or not, he'd recognize that body. Who did she hope to outfox? He herded her to the truck, curious if tomorrow would bring good or bad news once he received the fingerprint results.

Tomorrow would be soon enough to worry about that.

In the four miles to the restaurant, the scenery deteriorated from snazzy to shabby. While he described how the area had changed in a mere three years, Angel rode in silence, hands in her lap touching nothing. Her discipline was impressive, but at the same time disconcerting.

He wheeled into a run-down strip mall with one big store in the center surrounded by small eclectic retail shops. Once a high-end grocery store, the cavernous anchor of the center now housed a sprawling flea market. Zane parked in front of De Nikki's. He opened her door and she stepped down, her eyes cautiously flicking about.

Inside the restaurant, a rotund Nikki, with a salt-and-pepper handlebar mustache, greeted Zane like a lost cousin. The crowd was heavy for an early Thursday night. Must have something to do with it being just before Labor Day weekend.

As Nikki directed them to a small table in the back, Zane almost ran over Angel, who abruptly ended her forward progress. He caught her shoulders to keep from knocking her down.

"What's wrong?" he asked.

Something had pricked her attention. He scoped the entire room of people in a matter of seconds, but nothing appeared out of place.

The smile she offered him was counteracted by the apprehension in her eyes.

"Sorry. I stumbled." She turned to Nikki. "Where's your ladies' room?"

Nikki pointed to the far side of the entrance. "To the left of the front door, next to the hostess stand."

Zane didn't want to let her out of his sight, but what could he do? He'd sound ridiculous telling her not to go, especially while Nikki listened. When she backed away, he caught her by the arm.

"Are you okay?"

"I'm fine." She didn't look fine. Something had rattled her. Or someone.

"Please, Zane, people are staring." Angel slipped from his hold and walked quickly back the way they'd come then scooted around the hostess stand into the ladies' room.

He gave the dining room another once-over before going to wait for her at the hostess stand. Nothing unusual stood out. Who knew? Women always had something going on men didn't understand. He might be reading more into this than he should.

Nikki waddled up to Zane. "Is there a problem, Mr. Zane?"

Before he answered, Zane waited until a stockily built middle-aged man in a gunmetal-gray suit stepped past them on his way to the front door. He gave the man a second look then grimaced at the direction of his thoughts. Here he was acting suspicious of Nikki's clientele when in actuality Angel was the dubious one. He turned to answer Nikki.

"No. My friend hasn't felt well and I'm a little concerned. I'll wait to see how she's doing before we sit down."

"Oh, poor thing. Not a problem. You just tell me if you want something to go and we fix it up for you."

"Thanks, Nikki. Oh, one more thing. Is that the only door in and out of the bathroom?"

Nikki gave him a quizzical look. "Yes. That is it."

Ten minutes later, Zane's patience was spent. He asked Nikki to send a waitress in to check on Angel.

The woman returned immediately, wide-eyed and confused. "The bathroom is empty."

Chapter 6

Zane pounded the steering wheel in his truck.

What could have spooked Angel?

He'd been confident she couldn't get past him. He knew the men's room had no other way out than the door used to enter. Unfortunately, an exterior wall on one side of the ladies' room held two old-fashioned crank-out windows, which she'd managed to slip through.

His chest tightened at the thought of her alone again on the streets. The change of clothes helped to camouflage her, but she'd been worried about spending money on food. How far could she travel on limited funds?

Another aggravating thought hit him.

He still didn't have a fingerprint. Damn.

Zane started methodically cruising streets around the area. Maybe she'd run a sufficient distance to feel safe and stop. If she saw his truck, he wanted to believe she'd trust him enough to come out from hiding.

Trust him? She didn't trust him at all or she'd tell him who was chasing her.

He drove slowly through the residential sections near the restaurant, up and down backstreets. Solitary streetlights illuminated crossroads, but not much else. She could be anywhere within the unlit maze of thirty-year-old homes adorned with enormous vegetation.

No lost female flagged him down.

An hour later, he quit the hunt, frustrated at losing her a second time. His own stomach growling, he picked up a pizza on his way home. A mild wind blew through the silent parking lot of his complex as he locked the truck. He stepped into the breezeway covering his apartment entrance and froze.

Slumped on the mat next to his front door, asleep and unharmed, was Angel. For the second time that day, relief flooded through him.

He should shake her until her teeth rattled for the anxiety she'd put him through. Curled up in a ball with her cap halfcocked, she looked so vulnerable that all he wanted to do was wrap her in his arms, tuck her close and keep her safe.

Placing the pizza on the ledge beside the door, he eased down next to Angel. He ran the back of his finger lightly along her baby-soft cheek, inhaling the fresh smell of shampoo, no mousse, no spray, just plain shampoo—a sexy scent on her.

She stirred. Two exhausted amber eyes peered up at him, looking as relieved as he felt.

He spoke softly, not wanting to startle her. "I was worried about you. Where did you go?"

She mumbled something that sounded like, "A guy stared. Didn't know, um, had to go. Sorry, don't worry."

Her eyes fluttered a couple times. She was beat. There was no run left in her. She must have traveled the four miles back on foot. He snaked his arm around her waist to lift her to a standing position, grabbing the pizza with the other hand.

"Come on, Angel, you need to sleep."

She let him lead her forward, but once inside she stopped, shook her head and said, "I'd really like another shower."

The back of her blouse was damp from her exertions. He'd seen no other clothes than the running outfit she'd worn when he first met her.

"Sure. I'll give you one of my T-shirts to sleep in and we'll throw your clothes back in the washer," he said.

"Thanks. I'm sorry to be so much trouble."

"Honey, it's no trouble, but I wish you'd tell me what's going on."

She smiled, the shy expression too sweet to be criminal. "I don't want you to get mixed up in this mess. You've been so nice to me. I owe you that."

He sighed. She was whipped, and he hadn't slept much during the last two weeks. Any questions would keep until tomorrow.

"I'll get you the T-shirt."

Zane sat at the counter sifting through mail when Angel walked into the kitchen fresh from her shower. She wore his pale blue cotton T-shirt with a redfish busting a wave on the front. It hung halfway down her thighs.

Nothing else, just her and the T-shirt, he knew it.

Warning signals screamed from his professional side. No one wiped their fingerprints clean everywhere they went. She ran from a rough group. He'd caught her digging through the storage room looking for something he'd bet played a major role in her tenuous situation.

His mission should be clear—determine her identity and find out if she was tangled up in anything illegal.

He visually skimmed the creamy skin not covered by the T-shirt, wanting to cover the same area with his hands.

She didn't fit the picture of a felon. Damp hair framed her face. A soapy-clean fragrance filled the air between them. His eyes trailed down the two enticing legs that spanned the break between shirttail and floor.

There were dozens of reasons he should keep an emotional wall between the two of them.

But right now he didn't want a wall between them.

Hell, he didn't want that T-shirt between the two of them and couldn't ignore the inappropriate thought pounding in his brain.

The only thought firing every cell in his brain.

He wanted her. Bad.

"Pizza smells good." She raised her eyebrows, waiting to be invited.

"Sure. Here." He fumbled with the box like a schoolboy caught staring. "Want it heated?"

"Nuh-uh. It's perfect." She picked up a slice and proceeded to devour it as if he'd served her beluga caviar. She licked her rosy lips after each bite, the pink tongue destroying his state of mind.

He finally broke loose a slice and lifted it to his mouth to save himself from any further fantasizing. She'd wiped out three slices by the time he finished one, but he'd lost his appetite—for pizza.

"I'm ready for bed," she said.

Dangerous visual. He was also tired, but had serious doubts that he'd actually rest knowing she slept within the same walls—wearing next to nothing. Before he could dislodge that image, she interrupted his thoughts with a suggestion.

"If the foldout has sheets, I'm set."

No way. If she slept that close to the front door she'd turn into smoke and float out through the keyhole.

He cleared his throat. "You sleep in the bedroom. I've got buddies who come by unannounced sometimes. You don't want to be out here if one of them shows up." He could tell she didn't believe him, but what argument could she offer?

Angel finished her pizza and cleaned her area with the efficiency of a compulsive cleaner. Could that explain the neatnik personality? Maybe she had a germ phobia.

Yeah, sure.

At the door to his bedroom, he watched her climb between the sheets. Silky hair trailed across the pillow as she rolled onto her side with a whispered "Good night."

A painful throb pumped in his groin. Zane drew the door almost shut.

How in the hell was he supposed to sleep with that image crawling through his spent brain? He rolled his shoulders, loosening taut muscles. Did nothing for the one part of his body that needed it most. Fatigue would save him. He always slept hard the first night home.

Not tonight.

He got up and down during the night to confirm she still slept in his bed. With each check he made she'd shifted to a different position, leaving less and less sheet covering her.

The last time he peered through the slightly ajar door, a band of moonlight beamed over her backside from the break in the drapes. She lay facedown on her stomach. The T-shirt had ridden up to her waist from tossing about.

Oh man, he'd been right. No underwear.

Feeling like some lowlife voyeur, he forced himself back to the foldout to struggle through the few hours left until daylight.

Mason answered his cell phone. "Lorde."

"M.L., I've got some news."

"Good news, I hope." Mason was in neither a patient nor forgiving mood. But one man had never failed him. If anyone could find his gold coins and the bitch who stole them, C.K. could.

"It's all in how you look at it. The hot little number I'm tracking for you has gone south."

"How far south?" This *was* good news if his bounty hunter had Angel's trail. Mason could always depend on him to find anyone, anywhere. Would love to know how he did it, but didn't particularly care as long as the tracker didn't fail.

"Way down, but not quite to the Keys," C.K. answered.

Florida. Why would she go there? Her background checks had been thorough. Angel's parents were dead. She had no siblings, didn't even list a next of kin when he'd hired her.

The year in jail had played in her favor, though she hadn't known it at the time. She'd been thrilled that he'd hired her in spite of a jaded background. Had told him so then proceeded to become his best employee, busting her butt above and beyond in every aspect of her job.

He'd been certain she'd play ball once he brought her into the organization. Who'd have expected an ex-con to possess an honest streak?

"M.L., you want the problem handled when it lands in one spot?"

"No. Just keep her in sight until we find out where she took my collection. Then I'll deal with her."

Mason didn't want anyone to touch her. She was his alone. He'd wanted her from the first minute she walked into his warehouse. Planned to take her at the compound, if she hadn't forced him to teach her humility after her first attempt to flee. Silly twit. Useless for days after that, she was unconscious most of the time. When he found her this time, he'd bring her to heel, but with enough restraint so she was fully lucid when he buried himself inside her.

"M.L., you there?"

"Pinpoint the exact location and confine the problem, then contact me. I'll deal with it personally."

"You got it."

The first glimmer of dawn burst through the separation in the drapes to wake Angel from a troubled sleep. Men with guns and dogs had invaded her rest. Her feet were tangled in the covers. Caught in her nightmares, she'd struggled to move beyond a snail's pace as Mason's ice-blue eyes and sneering lips floated through the terrifying scenes.

She climbed out of the gigantic bed, shivering at the repulsive thought of Mason touching her again. Angel arched and stretched her stiff muscles. Her roving gaze landed on a framed photo on the teak chest across the room. Using the tail of her T-shirt as a barrier against touching the frame, she carried the photo to the window.

She angled the picture under the light. A much younger Zane hugged a teenage Trish dressed in a graduation gown. Pride was evident in his wide grin. Trish had been blessed with the devotion of a protective brother. What would it have been like to be watched over by a strong protective male while growing up?

All Angel could credit her father with had been to feed and clothe the three of them. He'd been more a stranger than a parent. She'd never questioned his late-night security work. Not until a detective charged her with delivering drugs for her father, then snapped handcuffs on her wrists. A few months later she got a crash course in the desolate world behind bars.

Honesty had always been her policy, but the detective had shown her the fallacy in that way of thinking. She'd spilled her insides, answering every inquiry he put to her. Then he gave the tape recording to the district attorney who used her as another notch in his political belt.

Her first hard lesson in life had been simple. Don't trust a man, particularly if he wore a badge.

Angel replaced the photo and slipped through a door connecting the bathroom to Zane's bedroom. A haggard face stared back at her from the mirror. She twisted her hair into a knot on top of her head while she waited for the air-conditioning to kick on again. The pleasant hum of the cooling system would cover any noise she'd make attending to her personal needs and dressing.

Trish's large vanity drawer was filled with a stash of hair clips and lotions. When Angel found a bottle of plum-colored nail polish she had the sudden urge to primp.

The last time she'd dolled up had been in high school. As a lanky teen, taller than most of the boys, she'd been more at home on the track than on a date. Her one serious relationship had lasted two weeks. Just long enough to lose her virginity to the boy who first swore his love then revoked that decree by sleeping with Angel's only girlfriend.

Her nails needed help, but plum polish wouldn't save them. She hadn't worn makeup since getting out of jail, preferring to project a clear "not-interested" message to men in general.

As she looked back now, where Mason had considered her a challenge, most men had heeded her unspoken missive, allowing her a wide berth—until Zane.

Tall, sexy, imposing Zane.

More than once, desire flared in Zane's eyes. He worked to keep his emotions hidden beneath a professional facade, but some reactions were too strong for anyone to shield.

Other women might be put off by a man his size walking his eyes up and down their torso, but for the first time in many years she'd been flattered. Her feminine side wanted to know what those suggestive gazes offered, longed to meet him halfway.

A sense of purpose trampled her fantasies. Her attraction to Zane was blurring her sight of goals one and two—survival and vindication. She rolled her eyes. Wasn't it time to stop being a fool? A man had gotten her into this mess, getting involved with another one wouldn't solve her problems.

Enough daydreaming. She owed Zane for a good night's sleep, but she'd have to find a way to pay it back some other time. Staying would only expose him to Mason's retaliation.

She peeked out the door to the living room to confirm he still slept, before padding to the laundry room where she changed to the sunny-yellow running shorts, jog top and T-shirt. Angel plopped the limp hat over her ponytail-clasped hair.

Her Annie Hall look, as Zane had tagged her, had failed to

fool a middle-aged man in a gray suit at the restaurant. She'd barely caught his blink in surprise when they'd entered. His expression had shuttered back to bored so fast she'd have missed the minute change had she not been intentionally searching the room for a note of recognition.

She could have imagined the brief facial change, the surprise that lit his eyes for a second, but Angel didn't think so. If it *was* one of Mason's men and she hung around, Zane might get hurt.

Mason's gang of muscle showed no mercy to anyone who got in their way. Hopefully, the man in the restaurant had followed her instead of Zane, but he would have had to been fleet of foot to keep up.

More than fleet of foot, he'd have needed a faster marathon time than hers. Angel's last one matched the Tamarind Triathlon record holder, convincing her she had a shot this year. Just placing in the top three would begin to restore her ravaged self-esteem, let her believe in a future. Not now.

No triathlon. No future. Just survival.

She jammed jeans and shirt into the shoulder bag.

Zane had washed her clothes—twice. Such a small thing, but not to her. Not after living in a world with men who would scoff at performing that chore for a woman.

No man was like Zane. None she'd ever met.

What a welcome sight he'd been when she opened her eyes outside the apartment last night. He threw her off balance changing from roaring bear to the kindest male she'd ever encountered. A complete gentleman...until she'd walked into the kitchen clad in his shirt.

Then he'd stripped her visually.

For the first time since naively giving away her virginity, she hadn't wanted to run from a man's interest. Her skin vibrated when he entered her space, at the mere thought of his touch. The strong desire to kiss him yesterday scared her. Need was a dangerous weakness. She hadn't needed anyone's kiss, touch, help.

But one minute they were discussing Trish and the next all she could think about was what his lips would feel like. How would he taste?

Angel pinched the bridge of her nose. Go, go, go before she did something stupid like give Mason a reason to kill a decent man.

She tiptoed to the front door, running shoes in hand.

Zane slept with a white undershirt covering his broad chest, a mat of black hair curled at the scoop neck. One rope-muscled thigh poked out from under the thin sheet covering his lower half.

The man was pure sex wrapped up in a steel casing.

She smiled sadly then mouthed the words "You're sweet…. Bye," and blew a kiss.

Zane flicked one eyelid open just wide enough to catch Angel's air kiss as the door closed. He dashed to the bedroom, thankful he'd worn a shirt and shorts to bed for her benefit. Not having to dress saved him enough time to shorten the gap between them. He laced his running shoes and raced out the door.

He hit the sidewalk just in time to see her turn south down the main highway. Brilliant rays of sun pierced the ruby horizon above the ocean on his left, highlighting her slender shape in the distance.

Angel's stride lengthened to a loping jog.

Where could she be going?

He'd intentionally let her go, thinking he'd follow and find a clue to her situation. Keeping a safe space between them, his mind worked through the possibilities, starting with the obvious—criminal intent.

Was she meeting someone? He tried to convince himself she ran because of fear, but then logic would raise its ugly head to laugh in his face.

Hard as he tried, attributing the lack of fingerprints to a compulsive cleaner was a stretch under the best circumstances.

Sweat trickled down his back from the rising humidity. He maintained a steady pace over the first mile. Few people stirred so early. He ducked behind cars and bushes to stay out of view when she glanced around.

Angel's quick head checks changed his mind. She wasn't meeting anyone, but avoiding someone.

She cut across the street then took a sharp corner. Twice she made a complete loop to end up somewhere she'd already passed. He didn't understand at first, but finally grasped that she was backtracking to circle behind someone who might be following.

He had too much experience to be tricked that way.

Angel slowed near a heavy business district, rotating her head, definitely scanning her surroundings. The street traffic picked up on the four-lane–divided highway Zane traversed behind her. He was beginning to wonder how long she'd hold this pace, when the screech of tires against asphalt disrupted the morning peace.

At the sound of a vehicle braking hard, Angel stumbled and spun around.

A black Land Rover. No identifying logo on the side, but she didn't need a gold triangle to confirm she was in trouble.

Angel spun away. Pedestrians impeded her progress as she wove in and out of the small groups ambling along the sidewalks. Bumping bodies, she shouted curt apologies then dashed through the middle of an intersection, dodging cars as she sprinted against traffic.

She headed east toward the beach—wide space, hard to follow her by vehicle. Rounding a corner, she stumbled to a stop.

Either the buildings were lined up too tight, with one fence connected to the next, or the land was so sparse it offered nowhere to hide. She stood out like a caution flag in a car race.

Spotting an opening to the beach between two towering condominiums farther down, she decided to gamble and plowed through the soft dunes toward the surf. The hot breath of fear clogged her lungs. Wading through the deep sand conjured the image of sinking in a quicksand pit. She whipped her head around, expecting a black sport utility to fly airborne over the dunes, a la Hollywood.

On the other side of the dunes, the sand firmed under her feet. Better traction meant speed.

Miles of shimmering beach stretched in both directions bordered by the rolling ocean on one side and an endless row of skyscraping structures on the other. She churned her legs fast, heading south.

Flying along the packed surface, she could only hope to outdistance Mason's men. She certainly hadn't outwitted them. This would only last so long. She might outrun his goons, but no legs could beat the speed of radios and cell phones.

She passed a group of shirtless old men surf fishing. A loose shoelace slapped one ankle. Way down the beach, tiny people speckled the wide shoreline. None were running toward her with guns drawn. She stopped and squatted to retie the shoelace, sucking in air, preparing for the next sprint.

Her fingers deftly performed the task while her eyes swept over the beach. She started to rise, when a *ping* sounded. Sand blasted up next to her foot.

That was all it took to turn on her afterburners.

Angel charged away from the surf with the speed of a missile seeking a target, angling toward the protection of the buildings and highway. She hadn't moved this fast since the last time she'd been in a dead-heat finish at a 10K road race. Her heart beat painfully against her breastbone, but not from exertion.

No, this was bone-deep fear.

Would Mason kill her without getting the coins back first?

She'd never considered that possibility, but hadn't thought his men would take a shot at her—unless they assumed she carried the coins on her body.

At the ocean side of a high-rise condominium, she slowed to work her way around the fence circling the pool area. A driveway separated this condo from the next one. She scampered down the paved path to a connecting parking lot.

At the only obvious hiding spot, between a tour van and a late-model Cadillac, Angel ducked low to hide while she got her bearings.

She forced herself to breathe slower, to quiet her panting.

A car cruised by slowly. She raised her head above the sedan hood to see a two-lane road with vacant structures and local retail businesses scattered among souvenir shops. None were open for business yet.

She had to keep moving until she found a suitable place to hide. An abandoned building was her best bet for cover until nightfall.

Three well-tanned senior citizens picked their way down the sidewalk, a block south from where she hid. From the north, a cocoa-skinned teenage girl in tights pumped weights, speed walking toward Angel on the same side of the street.

As the girl passed her, Angel casually slipped in behind, then dashed across the thoroughfare at the nearest intersection.

She turned down an alley next to a long derelict brick building and grabbed the first door.

It was locked tight. She rushed farther down and tried two more. No good. The last one gave when she yanked. With a quick look behind her, she stepped inside.

She stumbled through debris on the floor until her eyes adjusted. Angel wrinkled her nose at the mildew-tinged air. Shafts of light pierced through cracks in the disintegrating roof. This had potential.

Noises echoed through the hollow structure. She stopped.

Potential, but maybe not ideal.

Scurrying sounds wafted through the stagnant air from different directions. The place was probably a breeding ground for every imaginable critter. Domestic animals weren't a concern, but her time in jail had only amplified a healthy fear of rats.

Flashes of light beaconed from a door swinging half off of squeaking hinges on the far side of the narrow building. Every noise encouraged her to search for a better hideout. She picked her way to the opening, waited for several heartbeats and peeked out to make sure the coast was clear. Then she was moving again.

A narrow street ran adjacent to the rear of the buildings like a back-door access road. Two boxy produce trucks were being unloaded at a grocer's a block away to her right.

She eased to her left, away from the activity. A wooden barricade connected the next two buildings, blocking any exit there.

Her pulse raced at staying exposed so long. It would take a helicopter to keep up with her twisting route, but she still felt like an exposed duck on opening day of hunting season.

Single-story homes, knitted together with chain-link fences, filled the other side of the backstreet.

A German shepherd barked from inside a boundary.

She jumped, cursing her case of rattled nerves, but the last thing she needed was an animal pointing out her position.

The sound of footsteps on gravel nearby froze her. She started to go, then stopped.

Which way should she go? Her pulse spiked. The longer she stood paralyzed in indecision, the better chance of being captured.

Survival instincts took over. She ran in short bursts, casting a hasty look over her shoulder, and paused behind a stack of tires at the rear of an abandoned gas station. Her heart raced, every breath coming in painful bursts.

She fought to keep the panic at bay, but couldn't ignore the truth.

Mason would eventually kill her.

Her options were disintegrating into thin air. She didn't have a clue where she was or how to get out of Ft. Lauderdale. Her hands shook as she swiped perspiration away from her eyes. The hat had flown off, somewhere. She could feel her hair hanging loose on one side.

It didn't matter. She hadn't fooled the gunman.

Her heart pounded a jungle beat. Hands shaking, she picked her way around the garbage-strewn rear of the gas station and peered down a wall shrouded in thick green ivy vines. Next door, clumps of thorny sandspur plants covered the vacant lot, offering no protection.

The derelict gas station looked to be her best choice for a hideout. There were several doorway openings not completely overtaken by the verdant growth of vines spidering over the whitewashed concrete block structure. She felt her way along the wall with trembling fingers, eased toward the street, sticking tight as a shadow to the building.

Yellow shoes and a bright yellow shirt—some shadow.

As she passed the first two openings—dilapidated exterior bathrooms—she gave each an obligatory glance then held her breath against the urine stench and moved on.

She considered ducking into the next open doorway to what must have been the waiting area of the service station at one time. Tall half-broken glass windows stretched from the other side of the doorway to wrap around the front.

Damn. She couldn't hide there.

In her haste to reach the street, she assumed no one would stand inside, exposed by the glass.

She was wrong.

Just as she cleared the door, a massive hand covered her mouth. A powerful arm encircled her chest and jerked her inside.

He had her.

Chapter 7

"Shh. It's me, Zane."

Angel slumped against his chest.

Zane switched his hold from one of capture and restraint to support and comfort. He moved his hand away from her mouth to cup her face, lowering his thumb to stroke along her neck.

Her heart hammered under his arm. Her breathing rushed out in gasps.

She'd had the hell scared out of her.

He'd had the hell scared out of him, too.

Following her had been challenge enough. His heart had lurched up into his throat when the bullet barely missed her. It took everything he could muster to catch her when she'd torn away at world-class speed.

Why hadn't the shooter gone for her body? The shot hit too far in front of her to have been aimed for the bulk of the target.

Had the shooter meant to kill or only wound?

Who in the hell was after her? The bullet could have just as easily entered her head as the ground next to her shoe.

Her body quaked against his chest. Trying to calm her, he rubbed her arm, still glistening from her exertion. Before he thought, Zane brushed his lips over her hair. He'd love to bury his face in the soft mass, a welcome improvement over the dank room they hid within. Weeds fought refuse for floor space.

Zane expelled a breath of pent-up anxiety.

An eternity had passed after seeing her head toward the gas station. He'd hurried to reach it first then stood in the doorway, worried he'd guessed wrong and she was gone, permanently. His usual calm had almost deserted him. He'd been seconds from bolting out of the building to search for her, when the flash of yellow passed the doorway.

Zane folded her closer, enjoying the feel of her body next to his, safe and alive, for the moment.

Just as soon as he got her somewhere secure, she'd get an earful from him. Expecting patience at this point was too much. She'd tell him who was chasing her and why. No more cat-and-mouse games.

The thought of anyone harming Angel raised his ugly side. He'd left his share of casualties over the years, but he'd never intentionally hurt anyone who hadn't deserved it. The next person to put a mark on Angel would land on top of his physical-retribution list.

First he had to get her out of here—alive.

It took him a minute to realize she struggled against his hold. When he loosened his grip she turned to face him.

Fear for her life had him ready to unleash his frustration, until she raised tear-rimmed eyes to him. She shook from head to toe. One side of her hair drooped to her shoulders, while the other remained in a badly twisted knot. Her crimson face attested to the effort she'd expended in flight.

Her eyes searched his. She obviously waited for judgment, a naked plea for understanding written across her face.

His heart twisted. He lived in a world of good guys and bad guys, mostly bad. Until he met Angel, knowing who wore the black hats had been a simple process.

Every logical neuron in his being placed her with the bad guys. His heart begged to differ and defend her honor.

Therein lay the problem. His heart didn't have a good track record.

Her bottom lip quivered.

Ignoring the debate raging between intellect and emotion, Zane pulled her protectively to his chest. Her sleek body fit perfectly next to his.

An old man, leaning on a cane, strolled past the front of their hideout, tapping the ground as he went.

Zane shifted her deeper into the shadows. He scanned the surroundings beyond the dingy glass windows for any sign of threat. When nothing ominous moved along the silent street he returned his attention to Angel.

She tilted her head back. Her lips parted as though she meant to speak, but she nibbled on her bottom lip instead. Her breathing eased to an even rhythm, rubbing firm breasts against his chest with each inhale.

Heat bulleted through him with each slight movement.

He swallowed.

Her lips parted a tiny bit more. The pink tip of her tongue left a wet trail across the cinnamon lips. He stared into the depths of eyes the color of fine bourbon. Time slowed.

At that moment, nothing could have stopped him from dropping his head down.

He kissed her, gently, tasting the salty sweetness of Angel's lips. She hesitated at first then moved into his arms. Her hands pushed up his back to hook around each shoulder, anchoring him tighter.

The simple action was trust of the most basic level and it fed his hunger for her.

Teasing and experimental at first, the kiss turned bolder

when his tongue slid in to caress hers and explore the smooth inside. She tormented him with her delicate tongue. Muscles along his shoulders rippled with each needy grip of her fingers.

His fingers roamed under the back of her damp shirt to caress every creamy inch of smooth skin. He slid a hand down to her waist, snugging her closer into him.

Desire pounded in his brain, pulsed in his groin, but something deeper clawed around inside him. A primal need to protect and care for a woman?

Maybe. Not just any woman. *This* one.

Why this one?

Damn if he knew and right now didn't particularly care to examine why.

He tore his mouth from hers to explore the sensitive skin along her neck. She purred against his chest, flexing up like a kitten in need of cuddles.

With one hand, he pushed under the front strap of her tight running top to graze her nipple with his thumb.

She arched forward against him, igniting a fiery blaze that threatened to engulf both of them. His arousal throbbed against the two thin layers of nylon separating them, sending a clear message.

He wanted her.

A horn blew outside, startling both of them, and broke through the erotic haze.

Zane gritted his teeth. Dammit all. What the hell was wrong with him? Some maniac stalked her and he'd dropped his guard.

Another minute and he'd have dropped his pants.

His self-control was disgusting. No, his lack of self-control.

He withdrew his entangled hands, but held her by the shoulders when she swayed. Passion glazed over her eyes. Damn if that didn't stroke his ego, repair the dent she'd put there by not trusting him to help her.

Her lips were soft, puffy from being kissed, begging for another round.

She blinked, pushed away. Both confusion and surprise darted through her eyes. When her lips parted to speak, he shook his head.

Her delicate eyebrows knitted together in irritation before she finally nodded her understanding to be quiet.

Blowing out a frustrated breath, he scoped the exterior activity. By the amount of daylight, he guessed the time to be around seven o'clock. A young boy rode past on a tangerine bicycle, oblivious to any danger lurking nearby.

Zane leaned close to her ear, his lips in her hair when he spoke. "We're moving out. Stay close to me."

"No."

Wrong answer.

"The last time you said that I had a gun shoved in my face. Do as I say. We'll discuss this later."

He pinned her tight against his chest in an unspoken order to cooperate. Until she was safe, they did it his way. No discussion.

She yanked hard on the back of his shirt. The scowl he gave her didn't seem to deter her at all, because she pushed up on her toes. The stubborn woman seemed determined to say her piece.

Zane lowered his ear close to Angel's mouth, fully expecting the berating he deserved for behaving like a hormonal teen.

"Let me go ahead," she whispered. "I had an…incident on the beach. Someone is following me. It's risky for you to be with me. I'll meet you somewhere."

Zane couldn't believe his ears. Unarmed, wearing clothes bright enough to stand out in any crowd, she was trying to shield *him*. He'd left the apartment without a weapon, but, armed or not, he was trained to deal with any situation.

Unfortunately, she didn't know that and he couldn't risk blowing his cover to tell her.

Now what?

He tucked her head close to his shoulder and whispered, "I know all the back ways out of here. If someone is following you, they won't see us. Trust me."

Angel drew back. Myriad emotions crossed her face, none of which appeared to be trust. What had she been through not to trust the man who'd come to her aid twice, expecting nothing in return?

Liar. He'd been seriously close to undressing her only minutes ago.

Zane rubbed her back lightly and gave her shoulders a reassuring squeeze. He took her hand, leading her outside before she could resist his help.

She never stumbled as he scuttled them through a maze of narrow passageways, taking several diversions in and out of vacated buildings. Though he'd traveled miles following her, she'd circled so much they weren't far from his apartment. In less than an hour, they stood at his front door.

In his rush to leave, Zane left the apartment unlocked. Any other time he wouldn't be concerned, but that was before someone had taken a shot at Angel.

He hesitated with indecision for several seconds. The last thing he wanted was to expose Angel to a hidden danger, but he'd learned better than to let her out of his sight.

Pushing the door open slowly, he glanced around the corner at his unmade foldout bed. Frigid air seeped from the opening. When Zane stepped inside, Angel tried to move next to him, but he swung her close to his back and kept an iron grip on her wrist. Room to room, he eased through the house until he was convinced no one waited inside for them.

In the living room, he rounded on her. Arms crossed, feet apart, he was ready for answers. "Okay, enough of these charades. What's going on?"

"I told you."

"You said you had an arrangement that went sour," he pressed. "This looks much worse than a simple disagreement. Who is this guy and what does he want?"

Angel wrapped her arms around her chest and moved away

from him to stand in front of the terrace doors. "I can't tell you." She sounded as disappointed as he felt.

"Then explain why you can't."

She spun around to answer, hair swatting her face. "Don't you understand? He's a dangerous man. In fact, he's deadly. I *have* to go. If he finds me with you he'll—"

"He'll what?" Zane interrupted.

"He'll hurt us both. I couldn't live with it if I were the reason something happened to you."

Her distress was sincere. This hunted woman put his safety ahead of her own.

It happened again. The lines between black and white blurred a little more.

He'd always been the toughest kid in his class, never bested by an adversary, from football to martial arts training. He'd been his sister's protector, his squadron's leader and the front man in the High Vision drug-smuggling investigation.

No one had ever stood between him and the enemy.

He'd learned to defend himself at a young age both physically and emotionally with no one to rise to his defense. The depth of her concern pushed him into turbulent emotional territory, with no navigational charts.

In the same breath she refused to answer his questions—which aggravated him beyond reason—then confused him with her selfless consideration for his safety.

His world to this point had been simple.

Everyone was either guilty or innocent.

Not knowing on which side of the law Angel stood was giving him hell. If he could share his background, she'd understand he was better equipped to deal with the threat.

Somehow, he sensed it wouldn't change her mind, strange as that seemed.

Convincing her to go to the police might be his best recourse after all. The longer he delayed, the higher her risk was of injury or capture by the wrong people.

"Angel, since this guy is so dangerous, why don't you go to the police?"

Her eyes flashed an immediate negative before she said, "No! They wouldn't understand."

"*What* would they not understand? There are laws to protect women from men who stalk and brutalize them."

"It's complicated."

He got that bad feeling again, the one that told him she hid something not quite kosher. By the end of the day, he would have a fingerprint, if he had to tie her down to get it.

Zane's cell phone rang in the distance. "Don't move." He retrieved the palm-size phone. His pulse jumped when he recognized the task-force number set up as his charter-delivery dispatcher. This had to be a call to fly.

What was he going to do with Angel?

He stood where he could keep an eye on her from the doorway while he answered.

"Make it quick," Zane said.

"Sammy, here." Samuel Jenkins was the agent on his team who coordinated flights for the bogus Black Jack Airlines. "You've got a pickup at Bentley Field in south Georgia for High Vision this afternoon. Has to arrive in Ft. Lauderdale in time for a transfer to Miami by 1900."

"I didn't think they had a branch in that area."

"They don't. The chief financial officer has a home on Saint Simon's Island," Sammy clarified.

Zane checked the clock on the microwave. Making the run was no problem, but he didn't want to let Angel out of his sight.

"I can be there by one o'clock. Is this a *special* load?" Intelligence informed central office of any shipments that were suspect. If today's delivery was other than a standard shipment to keep his cover intact, he couldn't take her along.

"Negative. All we've been told is it's a hot shipment from the CFO's wife, something personal. They'll let you inspect it before loading. Supposedly it's smaller than a three-by-three crate, but based on the insurance binder, the cargo carries a high price tag."

Zane checked his watch. "I'll confirm delivery by 1700."

"Ten-four."

Zane snapped the phone shut.

Angel hadn't moved from the same spot, looking every bit a chastised child in time-out.

"I've got to make a run to Georgia just south of Savannah and back. You're going with me," he instructed.

"Why?"

"You did agree to translate, didn't you?" Zane gave himself a mental pat on the back for quick thinking.

She frowned. "Are you sure you'll need me to translate in *Georgia*?"

"There's a possibility." A rare possibility, but one never knew what to expect, he reasoned.

After he'd pulled that randy-boy stunt in the abandoned gas station, she had every reason to be suspicious of anything he said. What little gain he'd made toward earning her trust had probably been negated by his lust.

"Angel, another thing. I'm sorry about what happened in that building. It won't happen again. I don't want you to be concerned about staying here with me."

Her eyes drooped with hurt. She said nothing.

Great. Now he really felt like a snake's belly.

"Why don't you grab a shower," he suggested.

Angel rolled her eyes up and gave an exaggerated sigh. She was obviously not happy with him or the plan, but carried her bag of clothes to the bathroom. The door snapped shut. The lock clicked from the inside.

Not happy at all.

Zane bolted the front door then secured the latches on all the windows. Next he went to the alarm pad, bypassed the motion detectors and keyed in the code. He planned to return from his shower with her still present and accounted for.

Angel emerged from the bathroom wearing the only other clothes he knew she owned—the jeans and white shirt. At this rate, after a week of washing they'd disintegrate.

She'd dried her hair and twisted it up in the back with a clip he assumed she'd found in his sister's paraphernalia. The style suited her high cheekbones and slender neck, a soft kissable neck.

The memory of holding her in the corner of the dark building hadn't fled far from his conscious thoughts.

Desire wrestled with logic. For all he knew, she was wanted by the police. He'd better zip up any attraction and treat her the way he should have from the first—as a suspect.

With the apartment fortified against entry or exit, he could relax for the first time since meeting her.

Angel pivoted in the living room, her gaze tracking across every inch.

The sofa bed had been converted back to an overstuffed leather sofa, the area around it tidied. Her sweep of the room stopped at the flashing security keypad. She arched an accusatory eyebrow at him.

"Angel, I've alarmed the apartment so no one will enter without us knowing it."

"Or leave?"

Okay, so he hadn't fooled her. "Or leave. I'm grabbing a shower and then we'll go. Fix yourself something to eat."

She walked to the kitchen mumbling something under her breath about the male population that didn't sound flattering.

"Be out real quick," he called to her. No answer, which was a loud answer in some ways. Zane gave the perfectly clean bathroom a brief once-over, no longer surprised to find it that way, then showered and shaved.

Zane threw on a collared golf shirt and khaki pants. He slid his loaded .32 Smith & Wesson down the inside of his boot. The 9mm Glock stayed hidden within the false center of a hardback novel in his flight bag.

He walked into the kitchen to find Angel leaning forward on the counter with a slice of cold pizza in one hand. Her downcast eyes drifted back and forth across the front page of yesterday's paper. An almost empty glass of milk rested near the edge of the paper.

"You can have anything you want," Zane pointed out to her. "You don't have to eat day-old pizza."

"This is great. You have no idea how badly you miss pizza until you can't get it for a year." She'd mumbled her answer without looking up from the newspaper.

Where had she lived that she couldn't get pizza? He'd file that away for now.

Zane checked his watch. They had to get on the road.

"You ready to go?"

She didn't even hesitate as she cleaned up after herself, wiped down the counter and washed the glass. "Sure, if you're ready to unlock my cell."

That zinged right to the heart. "It's for your safety more than anything else."

"Just like a man to justify his action as it being for my benefit rather than admit the real reason. Fine." She hefted the linen bag to her shoulder. "I'm ready."

She made him sound underhanded. He hadn't turned her over to the police. He was keeping her safe. She had no reason to question him.

On the other hand, he supposed she had no reason to believe him either. Her resistance to sharing information left him few options. Until Zane knew who Angel was and what or whom she ran from, she'd just have to accept what he told her.

Then if he determined she was innocent of any wrongdoing, he'd have a professional help her deal with an ex-boyfriend, or husband.

Zane hadn't even considered the possibility of a husband— probably because he'd been thinking with the wrong part of his anatomy.

With his professional armor securely in place, he scooted her out to the truck. After three switchbacks on his way to the airfield, he had detected no one following them, but a bad feeling stayed with him.

Where would her pursuers show up next?

At Sunshine Airfield, Angel waited anxiously while Zane did a quick review of the maintenance log. She expected a black sport utility to block their exit from the hangar—more Hollywood influence—while Zane satisfied himself that the airplane was up to par.

After she buckled in, he taxied down the east runway, explaining they had to take off into the wind.

The Titan lifted effortlessly into puffy cotton clouds drifting through a sapphire-blue sky. At a thousand feet he settled back.

Hurt by the admission he considered the kiss a mistake, she'd hardly spoken to him since leaving the apartment.

She disagreed. To her, the kiss had been wonderful.

Of course, she had little experience to use for comparison. Based on that amazing kiss this morning, Zane definitely had more practice than her. She imagined groomed and sophisticated women flowing through his apartment.

Okay, so she was not sophisticated, but the kiss hadn't been that bad. If he had so much experience, he could have at least pretended he liked it, couldn't he?

Fine. If he wanted to act as if nothing happened between them, so would she.

Her nipples made a liar of her. The pair of traitors hardened just thinking about his touch. If he'd kept his hands on her another couple of minutes in that old gas station, her clothes would have combusted from the heat coming off her skin.

"Looks like a great day for flying." Zane's voice buzzed in her headphones.

"What?"

"Looks like a great day for flying," he repeated.

She shrugged.

"Have you flown a lot?" he asked.

"No."

"What type of work do you do?"

Let's see. What's a good answer? She'd worked as a courier when she'd been arrested for unknowingly delivering drugs for her father. After jail she'd worked as a maid in a filthy motel, shoveled refuse at the dump and waited tables in a strip club because a respectable restaurant didn't want an ex-con.

Oh yeah, she had it. She'd been hired by one of the largest import-export companies in the country. Two months in to her employment, she'd earned a raise and moved up to the position of inventory clerk. That job had come with opportunities for advancement from small-time jailbird to a maximum-prison resident.

Hmm. Maybe not.

"You could say I'm in between jobs right now." Good answer, even if it was a bit flippant.

Zane's mouth firmed into a straight line.

She couldn't read his eyes behind the aviator glasses, but figured he didn't appreciate her smart comeback. She didn't care. She was still ticked off about the kiss.

"Look, Angel, I'm just trying to make conversation. It shortens the trip."

She shrugged again and stared into space, literally, feeling like a brat.

"We're traveling north, just west of the A1A route. You can see the coast."

While Zane commented on landmarks along the way, a thought came to her. "How did you find me this morning?"

"I normally jog in the mornings. When I heard you leave, I slipped on my shoes to run with you, but you were way ahead of me by the time you reached the beach. Next thing I knew, you were running across the street like your life depended on it."

A call on the radio interrupted him for a moment. Zane continued. "I lost track of you and had just walked into that old gas station when I heard someone coming up the side and there you were."

"What made you take off so fast?" His hands moved over the controls automatically as he spoke.

She eyed him for a long moment. His story was a little too simple to believe. "You just saw me run across the road, nothing else?"

"Why? What spooked you?"

Being shot at? "I...saw someone down the beach coming my way and decided to change directions," she said.

He turned the dark glasses on her for a long moment; a vein in his neck pulsed. She expected him to challenge her statement, but he didn't. Instead, he opened an emotional artery.

"You're pretty fast, even to be running on adrenaline. Did you run track in school?"

Being reminded of high school for the first time in years was equivalent to having a dagger shoved through her soul. No one she'd graduated with had spoken to her again after the conviction. Thankfully, the people she'd trained around since then knew nothing of her history, only that her marathon race times were exceptional.

Zane had no way of knowing his innocent question peeled open a wound she thought had healed years ago. Seven years spent struggling to survive with the burden of a criminal record had given her little time to think about lost dreams. Over the past year, she'd committed the sin of dreaming again. Running the Tamarind Triathlon in Colorado in two months was to be her big chance at returning to the athletic community and regaining a margin of respect.

Thanks to Mason, that hope was gone.

"I ran in high school." She made a show of checking her watch. "How long is this flight?"

"Bentley Field is a little over two hours away. Where did you go to school?"

Her throat tightened. This sounded more like an interrogation than a conversation to kill time.

"I went to a podunk school. How long have you flown?"

"Fifteen years. I was a navy pilot until a few years ago."

"How long were you in?" Angel asked.

He shook his head and smiled. "Not fair. It's my turn to ask. If we're going to play question volleyball how about answering mine since I'm answering yours?"

She turned her shoulder to him, but being in close captivity made it impossible to dismiss him completely. Zane filled the cockpit with more presence than mere body space. *She* could ignore him, but her body had a radar system of its own that signaled when he entered her heat space.

Time for a new subject.

"Where's your family?" he asked.

Not that one. "No family. My mother died when I was twelve."

"Sorry. What about your dad?" Zane shifted his head her way, paused, his face expressionless.

Dead as far as she was concerned, the worthless dog.

"Haven't seen him in a long time." True. Any time in the next century would be too soon.

"Have you run competitively?" Zane started again.

Back to that, huh? Two national titles plus a roomful of regional trophies by the time she'd reached sixteen should constitute running competitively.

Oh yeah, now she remembered.

Her father had hocked her trophies for pocket cash.

Tears stung her eyes. She stared out the side window, straining to twist as far to her right as she could. Why wouldn't Zane leave it alone? Fidgeting, her fingers landed on a pair of sunshades in the side. She yanked them out and slid them over her eyes.

"I ran track in school and a few local races. Why did you leave the navy?"

His smile faltered. What? Mr. Got-to-know-everything doesn't like question volleyball all of a sudden?

She smiled, feeling a little smug.

"After our parents were killed, Trish began having problems. I was no help to her flying airplanes on the other side of the ocean. By the time I got back to Texas she was in the hospital."

Fingers on his right hand flexed in and out, gripping the throttle. Angel didn't think he was going to continue until she heard his low voice in her headset.

"Her best friend, Heidi, found Trish after she'd gone to a hotel with some guy, and he'd beaten her half to death. Trish told Heidi she screamed until she passed out, but no one helped. The place was full of crackheads."

Angel's shoulders sagged. Okay, they were even. Neither had intentionally forced painful memories on the other. Underneath the deep sadness in his voice, she picked up a thread of guilt, again. Why did Zane feel guilty about something he couldn't prevent? He'd been in the service. Trish was her parents' responsibility until they'd died.

Angel understood how it felt to carry misplaced guilt.

"Zane, you're there for Trish now. You can't change the past, but you can influence the future."

He didn't acknowledge her comment, but his features relaxed.

"It's your serve," she teased, hoping to lighten the mood, rewarded when his mouth quirked up on one side in a half smile.

"So tell me, what's your best time in a race?"

Angel hesitated, fiddled with her seat belt then lifted her chin to him.

"I've run sub six-minute pace." She said it matter-of-factly, but pride came through in her voice.

"No kidding? Did you get a track scholarship?"

She breathed deep, determined to continue and lance this emotional abscess. "Yes."

"Where did you go?"

"I didn't."

"Why not? With professional training, you might have made the Olympics," Zane said.

What should she tell him? That one of the most prestigious universities in the country rescinded their offer when they found out she'd be delayed a year while serving time?

"It wasn't my choice. They withdrew the offer," she said.

"You should have submitted to another college. For someone with your speed, there had to be plenty of universities that would have taken you…as long as your grades were up to par."

"I had the grades." She'd have carried better than a 3.8 average if training hadn't drained her time. "They just decided they didn't want me."

"Did you try to get into another college?"

The steady drone of the engines filled several minutes before she rubbed her neck then answered.

"I'm getting a headache. Think I'll catch a nap."

She wasn't as ready to examine that wound as she'd thought, and couldn't take a couple hours of this probing. If he didn't believe her headache excuse, at least he didn't say so.

Zane pulled a towel from his bag and handed it to her. "Sure. Here's something you can use for a pillow."

"Thanks." Angel peeled off her headset and settled back against the rolled towel.

If she had a headache, he was the pope.

Zane wanted to push for more, but knew at this point it would be fruitless. Better to chisel away than try to get it all in one chunk.

From her stiff body language alone, he knew he'd hit a major nerve—something to do with running.

"They didn't want me," she'd said. It wasn't the words as much as the cold pain behind them that struck him. How

could a university not want a talented athlete with good grades? If that was the truth.

Simple answer. She'd done something to warrant revocation of the scholarship.

A bigger question was, why hadn't she taken advantage of her abilities and found another school willing to offer her assistance? Maybe, as she said, it hadn't been her choice.

Sub six-minute pace? Yeah, she'd been some school's star runner. Her name had to show up in a database with cross-referencing race results and high-school track stars.

Based on what Zane had seen that morning, Ben could narrow the possibilities down by searching the top ten percent of women finalists across the country in the last ten years.

What would cause a school to reject a talented athlete? That was the meat of the question. Ben's network of information was limitless. There probably weren't a lot of prominent female athletes named Angel, if that was her real name.

She was definitely world-class level. He'd love to watch her fly through the end of a race and cheer her on as she led the pack. Those gazelle-like legs gracefully tearing across the ground. He'd be there to hug her when she won.

Where had that ridiculous thought come from?

Zane put things back in perspective and ticked off facts he knew.

She'd lost a scholarship.

Pulling information out of her was harder than dragging Imelda Marcos from a shoe sale.

She was a suspiciously compulsive cleaner who was trying to escape someone dangerous.

So what's the conclusion, Sherlock? A suspect. Had to be. But suspected of what?

She'd panicked at the mention of going to the police. That didn't prove she'd done anything wrong, but it sure as hell sounded suspicious. Handing her over to the authorities without verifying she was absolutely guilty of something really bothered him. Besides, alerting the local police would only put him in the position of having to explain more about their meeting than Zane was willing to share.

But if nothing panned out in Ben's search, he'd be forced to either let someone else get involved or turn her loose to fend for herself.

Neither option would give him peace.

He couldn't afford to lose any ground on the High Vision investigation. Not if he wanted to move from the field to a co-ordinator's position so he'd have more time for Trish. Cracking this case would ensure that.

Neither he nor Trish could touch a healthy inheritance until he reached the age of forty. His father felt a man should make his mark in life, before receiving free money. That will had been drawn up long before Trish was born, and had not been revised, in the meantime, Zane had to make the best of his skills for both of them.

Having a stable life where he was around on a daily basis was the only hope of saving his baby sister from her alcohol addiction.

With a few more pieces to the puzzle of Angel's background in hand, Zane sat back to enjoy the flight. Days like this were made for being airborne. Working nights, weekends and holidays were part of his job, but being able to fly had balanced out the loss of a personal life for a while.

Not a cloud in the sky for as far as he could see. The only annoyance was a northeast crosswind to deal with at landing. He'd just confirmed clearance to land, when Bentley Field radioed him.

"You must be getting big bucks working on a holiday weekend, flyboy."

"How goes it, Jason?" Zane had met the young mechanic on a recent stopover when the Titan had needed a minor adjustment.

"The same. Underpaid and overworked. You expecting company?"

"You mean the High Vision people?" Zane asked.

"Naw, they're here, too, but a big SUV's been sitting on the ramp for the last twenty minutes and you're the only bird we're expecting right now."

Not a good sign.

Chapter 8

Zane did a mental check of his weapons. He'd love to find out who was after Angel, just not at the risk of her being captured or harmed. If this were a planned operation he'd have backup, but no one in the task force could know about Angel.

He was on his own.

Keying up the mike, he said, "Jason, has High Vision shown anyone what the load is? My dispatcher didn't have much information."

"Oh, yeah, he told me. Poor dude they sent to deliver it was supposed to go away with his girlfriend this weekend. He wanted a shoulder to cry on."

"Must be a big deal," Zane said.

"Hey, you'd think it was the crown prince of Europe. You're the limo ride for a little white mutt headed to Miami for a weekend of R&R with his four-legged lady."

Zane flipped through his memory bank on the corporate management of High Vision. Their CFO and his wife raised champion bichon frise dogs, including a stud worth more than some people earned in a year. He understood the secrecy. The CFO was worried about the animal being stolen during transport.

"Okay. I'll see you in a few."

"Not me, flyboy. I just bought a new bass rig with a hot Mercury outboard. I'll be on the water by sunset. Catch you next time."

Angel snapped awake when the tires bounced on the runway. With her hair tousled and eyes half-open she could have just climbed out of bed.

One lascivious thought led to another.

Zane pictured her strewn across his bed lying facedown, his T-shirt halfway up her backside—with his hand covering her perfect bottom. He clenched the controls.

The plane bumped.

She whipped her head around in surprise.

He mouthed the word *sorry* and reminded himself to stick with the game plan, which didn't include erotic fantasies.

At the terminal side of the runway, he swung off and parked on the ramp then took in the waiting congregation. No one among a group of five standing next to a silver Suburban resembled what he'd consider a dangerous boyfriend.

Two elderly women, linked arm in arm, were dressed in matching flowered, short-sleeve dresses that fell midway of their chunky calves. Black ankle-high boots complemented their military buzz cut.

A wiry little man held down his dirt-brown hat against the wind swiftly kicking up dust. Standing next to him was a middle-aged, flame-haired woman and a height-challenged man almost as wide as he was tall. Sunshine glinted off the thin, brown hair covering his basketball-size head.

What the hell was going on here? Zane unbuckled his seat belt and slipped out of the cockpit. When he opened the cargo door to step down, loose sand blasted his face in a rush of burning air. A hand pushed against his back and he turned to find Angel climbing out.

"Where do you think you're going?" he asked.

"I'm your translator, remember?"

Yeah, he remembered. She didn't have to look so smug when she pointed out the flaw in his plan.

"If you handle this group anything like you did Mr. Suarez, you'll be lucky to stay in business through next week." She cocked her chin up at him, squaring her shoulders, positioned to do battle.

Keeping her within reach might not be a bad idea. "Stay close to me. I don't know who these people are."

Zane stepped past the nose of the plane, and the odd group advanced several feet. The skinny guy fighting to keep the crinkled hat on his head cleared his throat and spoke.

"I'm Earnest Earwood. We represent TAF, which stands for Treat Animals Fairly." Each word tumbled from his mouth like a telegraph operator reading a message. "We're here to protest your part in the mistreatment of animals."

One of the two gray-haired women, who resembled each other too much not to be related, spoke up. "I'm Berta Nielson and this is my sister, Valerie."

Valerie jumped in. "We don't think these poor animals you transport should be put through pain and suffering."

Berta pointed at Zane. "How would you like to be faced with their future?"

Zane's canine cargo was headed for a weekend of rousing sex with a ready-and-able partner.

Zane would love it. He smiled. "I could tolerate it."

Valerie's face screwed into the shape of a dishrag after heavy use. "That's appalling. What kind of man are you?"

One that hadn't been with a woman in a while, Zane thought remorsefully. "You don't think my cargo deserves to be used in an experiment?" He was trying hard not to chuckle.

Angel arched an eyebrow at him.

"No animal should be put through that kind of suffering." The redhead had a high-pitched voice, painful to hear. "We're the Thorntons and we've spent our life protecting animals."

Most of the critical shipments for High Vision were handled in the middle of the night, just to avoid TAF groups showing up to protest. The disorganized association was composed of radical protesters who rarely had their facts straight and generally caused headaches for the bona fide animal rights organizations.

Zane should end it here, but TAF had cost him a connection with an informant in the early stages of the investigation. He owed them one. Besides, he was enjoying himself and wanted to see just how deep a hole they'd dig if he handed them a shovel.

"Maybe this animal would enjoy this particular experiment," Zane suggested.

Eyes bulged and mouths popped open like hungry guppies. Zane smiled at the reactions.

The main four spouted off at the same time.

"You're a monster."

"How can you say that?"

"We shall call in reinforcements."

"How do you sleep at night?"

Mr. Thornton still hadn't commented.

Angel gaped at Zane as if he'd lost his mind. "You can't even keep people calm in English," she whispered tersely. "How *do* you stay in business?"

He narrowed his eyes at her.

Angel addressed the crowd. "Excuse me. *Excuse me!*"

The shouting died down to a rumble. Angry eyes surveyed her.

She pushed past Zane. "Black Jack Airlines would never do anything to harm an animal." She turned to Zane. "Right?"

When he didn't say anything, she bumped her heel into his shin. "Umph."

Angel must have taken his grunt as an affirmative. She smiled at the crowd and said, "What specifically is your complaint?"

Berta's thick eyebrows ran together in a straight line across her forehead. "TAF opposes unnecessary and cruel testing on animals. We have a report that Black Jack Airlines is transporting a test animal today."

Angel twisted sideways to Zane. "Is that true?"

He smiled and nodded, then almost busted up laughing at Angel's incredulous face.

"Just as we thought." Earnest choked out the words through a raspy throat. "He even admits to his dastardly ways."

When Earnest succumbed to coughing, Valerie took a shot at Zane. "You wouldn't be so happy if you were put in the same position as that poor animal."

Zane grinned. "Au contraire. If I had a willing mate waiting with bated breath for a romantic weekend with me, you'd probably have to remove my smile surgically."

The crowd stilled. Not a sound was heard over the whirring of the wind. Everyone stared at him in shocked silence until Angel squinted in concentration and pushed for an explanation.

"Zane, what are you talking about?"

So much for having fun. Zane sighed, resigned to explaining.

"Our cargo is a pedigree bichon frise being sent for a weekend of recreational sex. The evil testing he'll be put through is to determine if he can make little champion puppies. If it does kill him, that doesn't sound like a bad way to go, in my opinion."

Wild threads of silky hair escaped the bundle twisted on top of her head and blew across Angel's face. The corners of her mouth curled up. "You have a wicked streak."

For the first time since leaving the apartment, he was in her good graces again. Warmth spread over him at her pixie smile.

He had a wicked streak? She didn't know the half of it.

"Earnest, you said there was a monkey being shipped

today. Where's the monkey?" Berta wasted no time assault-
ing a new target. Poor Earnest was no match.

"Hold on, Berta. This isn't my fault. The Thorntons said
Valerie told them the same thing."

"Blast it all, Earnest. You're an idiot. Valerie heard you tell
me. That's why she told them."

Zane had enjoyed all he could stand. "If you'll excuse us,
I have a deadline."

No one so much as turned to acknowledge him as they
formed a circle of finger-pointers. The only person not shouting was Mr. Thornton, who looked at Zane and rolled his eyes.

Zane checked the area carefully while he directed Angel
toward the office. A single man in a green High Vision security jumpsuit waited outside the office.

"I'm Zane Black. Black Jack Airlines. Where's your
cargo?"

"Inside, where it's cool. I'll be right back."

The employee returned with a polished chrome animal
kennel.

Zane took the kennel from the man. "Who's picking up
Don Juan in Ft. Lauderdale?"

"Here are the transfer papers. I saw the TAF group delay-
ing you out there. Are you still on schedule?"

"Not a problem. This little guy should be popping his
champagne cork by sunset."

Angel chuckled at the silver Suburban full of unhappy
campers driving away in a dust cloud then followed Zane to
the Titan. He secured the kennel inside the cargo bay and had
just lifted the Titan off the ground, when a pitiful whining
filled the air.

She twisted around. Two soulful eyes peered through the
wire opening at the front. She couldn't stand to see a sad child
or a lonely animal.

"I think he's scared," she said.

"He'll settle down in a little while."

"What's his name?"

"It was like Sir something-something Chutney," Zane said. Another mournful sound emitted from the cage.

"Poor Chut."

She knew how he felt. Shuttled from one track-and-field competition to another as a teenager, she'd been exhibited like a circus act. Nothing had mattered—not the long hours she'd devoted to besting her last race time at the expense of no social life, not the physical pain or being put on display like a trained seal.

She'd been willing to endure anything as long as she got what she wanted in the end—four years at Stanford, training under the best track coaches in the country while earning a degree in physical education.

At one time, she'd dreamed of a chance at the Olympics before eventually going on to teach.

Instead, she'd been caged. The world she returned to twelve months later wasn't the same one she'd left.

Ignoring Zane's warning to be careful, Angel yanked off the headset and unbuckled her harness. On hands and knees, she came face-to-face with Chut. She sprung the cage door, opening it wide enough to slip her hand inside. The white ball of fluff shook harder than an out-of-control vibrator. He inched forward and sniffed her outstretched hand.

"Watch it, Angel. You don't know if that dog bites." Zane's voice boomed through the cockpit.

"He won't hurt me. Please don't yell. You're frightening him."

She sat down so she had the dog on her left and Zane on her right. When she opened the wire door wider, Chut made a couple tentative steps through the opening. In the next heartbeat, he straddled her lap.

Angel beamed a triumphant smile at Zane the next time he glanced at her.

She snuggled the terrified dog close to her chest and slipped back into the copilot seat. His animal scent was wrapped in a powdery shampooed fragrance. She ran her fingers across the gossamer coat, white as fresh snow.

Once her headset was back in place, Zane said, "You're going to be sorry if he gets real excited and makes a mess."

"No, I'm not. Everyone needs to be held sometimes. Isn't that right, Sir Chut?"

Zane's hand stilled for an instant when she spoke. She felt him studying her from behind the aviator glasses and could have kicked herself for the suggestive comment.

It just popped out of her mouth. Zane would use a statement like that to start another conversation delving into her past. Not somewhere she wanted to go. Any deeper prying would open more cavities filled with pain and details she'd rather not share.

She really liked Zane, too much, in fact, if her enthusiastic response to his kiss was an indication. A kiss he'd apologized for.

And she'd encouraged him, for goodness' sake.

She had nothing to attribute her careless behavior to except the dangerous situation she'd constantly been in since the day they met. Even though her body reacted with a will of its own from merely being in the same room with Zane. Sure, he had smoldering eyes and knew how to use his mouth to curl her toes, but she'd resisted men in the past. On the other hand, none of those men were anything like Zane. She'd never lived in close quarters with another man who was not family. That had to be the reason she lost her head when Zane touched her, looked at her, smiled.

Just a matter of too much time together.

That wouldn't be a problem once she found the coins.

Soon.

In the meantime, she wanted to steal this memory, enjoy his attention for what little time they would share. Even if it was only hours. Once she left, she'd have this memory to get her through what promised to be a dismal future.

The upside of leaving so soon would be that he'd never know the ugly details in history. If he did, he'd back away just as everyone else had. Watching the change in his eyes from caring to disgust would kill her.

Which is why she had no business daydreaming about him. She had to tell her heart to stop.

Sand continued to spill out of her invisible hourglass. She had to find out what happened to the package where she'd hidden the coins. Now was as casual a time as she'd get to investigate where Zane took it.

"I'll bet you've had a lot interesting cargo," she started.

"They're more high priority than interesting."

"Who are some of the companies that use your service?" If he told her the name of the custom curtain manufacturer, she could find out if they were notified of delivery.

"High Vision, Suarez and Associates, Wizard Computers. There are a couple others, but those are the main ones."

She chewed on her lip. How direct a question could she ask without tipping off what she wanted?

"Aren't there a lot of boat companies in Florida? Don't you get any of their business?"

"Not really. They aren't willing to pay my price for parts in a panic."

She noticed Chut panting. "I think Chut's thirsty. Got any water?"

"Hang on until I get the autopilot set."

After several minutes, Zane found a cup and a jug of water. He cut the plastic cup down to half the height and filled it with water then handed it to her.

"Thanks. Here, Chut, have a drink."

Chut lapped up the water, dripping it all over his coat and Angel's lap. When he'd finished, she swore he was smiling.

Zane lifted the cup from her fingers and said, "I've got a

cup holder on this side. We'll keep it handy in case he wants any more."

Chut stopped shivering. He reached his paw up to her gratefully, then squiggled once and settled into her lap.

With enough time, she felt certain Zane would slip up and give her a clue to the whereabouts of the package, but time was at a premium. While she cooed to Chut, another idea struck her.

"As long as I'm an indentured servant, I could help you get your business organized." That earned her a frown.

"You're not a servant," he said testily. "All you have to do is translate. And my business is just fine, thank you."

Oh, yeah. Zane had a business in south Florida but doesn't speak Spanish. He puts more effort into sparring with a radical animal rights group than calming an irate client. No wonder he had the storage room from hell.

"You can't possibly know where anything is in that storage room of yours. When we get back, I'll help you put it in order. Really, it's the least I can do," she said and answered his dubious expression with what she hoped was an encouraging smile.

"We'll see."

Not the resounding agreement she'd wanted, but not a rejection either. Somewhere in that hangar there had to be a clue or name that would help her.

"So what races have you won, Angel."

Ugh. "I'd rather not talk about running, okay?"

"Why? I don't understand your aversion to the topic. You're obviously good."

She sighed. "Because in my world today, it really doesn't matter how good I was at one time."

His forehead wrinkled at that comment, but he left her alone.

Nor did it matter that she'd lost it all after being convicted of a crime she'd naively committed. That was all behind her.

Now she only had to worry about staying alive and out of prison.

When the radio beckoned his attention, her eyes wandered over his profile. His strong chin and no-nonsense posture spoke volumes. He knew nothing about her past, but he'd accepted her, caring only for her safety. The man was good all the way through.

Nothing like her father, who'd put her in the middle of his criminal activities then sacrificed her to the district attorney, who refused to believe she had no knowledge of the drugs she'd been duped into transporting.

Zane was the kind of man dreams were built upon. A man she could believe in and depend on. If only she'd met him in another time and place. She would love to share her troubles with Zane, but not at the risk of implicating him.

To tell the truth, she wanted to share more than her problems with Zane. He awakened strong needs, desire she'd buried years ago. No man had interested her enough to take a chance, but Zane made her want to wish for things she'd never have—a home, a family, respect.

Zane called for clearance into Ft. Lauderdale airspace, breaking into her thoughts. Angel coaxed Chut back into his chrome shelter.

At the hangar, Zane refused to let her leave the Titan until he'd confirmed the van parked outside contained only High Vision personnel. He had her loaded into his truck, zooming down A1A, before the ink dried on the transfer papers. She didn't ask where they were headed and he didn't offer to explain.

Angel sunk low in the seat to stay out of sight. Zane must have understood her reticence to being visible since he didn't comment. From her angle, blue skies flashed past, interrupted by the occasional commercial sign.

The Gulf Winds Marina sign came into view.

She shot up in the seat.

"What are we doing here?"

She couldn't have been more surprised if he'd driven up

to the Taj Mahal. Excitement and anxiety tripped through her.
Had Zane loaded the package into the truck bed without her
seeing him? She calmly stretched her head up and around. The
bed was empty. Her palms dampened at the possibility of
finding the package of boat curtains.

"A quick stop," Zane explained. "Won't take more than ten
minutes." He parked the big truck in front of the dock for slip
eighteen and opened his door, saying, "Just stay here and I'll
be right back."

"No." She hadn't meant to snap at him.

"That's becoming my least favorite word. No, what?"

"I want to come with you, please." She smiled to sweeten
her request, elated to be at slip eighteen.

Zane shifted, subtle, but she caught the change from casual to alert mode. He scanned the marina lot. So did she. Two
empty, late-model pickups and a rusty Jeep sat in the desolate parking area.

"Okay, but—"

"I know, I know, stay close." She hopped out after him. It
took immense discipline not to run down the dock. Zane lum-
bered along, with her close on his heels.

The young man from the day before was nowhere in sight
and neither was *Wet Dream*. Empty water filled slip seventeen.

Next to it in slip eighteen floated a wooden cabin cruiser
Noah must have passed over in lieu of the ark. The ancient
teak deck was sun-bleached gray. What little varnish still covered the mahogany trim along the sides of the cabin sprung
out in peeled tufts.

Zane stepped down onto the deck of the archaic vessel ap-
propriately named *Hard Luck*.

"Should you be walking around on that thing?" Angel asked.
Zane grinned up at her. "Sure, this is my boat."

C.K. pulled the vibrating phone from the lower pocket in
his camo cargo pants. "Speak."

"Joe, here. Your girl and the pilot are back in town. They just pulled into a marina. No way to follow them inside without being seen, too open, but there's only one way in and out. Got a man ready to follow. Want a man on foot to go inside just to make sure they don't leave by boat?"

"Give it a little bit. They don't come out, send him in. Don't get too close. I don't want her spooked again," C.K. warned.

"You got it."

"Call me when they get back to the apartment. That's where I want them."

"Will do, boss."

Chapter 9

She couldn't believe her ears.

Zane's boat? Where was the package?

"Don't look so shocked, Angel. Pilots like the water, too. I plan to restore it. Bought it in Miami and hired a captain to bring it up here for me."

He cast an admiring gaze over the craft. "I won't be able to work on it for another couple months, but she'll be ship-shape by next spring."

Angel caught half of what he'd said. Her mind raced to figure out where the package of new canvas enclosures could be stored. This boat wasn't anywhere near ready for side curtains.

Zane stared up at her expectantly.

She realized he waited for her to say something about the boat. "It's, uh, nice. Lot of potential, roomy."

Right answer. He grinned like a man who'd won the lottery.

He'd need a big jackpot to make this thing into a usable watercraft.

Zane opened the cabin and stepped down into what appeared to be a living area. He opened small windows, pushed them out from the inside and lifted the hatch. She'd squatted on the dock to watch him, hoping to see a brown paper package miraculously lying around in the open.

No such luck.

She stepped around on the walkway extending from the main dock between the slips. Grasping the sidewall of the hardtop covering the cockpit for support, she jumped down onto the deck. At the cabin door, she found Zane digging through a small cabinet above a compact kitchen area. He pulled out two key rings, each with an orange plastic float attached.

She moved out of the way when he climbed out onto the deck and moved over to the right side of the boat, where a steering wheel and gauges looked like a cockpit area. Probably what lured pilots to boats.

Zane stuck the keys into the dual ignitions then moved to the center of the deck and dropped down on one knee. He raised a hinged section. With a flip of his wrist, he switched a silver toggle.

After standing up, he explained. "Have to switch the battery on."

Sounded reasonable. She had no clue what he was talking about, having rarely been on a boat, but he said it with such authority she assumed he was correct.

Zane moved back the wheel, gripped the handles mounted against the wall on his right and shoved them forward a couple times then returned them to the middle position. After several attempts, the right motor cranked with a throaty rumble. The left one started up on the first try, eliciting a triumphant grin from Zane.

Men and their toys.

He tinkered with the controls for a few minutes, then tapped one of the gauges and frowned.

She leaned in to see what concerned him. "Something not working?"

He shook his head, more to himself than to her. "No, that's the problem. It does work."

"I don't understand."

Zane studied the dash. "These are the fuel gauges. Both tanks are too low. Had a message from the captain that he ran into weather and arrived later than he'd planned, so he couldn't fill the tank before docking. I can't blame him, but I have to get the boat fueled soon."

"Why? Are you taking it for a ride?" If he went for a ride in this thing, low fuel should be the least of his worries.

A life jacket, flare gun, inflatable raft—those were items to be concerned about.

"No, it's for safety," he continued. "An empty tank is more dangerous than a full one. Gas fumes combust quicker than solid fuel." When he'd finished running the engines, Zane returned the keys to their hiding spot.

Leaving the ignition keys on board the boat amazed her. Attitudes in Florida were definitely more trusting than where she'd lived.

Zane snapped his fingers. "I forgot to grab the new bowlines from the truck and I need to see the manager. You ready?" He stood next to the side, offering his hand to help her back onto the dock.

She caught herself before "no" popped out of her mouth. "I'd like to wait here, if it's okay with you. I've never been on a boat like this." That was basically true since the closest she'd ever come to boating was riding a ferry.

Zane eyed up and down the dock, but few craft remained in port on the beautiful day. "Promise me you'll stay right here."

"Of course."

He appeared doubtful at her fervent answer, but left after another glance around. It would be hard for her to leave without him seeing her.

As soon as Zane stepped off the end of the dock onto the parking lot, Angel scrambled below to dig through cabinets and drawers. The air in the cabin smelled of mildew. Thank goodness he'd opened the windows and hatches.

Odd lures, matches in a watertight capsule and several sets of sunshades were in the first two drawers. A cabinet below the tiny sink held rags, a rusty battery-operated light that didn't appear operable, rolls of clear line and a green plastic divided container full of assorted hooks.

Nothing in the shelves above the large bed covering the front section of the cabin except a half-empty bottle of sunscreen. The nautical pattern on the tattered covers had faded severely in the center area where she figured the sun burned through the hatch when it was open.

She'd just discovered compartments under the bed cushions when she heard, "Make yourself at home."

Angel swung around to face Zane standing at the top of the steps to the cabin.

"Sorry, I was just curious." She took a deep breath. "Boy, is there a lot of storage in here. You really picked a good one." She nodded her head as she made that declaration.

Zane's narrowed visage had her thinking he didn't quite buy the act, but he didn't challenge her.

"I'll change out the bowlines and we'll go."

Light showered back through the door once his massive body shifted out of the way. She could hear him on the front, shuffling around, and decided she'd be better served to come back alone to dig through the boat.

Leaving with the knowledge the coins might be within reach strained the limits of her patience. As a child she'd been impatient, but twelve months in a jail cell had taught her diligence. Waiting for the perfect opportunity to escape Mason had paid off and, so far, his men hadn't captured her.

She had no doubt about finding the coins again. Her life depended on it.

Out on the deck, Angel found Zane waiting for her on the walkway beside the boat. He towered over her when he reached down to offer her a hand up. Their gazes locked as he wrapped his fingers around both of her forearms and lifted. His strength amazed her as she flew up into his arms.

The air sizzled between them.

Tall, with a thin athletic body, Angel had never thought remotely of herself as petite, but sometimes Zane made her feel delicate.

Like now.

His hands rested on her shoulders, softly rubbing her tight muscles. His eyes bored into her.

Standing so close to him, her body refused all input from her mind. When his arms slid down around her back, she leaned into the embrace, unable to resist the comfort offered. He raised her up until she stood on her toes.

She held her breath, anticipating another sensual kiss.

Instead, he dropped a quick peck on her forehead and loosened his grip to go.

The man was making her crazy. She refused to be dismissed so easily, and pushed up another inch to nip his lower lip. Her fingers wrenched his shirt, tugging his chest to hers.

Heat banked his eyes. The storm brewed.

She had no time left for subtle. The coins were near. Once she found them, she'd be gone.

He shifted away, but she held firm.

Angel gave it one beat and ran the tip of her tongue over his lips.

He growled, tightened his grip and kissed her as if he meant it. No more teasing, his tongue danced a fevered volley with hers.

One notion chased through her mind.

If he apologized for this, she'd push him overboard.

Vaguely aware he'd moved from her mouth to her ear, she knew exactly where his hand was when his palm skittered over her breast. Her knees threatened to buckle.

She moaned.

He cursed. His hands stilled, robbing her of all the sultry sensations she'd been enjoying.

Glaring up into his mahogany eyes, she warned, "Don't you dare apologize."

Long seconds swept past. She braced herself for whatever irritating response he'd have this time.

A feral smile spread across his face. "What am I going to do with you?"

She had a few suggestions if he couldn't come up with any. Angel lifted her chin in a silent challenge.

Zane shook his head. "You have no idea how close you are to real danger. Let's go before you find out."

She groaned out a frustrated sigh.

He kissed her quickly then grabbed her hand and led her up the dock. Once they were both inside, Zane cranked the engine, but didn't shift the truck into gear.

"You're not talking. That's a bad sign for you," she teased.

"Angel, I like you, but—"

"Stop." *I like you, but?* That sentence could only end with a knife to the heart. She liked him, too. A lot. Too much, which was real stupid considering her situation. Regardless, she didn't want to hear the rejection. She'd heard enough in her life, too many.

"Look, just forget it. Didn't mean to make you feel uncomfortable."

"Angel, it's not that—" He gripped the steering wheel, not looking her way.

"Please, Zane, don't. Let's just forget about it." Easier said than done, but she could handle that better than hearing that he wanted no part of a woman who lived like a homeless indigent. The air thickened with discomfort. She searched for something to change the subject and noticed the large rope still piled in the back.

"You forgot to get one of your ropes."

"That's for the anchor." Zane shoved the gear shifter and the truck moved forward. "I'm not changing it today. That takes a while."

They left the marina heading in the direction of his apartment. He drove down the beach highway, his profile stern, distant, as if heat hadn't just flashed between them.

Worse, as if he'd judged her and she came up lacking. He ran hot, cold, hot. She'd figured out little about him.

Why was she even trying? Where would it lead?

Nowhere. Heartache.

Forget about what you're supposed to be doing? Men with guns, coins, Mason—any of that ring a bell? She fisted her hand. Get back on track. Wanting more out of life is what made Mason's job so appealing.

Find the coins. Nail down an alibi. Contact the FBI.

No room left for lusting after a pilot she'd never see again.

Angel pressed the window button, lowering the glass. She never could get enough fresh air after the stale atmosphere inside the prison. She snuck a peek at Zane.

His window was down as well. He drove one-handed, thumb tapping against the steering wheel.

She cut her attention back to her surroundings, noting the main roads she'd seen in the past two days. Marathon training had taught her to quickly pick up directions and landmarks along any route. Locating the marina again would be no problem.

Warm air coming off the blistering pavement blew through her open window as Zane slowly wove through the thick Labor Day traffic.

With her arm outside the window, she waved her hand against the force of the wind, enjoying a childhood practice. Her eyes roamed over the passenger-side mirror. She saw a dark sport utility swing wide behind a van four cars back.

Hair stood along her spine. A gut feeling triggered her antennae to danger. Traffic slowed to a stop. She got a better view of the suspicious vehicle when Zane moved his truck over to the left lane. The make was a Yukon, not a Land Rover.

Paranoia must have her imagining every dark sport utility followed her. But when she noticed the vehicle sliding over into Zane's lane in what appeared to be a late decision, her heart began to pound against her chest.

No other cars moved around in the two lanes to her right. Heavy traffic chugged forward, moving a few feet at a time, clogging the flow of vehicles through the huge intersection.

What would be the point of jockeying across lanes?

The driver could just be antsy, but what if she was right? Would someone dare to walk right up to the truck while she was caught in a traffic jam?

Zane moved into the left-turn lane.

She spied into the side mirror.

The navy blue Yukon was now two cars back—in the turn lane.

Panic sucker punched her.

Zane reached over and pressed buttons on the radio. Late seventies rock and roll poured out in a low volume.

"I hate traffic the Friday before a holiday," he mumbled.

Breathing was difficult. She couldn't answer him. They inched forward as the gap between cars tightened. Their truck sat in a virtual parking lot with nowhere to maneuver if they had to get away.

She chewed on her bottom lip. If whoever it was took a shot at her, Zane might be in the line of fire this time.

"Angel, are you okay?"

She jerked around at the question. "Fine. It's the traffic. I hate it, too." The longer he studied her, the more nervous she became. She had a strange feeling he anticipated her movements.

Zane had found her too easily this morning. He must have had some special training in the navy. Getting away from him was becoming a bigger challenge than the mock-survival weekends she'd endured to gain an edge for triathlon training.

One more glance in the side mirror threw her into full panic. The passenger door swung away from the Yukon. Someone stepped out, all but his gray pants hidden by the door.

Blood pulsed through Angel's chest.

"Oh my God, Zane! Look at that!" she yelled in a panic, pointing to his left. The second his head swing away, she hopped out of the truck and ran.

Alarmed, Zane had hardly turned his head when the passenger door slammed.

Spinning back around, he found himself alone in the cab.

Damn! She was gone again.

He jumped out to search the sea of cars for a female in flight. Beyond the three lanes to the right of his truck, a dash of white shirt dissolved into a gaggle of sightseers ambling along the sidewalk. Seconds behind her a gray blur arrowed into the same crowd.

Had the gray shirt behind Angel been someone chasing her or a teen on skates?

He slammed an open palm on the hood.

Unbelievable! Absolutely, un-damn-believable!

An enclave of horns honked as soon as the turn signal changed to green. Zane dived into the truck and threw it in gear, amazed he'd managed to lose her once more.

"Not very impressive for a seasoned undercover agent," he lambasted himself.

But this time, he'd gotten a break. She'd been too involved with the dog on their way back from Georgia to notice he'd taken the cup she'd used to serve Chut water.

With one good fingerprint he'd finally know who she was—*if* he found her again.

Angel fought her way through sidewalks strangled with tourists. She cut across an intersection then turned against slow traffic to run down the centerline, receiving appreciative honks from male drivers. She switched back and forth through cross streets that all ran in square patterns.

When a bus shelter came into view, she dived inside, completely lost. A man in a gray T-shirt and jeans had jumped from the Yukon. After the first mile she hadn't seen him again, but felt as if every pair of eyes she passed watched her. Cars flowed along the secondary streets, slowed next to the bus shelter. Nerves drove her back out to the street. She darted into the midst of sluggish traffic once more.

A cabbie slammed on his brakes and his horn at the same time.

She jumped as if a rattlesnake had struck at her.

The driver added a flurry of hand gestures to the garble of blistering Spanish muffled inside the car. He was in the process of sticking his head out when she dashed over and climbed into the empty rear seat.

She whipped out a ten-dollar bill, apologized in Spanish and gave him an address. Spending the money galled her. She could easily cover the distance on foot, but outrunning a vehicle wasn't possible.

The cabbie's anger appeased at the sight of cash. He hit the gas pedal, throwing her against the back of the seat. She'd given him a street crossing near Zane's apartment and could only hope the wild man knew where she was talking about.

She kept watch out the back window, but it would take someone with a death wish maneuvering a race car to keep up with this guy.

Zane drove straight to his apartment. The last time Angel vanished she'd gone back there, but the route had been shorter and easy to remember. Eight miles of turns and bridges separated his home and the marina.

He swung into the first parking spot and wished with every breath he took she'd be waiting at his door.

Negative.

Regardless, he dashed into the house just to make sure she wasn't magically sitting at the kitchen counter eating cold pizza. The farther he searched, the deeper his disappointment.

His immaculate apartment appeared undisturbed. There should be no trace of her. However, the perfectly tidy apartment was as strong a reminder of his compulsive-cleaner houseguest as her yellow running shoes would be if they sat in the middle of the floor.

Regret coursed through him. He hadn't meant to hurt her feelings after he kissed her on the dock, just not step further over the line of being a professional than he already had with her. His logical side warned him to be careful where she was concerned. There was too much at stake to risk losing it over a woman who wouldn't even tell him her last name.

He knew that, knew all the arguments he'd give someone else in his predicament.

On paper, it made perfect sense.

Deep inside, where feelings overruled logic, nothing made sense.

She was hurt when he withdrew in the truck, battled with what he wanted to do and what he had to do. He was searching for a way to help her, to help himself.

He had to find her for his sanity if nothing else.

Grabbing his keys on the way out, he punched in Ben's number and jogged to the truck. The fingerprint specialist might give him guff, but he'd always come through when Zane had to have a name.

C.K. needed to do some housecleaning when this job was finished. Joe was one of his best men, but one more mistake and he'd be demoted.

Demotion in C.K.'s world was permanent, all the way down to the bottom of a lake or a six-foot-deep hole.

"C.K., I don't have wings." Joe's exasperation came across the phone line. "She takes off on foot through six lanes of traffic, not much our men could do. I'll find her, but we got company."

"Who?" Had Mason gotten nervous and hired a backup group?

"Don't know, but I think that's why she ran. Some guy jumped out of a dark blue Yukon right behind her. His buddy drove the truck across the median in the other direction before we could nail a tag number."

Joe just added another demerit point to his next evaluation. CK couldn't believe this bitch was outmaneuvering the best men in the business.

"Cover all the bases. Keep a tail on the pilot. If she doesn't turn up quick, we'll have a chat with him." C.K. flipped the phone shut. The pilot had a bogus address. The apartment in Kendal had a few pieces of furniture, enough to fool most people just tracking down a paper trail, but not a professional. Mason's girl had teamed up with a cagey character who had something to hide.

His men would locate the correct address by this evening. C.K. grinned. No one hid from C.K. for long.

Angel watched from a fast-food restaurant as Zane drove away from the apartment complex. She'd been lucky to arrive ahead of him. Catching a ride with a man on the edge had helped. No one had followed Zane in or out of the parking lot. Good. At least he was still safe. She waited a little longer before hunting a way into the apartment without attracting undue attention.

It took her fifteen minutes to zigzag a half mile, but she finally managed to slip around to the rear of the apartment. Hunched over most of the time, she worked through the thick foliage, hesitating when tenants strolled by on the paths.

When she found the patio belonging to Zane's apartment, Angel rolled over the concrete railing onto the tiled floor. The cool surface offered a better hiding place than his comfortable chairs. She had no idea where he'd gone and probably had a long wait. That being the case, she had no intention of spending it perched up in plain view.

The longer he was gone, the better.

She'd use the time to figure out what to tell him. No matter what she said he wouldn't be happy. Angel eased back into a semicomfortable position.

A muffled two-tone chime sounded from Zane's front door then *tap-tap-tap*.

Her pulse jumped into high gear. She struggled against the urge to flee. The only thing stopping her was the fear there could be more than one person watching the rear who would intercept her. She crawled around behind the chairs to hide, as far out of sight as possible.

A shiver raced down her spine as she watched the front door handle turn and the deep blue barrier inch open.

Chapter 10

A piercing security alarm screeched as soon as the connection at the door was broken.

Angel scrunched down so low in the corner of the patio that her knees and chin met. She needed an escape route if the intruder proved to be a threat, but where would she go at this point? Her eyes darted back to the front door.

A hand slipped inside.

It punched several numbers on the flashing panel, quieting the searing noise. A pile of dark curls bobbed around the edge of the door, followed by an impish face peeking into Zane's apartment. His sister.

Trish leaned in farther and called, "Sugar, are you home? If you are, get your drawers on 'cause I'm coming in." She calmly entered, then closed the door, turned and walked to look down the hallway toward Zane's bedroom.

"Za-ane." She shrugged and strolled into the kitchen.

Angel expelled the breath she'd been holding.

How long would his sister stay or, worse, what if she wanted to sit outside? She mentally ticked through a selection of possible scenarios, all of which ended with being found hiding on the patio.

One of the few lessons she could attribute to her father was, "The best defense is a good offense."

And the truth be known, Trish had no idea what type of relationship Angel and Zane shared. Finding her there without him might not look unusual.

Even better, maybe Trish knew where he'd stored the canvas boat curtains.

Angel stood up, straightened her clothes and twisted all of her hair back up into a tidy knot. She flicked a look around to see if anyone watched her and tapped on the glass door, waited a minute then rapped harder the second time.

When Trish stuck her head out of the kitchen, she immediately cocked it to one side in that confused-dog look before her eyebrows shot up in recognition. A cheery smile popped into place as she hurried across the room to unlock the glass doors, chattering the whole time.

"Oh, sugar, I'm so sorry. I didn't see you sitting out there. Did you lock yourself out?"

That works. "Yeah, I was locked out. Good to see you again."

She hadn't noticed Trish's soft southern accent the first time they'd met, but caught it now.

"Come on in, sug, it's too hot to sit out there. I don't know how you and Zane stand the heat. The man loves his fresh air. Let's close the door and enjoy the AC."

Trish's ankle-length fuchsia dress dotted with yellow squiggles blared in stark contrast to Zane's coffee-brown and forest-green decor. The dark-haired beauty circled the sofa carrying a glass full of a cola-looking liquid, before sinking down into the soft green leather.

"Want something to drink, sugar?"

"No, I'm fine. Thanks for letting me in."

"No problem." Trish eyed her curiously and said, "I hadn't even heard of you before yesterday. So, where did you meet my brother?"

A reasonable question under any other circumstance, but not one Angel had anticipated. Telling Zane's sister he'd helped her escape armed men didn't sound like a good idea.

"We met in North Carolina. I was in a hurry to leave, so he gave me a ride to Charleston." Basically true.

"How did you end up in Florida? Do you live here or are you just visiting?"

Though Angel knew his sister's intent was not to put her on the spot, it didn't alleviate her discomfort. The fact that they'd never meet again didn't change the way Angel felt about blatantly lying to her. Funny how honesty had gotten her where she was today. Still, she resolved to stay as close to the truth as possible, with a little creativity.

"Actually, I'm visiting. I plan to relocate in the future, but haven't made up my mind where yet. How long have you been here?"

"I moved here three years ago when Zane did. Before that I lived in Houston, Texas. We grew up just outside the city limits. Our parents died while Zane was in the navy so he opted out early. He didn't feel a real tie to Houston. I'd missed him terribly. When he picked Ft. Lauderdale, so did I."

Trish's deep brown eyes softened every time she mentioned her brother.

Angel envied the close sibling relationship. Zane's love for his sister had been written all over his face when he'd hugged her the day before.

Before Trish could ask another question she'd have to dodge, Angel said, "Zane tells me you have a gift shop. Sounds like a fun business. Tell me about it."

"We've only been open for three months. It's doing okay.

Takes awhile to get going. Like I tell Zane, the winter season is the best because the snowbirds show up."

Trish grinned and Angel smiled back. Who could *not* like this woman?

"Zane's been a tremendous help." Trish spoke, face animated, hands moving in tandem with her excitement. "He's amazing. I had no idea where to start, but I'm getting the hang of it. Everywhere he goes he finds the most amazing things for the shop. He takes care of all the real business and I work with the customers."

Angel considered the "tough breaks" Zane had mentioned. What a shame that she'd been an inconvenience, a mistake in her parents' life. Trish was bright and pleasant, obviously loved her brother and worked at her shop. Sometimes. She seemed to keep odd hours, unless someone else was covering for her when she showed up at Zane's unannounced.

Trish waved her hand from side to side. "Yo, Angel, back to earth."

"Sorry, what were you saying?"

"I asked you where Zane is."

Hmm. "He didn't tell me where he was going, but he'll probably be back before you know it." Good answer.

"He doesn't even have an answering machine. Can you believe that? He grouches that ours doesn't always work, but that's because my friend Heidi turns it off so she doesn't miss any calls when she's home then forgets to hit the button on her way out."

Trish downed a slug of her drink. "Doesn't want me to call his cell unless it's an emergency. I called earlier to see what his plans were but missed him," Trish said, jiggling her glass. "So anyhow, I jumped the bus and took a chance he was here. Just as well. I'm getting to know you. Can't say that I've met any female friends of Zane's since he moved here."

That's interesting. "Why not?" Angel asked.

Trish's thick black lashes met when she smiled. She shoved her shoulders up in a shrug. "He's never had a problem meeting women. They fall all over him, but a girl in Texas burned him years ago. They were intense for two months, until he found out she was engaged to be married."

Zane's sister continued swishing the cubes around in her glass and rambled on. "I don't think he ever got over it. He sees everything in black and white, right or wrong. If there's one thing my brother hates it's being deceived. Personally, I was glad to see the gold digger gone. My brother's generous to a fault and I can't stand anyone taking advantage of him."

In spite of all Trish's flighty mannerisms, she exhibited core strength where Zane's welfare was concerned. A strength that maybe even her brother didn't realize.

The smile of a charming young woman replaced Trish's vexed reaction over the gold digger. She glanced at her jangling bracelet watch.

"I can't stay long. Heidi is picking me up after she gets off work." Trish bounced up, holding her glass out for examination. "Looks like I'm empty. Hang on. I'll be right back. You need water or a drink or anything?"

It wasn't bad enough she was becoming attached to a man she'd never see again, but Angel wanted to get to know his sister better. Some people fantasized about winning the lottery and living a life of leisure.

She fantasized about having a respectable job, a real home, though not elaborate, with a man who loved her who would give her children. Now that she'd met Trish, she wished she'd had a sister as well. Not much of an imagination, but the odds of having her dreams fulfilled were more obscure than winning a lottery.

In the less-than-ideal household Angel grew up in, she kept few friends. She never brought guests home to be around her mother's drinking. It took a long time after her mother died to start making friends. She built a few running friendships, looked forward to a new life once she left for college.

Once news of her arrest hit the papers, everyone deserted

her. Angel eschewed all female relationships after the year she'd spent in a cell trying to survive among women who'd trade a life for a pack of cigarettes.

She must have been born under a dark star to have such lousy timing.

After years of bitter disappointments, she'd met a man dreams were made of, with a sister she was beginning to genuinely care about. Creating space in her life for either one was an indulgence she couldn't afford.

Life continued to wave her heart's desire in front of her then snatch it away when her fingers touched the brass ring.

Trish hummed as she passed in front of Angel's chair until she bumped the coffee table and lost her balance. Angel leaped up to grab Trish's drink before it hit the glass surface. When the now-full drink hit the floor, ice and cola splattered across the carpet.

"Hang on, I'll get some towels."

Snagging a rag from the laundry room, Angel scrubbed the sandstone-shade rug. She sniffed a sweet whiskey scent but kept her thoughts to herself. Once the ice was picked up, the damp area was hardly noticeable. Amazingly, the drink had left no stain.

"Hey, thanks," Trish said, rubbing her eyes with the heel of her hand. "You should move here. Maybe Zane would stay home more often."

"That would be nice, but I've got a small problem I need to take care of before I can figure out where to live." If she was here, Angel might be able to help Trish, reach out to the young woman where no one had offered help to her mother.

Alcohol could numb the pain for only so long before it got out of hand.

Wavy black hair framed Trish's perfect complexion. She checked her watch. "Heidi's running late. Better go catch the next bus before I miss it." She stood then checked her watch again and sat down.

"Got another minute or two," she explained. "I hope you two keep seeing each other. I really like you, and my brother's the best. We're a lot alike, you know."

Angel decided to sit back and see what Trish could tell her about Zane. "I'll admit you two can't deny being brother and sister. Not with all that black hair and dark brown eyes."

"Well, yeah, that too, but he's restless like me," Trish noted.

"Really? What do you mean?"

Trish warmed to the new topic. "He never does the same thing for long. Jokes that he's a jack-of-all-trades but a master of none. I think he just gets bored. I call him the mystery man."

Before Angel could ask what she meant there was a knock at the door. Trish rocketed up from her chair. She rushed to the door and swung it wide open with no consideration of who stood on the other side.

Angel had leaped to her feet as well, heart slugging her chest bone. It wasn't Zane. She'd have heard the rumble of his diesel engine.

Two arms decorated in bangles and rings wrapped around Trish's back. A head of spiked blond hair hugged over her shoulder. Trish turned to Angel.

"This is my friend Heidi. Heidi, this is my friend Angel. Zane's, too."

"Nice to meet you." Angel let out a choked breath of relief and walked over to shake hands.

"Same here. Wow, you're taller than Trish. I think I'm living in the land of giants."

An understandable observation from someone who only reached Angel's shoulder.

Trish's uninhibited grin radiated happiness.

Angel swallowed back a lump of jealousy over the noticeably close friendship. No brother, no sister, no girlfriend, no man in her life. Angel's fantasy dropped to a lower notch.

One. Why couldn't she be cared for by at least one person? Was she destined to spend her life alone?

"Tell Zane I had to go, but I'll see him later." Trish gave Angel a big hug and whispered, "Thanks. I owe you for cleaning up my mess." In a flurry of chattering, Trish snatched her purse from the kitchen and closed the door behind them as she followed Heidi out.

Angel smiled, wishing she didn't have to leave. Wishing she could be like any other normal person with an average life. She wanted to stay in Ft. Lauderdale, wake up tomorrow morning with no criminal record and no Mason. But staying would only jeopardize Zane and Trish. Once she found the coins, she'd never see them again.

She smacked her head. "Stupid, stupid, stupid. I cannot believe I didn't ask her about the damn boat curtains. Next time, I need to keep my nose stuck in my own business," she complained to the empty room. She sank into the dark green leather chair. What had Trish meant by mystery man? Angel assumed he'd always been a pilot.

Zane was definitely a mystery man. The biggest mystery Angel found with him was his hair-trigger mood that ran from sizzle to chilly in the blink of an eye. One minute he couldn't keep his hands off her, and the next he kept her at a polite distance.

What did she expect, turning up in the least likely place every time the man saw her?

There was also the *small problem* she'd told Trish about. A small problem would be if no one showed up in a week to pay her rent. Staying away from Mason and locating the gold coins ranked as huge obstacles.

What few worldly possessions she owned would soon be set on the street, including a used racing bike and her acceptance notice to compete in the Tamarind Triathlon.

All the hard work she'd invested to compete in the high-profile event had gone down the drain. Her one opportunity to redeem her name in the athletic community had been thoroughly crushed.

What name? If she didn't figure a way out of this mess and Mason didn't kill her first, she faced a stretch in prison to add to her illustrious reputation. Or a life on the run.

Zane might be a mystery to his sister, but he'd been nothing short of a lifesaver since Angel had met him. As if it hadn't been enough to rescue her the night she escaped, he'd shown up in the abandoned gas station out of thin air after someone had taken a shot at her.

Questionable, yes, but she'd been damn glad to see him.

Mysterious or not, he was a godsend. Zane's caring and protective attentions chiseled at the icy barrier she'd built around her emotions. His first kiss had surprised her, but his hands had awakened needs she shouldn't even acknowledge.

She licked her lips remembering his taste.

Years of debilitating setbacks had hardened her soul. As a woman with a jaded past, she'd long since given up on ever believing someone decent would care for her or that she'd ever want anything from a man but a job.

She knew better than to trust a man with her life, but trusting one with her heart?

Now, *that* was a stretch.

Her throat tightened. Dreams were for other women. She didn't have a future and not a chance of one with a man like Zane. Even if she found a way out of this mess, nice guys didn't want a convicted criminal for a girlfriend.

Nothing could change the past.

Angel never indulged in self-pity, but a tear managed to slip down her cheek. She was falling in love with Zane. It must be her lot in life to want only what she couldn't have.

Another tear trickled down the side of her nose.

Of all the things she'd lost in her life, losing him would be the hardest.

C.K. pushed the long thin blade across the cool whetstone, enjoying how the smooth stainless steel ground to a fine edge

under the pressure of his forefinger. He wondered if the blade
would split a hair. Hadn't someone once told him a perfectly
sharpened knife would split a hair?

Silky, auburn hair would be a good test.

His cell phone vibrated. Right on time. "Speak."

"Joe, here. No sign of her yet. Got a tail on the pilot. He's
driving around, stopping at places and leaving right away like
he's looking for her, too. But we found his apartment."

Some jobs were simpler than others, but C.K. didn't care.
Diligence always paid off. He'd get her.

"Double the coverage," C.K. instructed.

"Will do, boss."

Chapter 11

Zane dialed Ben's lab number while he whipped his truck around the marina parking lot to head for the exit.

After ten rings he hung up and dialed his lab technician's cell number.

"Hello, this is Ben."

"Hey, bud, it's Zane. Where are you?"

"I'm at the hospital. Kerry went into labor about two hours ago."

Zane was torn between being thrilled for Ben and disheartened he couldn't ask his friend to run the prints.

"What's up, Zane?"

"It'll wait."

"Don't tell me you finally got prints?" Ben razzed.

"Yeah. I've got some data to run, too."

"You don't sound too thrilled. Why do I get the impression something's not right?" Ben asked, no longer in a teasing mode.

"You could say things have gotten more involved," Zane said.

"I don't like the sound of that. Why don't you turn this over to somebody else? You're way too close to moving up the ladder in the task force after this bust, and getting off the streets, to take an unnecessary risk right now."

Ben was right. With the High Vision ring broken, he'd be offered a rank that came with a normal life. If Zane had any hope of helping Trish, he had to be home more often.

Worse, if it turned out he'd been hiding a criminal, more than a promotion would go down the drain.

But he couldn't walk away until he knew for sure. That's why he trusted no one but Ben to check out the prints without stirring up problems. He could only follow his gut feelings. Turning his back on Angel at this point would be no easier than abandoning his sister.

Angel needed him. She was too stubborn to accept his help. Too bad. She was getting it anyhow.

"It's complicated, Ben. I'm not going to drop the ball with the High Vision case, but I have to find out this woman's background," Zane admitted.

"What if she's a criminal?"

"Then I'll deal with it," Zane stated emphatically.

"You may be getting in over your head on this one, bud," Ben warned.

"Maybe, but I'm past the point of no return."

"Oh, buddy, this doesn't sound like business anymore, but I'm not going to pry. Drop off everything you've got. I'll run the fingerprint through as soon as I get back to the lab, but I'm telling you I won't sugarcoat the truth."

"Thanks, Ben. Give my love to Kerry."

Two more turns before Zane reached his apartment.

Streetlights flickered on along the highway in the dusky early-evening glow. The western tree line swallowed a tangerine sun. Three hours had passed since Angel vanished.

Sick disappointment settled in his chest.

She hadn't been at the airport or the boat. He couldn't think of anywhere else she might go.

With Ben and his wife in the delivery room expecting their first child, Zane wouldn't get a rundown on the fingerprints for at least a day or two.

By the time he found out who she was, it could very well be a moot point.

Angel would be long gone, maybe permanently.

His stomach churned at the idea that someone wanted to kill her. He forced his thoughts away from that possibility.

She'd been a frustrating puzzle from the minute he'd met her—a multilayered, three-dimensional puzzle with danger-ous, razor-sharp pieces missing. Where had she been kept against her will and why?

All he knew was she had the talent of an elite athlete and had lost a scholarship for some unknown reason. Everything came back to that one word—unknown.

He wanted to shake some sense into her, make her under-stand how much she needed his help. She'd been tagged with a transmitter like a banded bird and placed under armed guard. The thugs he'd met in Charleston were dressed in thousand-dollar tailored suits.

Against an organized and financially robust lethal group, how did she expect to protect herself, much less him, too?

He couldn't recall when a woman had put him first in her life. Certainly not Sylvia, the dazzling jewel he'd fallen for in Texas. She'd been anything but what she presented. Truly a woman who planned for her future by covering all bases, Sylvia was engaged to another man while dating him.

Just when Sylvia had convinced Zane she loved him, he discovered she had a clueless fiancé who couldn't wait to marry the lying witch.

Good thing Ben still lived there. Observing Sylvia with ob-jective eyes had given Ben cause to run a very revealing back-ground check.

All Sylvia really sought were the material proceeds Zane's family name and eventual inheritance would offer. Basically a businesswoman, Sylvia had been shopping her engagement deal to see if she could improve her investment. Since then, Zane gave few women little more than casual interest. Others had proved to be just as materialistically driven.

Except for Angel. For someone who desperately needed help, she refused his every offer.

He trusted few people in his life, understood Angel's reticence to share her private problems. But he didn't believe she'd survive on her own for long. Not without a lot of luck and a chunk of money. Neither of which appeared readily available to her. What would it take to convince her she could depend upon him? He might never find out.

She was gone, maybe forever.

Out of sight, out of mind?

Whoever came up with that saying never met Angel. Auburn hair and mile-long legs remained emblazoned as a header to all his thoughts.

As he made the last corner into his development, images of Angel clicked past his mind's eye in slow motion. Wide-eyed and terrified in his airplane, then curled up, sleeping against his front door.

She'd danced her fingers through the wind as she'd ridden beside him in the truck. Shampooed and showered, draped in a single towel next to his laundry. Zane smiled, remembering the look on her face when he'd found her.

Half covered in his shirt, she'd slept in his bed.

Her hazel eyes flashed with fire when he annoyed her, but they were pure whiskey—warm and intoxicating—when he kissed her.

He shook his head at his wandering thoughts. A dial in his brain flipped to his professional conscience, jeering at him to admit the truth.

Black and white, right and wrong battled in his mind. When had the lines blurred?

Angel behaved as a fugitive.

That's the real reason he should be hunting her. With a little more time, once he uncovered her identity and knew why someone chased her, he could help her. But, if she's not a criminal, why did she refuse to bring in the police?

If he did corral her again, he'd turn her over to the authorities. They had more time to deal with an uncooperative female in trouble, he reasoned.

Right?

He parked the truck just outside the door to his apartment and sat there, watching the halogen parking-lot lamps begin to brighten.

Who was he kidding? Zane snorted at his lack of honesty.

Hand Angel over to a bunch of strangers? No way. If he found her, he knew what he'd do—drag her into his arms and taste her lips. There'd never been a woman he'd been driven to have in the way he desired Angel.

If he got his hands on her one more time, he'd…

Mason answered the private line in his Manhattan office. "Lorde."

"Sir, this is Richardson." Richardson oversaw Mason's warehouse as head of security. He knew about all shipments, legitimate and otherwise.

"Is there a problem?" Mason asked.

"Possibly. An auditor from the underwriting group for the warehouse insurance came by."

"What's the problem?"

"Smelled like a fish," Richardson said.

Mason gritted his teeth at the nickname his group used for the FBI.

"What did he want?" Mason demanded.

There was a slight pause on the other end of the line before Mason heard, "Most of his questions were standard until he asked for the inventory clerk."

Weiland, one of Mason's best men from his private compound, had replaced Angel when she'd been *removed* from the operation.

"What did Weiland tell him?"

"Uh, Weiland didn't speak to him. The auditor asked specifically for Angelina Farentino. Said she was listed as the contact. I told him she no longer worked for Lorde Industries. He asked a couple vague questions and left."

A prick of concern crept along Mason's neck. Richardson was right. The auditor smelled like a fish.

"Did you get his card?"

"Yes, sir. I called the underwriters. They confirmed he was a freelance auditor."

That meant nothing. The FBI was capable of infiltrating anywhere they needed an operative.

Mason was sure he'd convinced Angel that she'd played a role in the smuggling operation, and that with her record no one would believe she was innocent. As long as she ran, he felt certain she'd avoid the authorities, but if they picked her up first, she could be used against him.

And the minute she tried to sell those coins, she'd be arrested.

He ended the call and dialed his bounty hunter's number. The receiver clicked on the other end then he heard, "Speak."

"C.K., I want an update," Mason said.

"I've nailed down the city. Think we've got an address."

"Think? Not good enough." Mason's fingers strangled the phone.

"M.L., hold it a minute. The pilot who moved your problem last time is still handling the package. That's the address. I'm checking it out."

"Your sources aren't working fast enough," Mason charged.

"We'll get her, but looks like somebody else has an interest. You don't have another team down here, do you?"

"No. What are you talking about?" Mason said.

"Had another group try to intercept her, but she ran from the pilot's truck. Better not be another contractor. If they get in my way, I'll remove them," C.K. warned.

"You're the only one on my tab, but we may have interest from the government."

Time was no longer on Mason's side. C.K. had to pick her up before the feds did.

"Secure the problem somewhere out of the way, then call me," Mason said.

"I expect some resistance."

"Don't damage *my* merchandise."

"What about the pilot?" C.K. asked.

"I don't care what you do with him. Just don't leave a trail and don't draw attention."

Mason hung up and dialed his favorite reporter, the one who owed him for a favor.

Zane parked the truck then trudged to the apartment, hating the emptiness that awaited him inside. He unlocked the door. When the alarm failed to sound, he tensed.

Reaching down in his boot to retrieve the .32 Smith & Wesson, Zane eased the door open. Through the dark shadows cast across the room he could just make out a figure silhouetted against the hazy light beyond the glass doors.

A woman stood with her arms folded against her chest, staring out at nothing.

His throat closed up.

Angel. He couldn't believe she was here.

Zane stepped in, closed the door and dropped the gun back down in his boot. He moved gradually into the room, afraid she'd vanish into thin air. His lungs struggled to draw oxygen.

She was really here.

An arm's length away, he stopped. She hadn't moved to acknowledge him. Scattered thoughts raced across his mind, but only one broke through to the surface.

She'd come back to him.

He swallowed and whispered, "Angel?"

A soft glow emitting from a single bronze lamp tinted the room. Turned away from the light, her face was hidden in shadow until she lifted her head. The sight of her tear-streaked cheeks ripped his heart to pieces.

He opened his arms and she came into them. Zane wrapped her in a close embrace, so very glad to feel her warm body next to his.

"I thought you were gone," he said, his voice raw with emotion. "Forever."

She shook her head against his chest. Her tears dampened his shirt.

"Are you okay?" he asked.

She nodded against his chest, hugging him around the waist.

He stroked up and down her back, his fingers massaging along her spine. His chin rested against her silky hair. A lump of gratitude formed in his throat. She was alive.

Angel tilted her head back. Sad eyes beseeched him through wet lashes. "I had to get them away from you." Her fervent words, spoken quietly, floated through the still room.

He breathed out a deep sigh and leaned his forehead against hers.

"Honey, I wish you'd trust me enough to tell me what's going on," he pleaded in a whisper.

She pushed her hands up past his chest to each side of his face, stroking lightly until two fingers rested on his lips.

He kissed the soft pads.

"Zane, you're the one person I do trust," she admitted.

Her sheer breath flowed against his neck. She trailed her fingers across his face and neck, tormenting him with the wispy touch.

"I'm sorry. I shouldn't have come back here, but I had nowhere else to go," she apologized. "My being here puts you at risk. I never meant to cause you trouble. I don't want anything to happen to you."

He hugged her close. From *what* was she trying to protect him?

"Who is the guy that's after you?" he urged.

She shook her head no against him.

He'd have laughed at her favorite word if he weren't so worried.

"I can't keep guessing. I need to hear it from you," Zane said. "He's not your boyfriend or husband, is he?"

"No," she said, barely above a whisper.

"Then you either did something to make him angry as hell or you have something he wants," Zane said.

"Yes."

"Which is it?"

"Both."

What did she have? Zane had the compass, but that couldn't be it. Could it?

"If you give it back, will he leave you alone?" Zane asked.

"No."

"Why not?"

"It doesn't belong to him," she explained.

Zane drew his head back. She was killing him. None of this made sense.

All his questions fled when she blinked wet lashes up at him. He realized she wore one of his T-shirts. Her hair was damp. She'd showered, which told him she'd probably covered some of the distance by foot, if not all.

He ran his fingers up her back, combed them through her hair, fine strands lacing around his hand.

Nothing mattered at that moment. Not her past, not his future, nothing but the luxury of her in his arms.

Zane lowered his lips, gently raked across hers. He kissed her cheek, her nose, her eyes, tasting the salty tears.

She twined her fingers around the back of his neck, snuggling herself up against him. His lips swept softly over her warm mouth until she returned his kiss with an intensity that rocked him.

Of its own accord, his hand moved down along the smooth contour of her back. He scooped her bottom, his hand meeting with soft bare skin, and lifted her against him.

His tongue arrowed between her lips, delving again and again for the exquisite taste that could only be Angel. A taste as narcotic as those he kept off the streets. Her fingers clutched his shoulders and, with a shift of her hips against his throbbing arousal, she sent shock waves through him.

Caution sirens screamed in his head.

Her scent overrode them.

Zane moved his lips along her chin up to the crest of her ear. He buried his face in her hair, inhaling the wonderful fresh smell.

She crooked her head to one side, allowing him to scorch a trail of fevered kisses down her slender neck. Feather-soft hair flicked over his fingers as his hand roamed across her shoulders.

With one arm supporting her, he leaned her backward to enjoy the sweet access of her throat. Her purred moans drove him to the brink of no control. He'd never sate his taste for her. Covering her mouth with his, their lips joined in a sexual dance.

In the recesses of his mind, a voice pleaded with him to slow down, don't act irrationally.

Her fingers combing through his hair silenced the voice.

A chirping noise broke through his fervor, annoying him. *What the hell was that?*

She tugged on his hair when he tore his mouth away. He sprinkled kisses along a southern path to her shoulders. She stretched up on her toes, a feline leaning in to be stroked.

The chirping grew more constant.

Damn. What was that?

With deft movements, the oversize T-shirt rose to her chest. He cupped a breast, just the perfect size to fill his hand, sent two fingers across the areola.

She sucked in a sharp breath, expelling the air in a long pained moan.

The chirping was back.

It finally dawned on him his cell phone was ringing. He didn't want to answer and thought seriously about pitching it out the door.

With each loud chirp of the phone, consciousness hammered his aroused senses back to reality. He was in the middle of an investigation. His sister and Heidi had the number for emergencies.

For once in his life, Zane wished he was undisciplined enough to ignore his responsibilities.

Every nerve in his body stood on end. He was so hard the zipper outline had to be embossed on his erection.

And he was seconds from stripping the woman in his arms.

That woke him up.

What the hell was he doing? For the second time, he'd completely lost his grip.

Resigned to his fate, Zane pulled his hand from her breast. He stroked her shoulder, shifted the shirt back down to cover her and kissed her face.

He didn't want to take his hands off her.

"Honey, I'm sorry," he whispered.

Sorry they weren't in his bed, sorry his life was not his own, sorry some jerk had invented cell phones.

Angel lifted her head. She stared at him as though he'd said there were elephants coming at them. Dazed and mussed as if she'd just been loved, her lips were puffy, waiting to be kissed.

If their lips touched again, he wasn't sure he could back away.

Quiet reigned for several seconds once the phone ceased, but then the irritating sound resumed.

"Damn." He kissed her forehead. "I've got to take this call." He eased her out of his arms and jerked the phone from the clip on his hip.

"Zane," he snapped, anger, frustration and self-disgust wrapped around the short salutation.

"This is Heidi. Sorry to bug you, but you said to call if Trish ever needed you." As his sister's best friend in Texas, Heidi had decided to stay in Ft. Lauderdale after one visit. She was the closest Trish had ever come to having a sister. Her concern for Trish rivaled Zane's, the reason she was the only non-agency person besides his sister who had his cell number.

"What's wrong? Where is she?" Several possible situations crossed Zane's mind, all of which soured his stomach.

"She's okay, but she's at the Pink Baby and some guy is giving her a hard time. I dropped her at the shop earlier and was supposed to meet her at the bar. I went home to let Dazzle out in the yard and my car won't start. I know you don't want her walking to a bus at night," Heidi said.

Zane groaned.

"Trish heard from one of the other girls he's into weird stuff, and I think he scares her. Trish didn't want to bother you, so I told her I'd get a ride and come get her, but you're only fifteen minutes away. I'm close to an hour once I get the car started."

Zane looked at Angel. In the minute since he'd answered his phone she'd withdrawn. The distance between them felt as wide as the ocean crashing against the beach outside. She'd turned to him for comfort and he'd practically mauled her.

"Okay, Heidi. I'll get her."

He snapped the phone shut. "Angel…"

She held up a hand to stop him. "I shouldn't be doing this. I'm sorry. Really. It won't happen again."

He closed his eyes then opened them. When would his life get any easier?

"Look, Angel, it was my fault, not yours."

"Then let's just call it even and drop it."

Not sure what to say without making things worse, he decided to take her advice and let it go, for now.

"I've got to go pick up Trish. Do you want to come with me?"

"No. I'd rather stay here," she said.

Zane sighed. Trish had to be picked up before she got hurt.

"Will you promise me you won't leave the apartment?" he asked. "I don't think I can take too many more surprises today. When I get back, I want you to tell me why you took off earlier."

"I won't leave," she said, then added, "I promise."

Based on her posture—arms crossed, back straight, chin high—a casual observer would think her confidence had returned. Not Zane. He'd noticed her habit of chewing on her bottom lip when she was nervous. The nibbling gave her away.

Disappointment filled her eyes when she licked her lips and said, "I can't tell you the truth about why I left earlier, and I'd rather not lie to you."

She still didn't trust him.

After what he'd just pulled, she'd probably never trust him. He huffed out a harsh breath. They'd tackle this when he returned.

He changed the subject. "After I get Trish, I'll pick up something to eat on the way home. What would you like?"

"Pizza?"

Her predilection for one food group amused him, but his heart was in his throat, making it tough to smile.

He hated walking away from her right now, but knew better than to leave Trish for long when she was partying hard.

Angel must have misread his reluctance as concern that she'd disappear.

"Don't worry. I'll be here."

Would she?

Chapter 12

Angel dug through the basket full of clean clothes next to the dryer. Not enough that she was wearing his clothes, but she'd spilled soda down the front of the white one she'd had on and needed a new one. She found a blazing-red shirt with a chest pocket.

Perfect. It suited her blazing fury. She hadn't quite figured out who she was angrier with, herself or Zane, but red covered all bases.

Had she completely lost all sense of priority? Okay, be honest. She wanted him as bad as he obviously wanted her, if that hadn't been a gun in his pocket. A big-barreled gun.

Desiring him to touch her in ways she could only imagine was bad enough. Letting him take her physically to a place she'd never reach again would destroy her emotionally.

Where would consummating the heat igniting between them leave either one?

She stalked into the bathroom and jerked off her clothes.

She scowled at her puckered nipples, annoyed over her body's inability to quickly dismiss his touch. On the other hand, she was equally annoyed at him for keeping her in a physical state of habitual frenzy, while apologizing at the same time.

Chilled from the frigid air coursing through the apartment, Angel cranked the shower lever to one degree before scalding. The boiling water charged over her screaming muscles, drawing out the tension. Surely the residents of this humid state ran up a huge water bill from showering. Twice daily would be a minimum.

She sometimes showered three times a day since leaving prison. Didn't care as long as she showered without a group of women present.

Refreshed from the shower and calmer, she dried her hair quickly before relaxing on the leather sofa. There was no point in continuing with her habitual cleaning at Zane's apartment. What would a pilot care if she left a fingerprint?

She found the television remote on the bottom shelf of one end table. Local news trailed across the screen, spouting the latest stock-market concerns and weather before moving to national interests.

Curling up against the wide armrest of the sofa, she'd almost drifted off to sleep when a news report broke through her slumber.

"The body found in a Dumpster near Raleigh, North Carolina, has been identified as Jeff Jurnowski," the news anchor announced. "Initial report on cause of death is a gunshot wound to the head. The police have several leads, but are not discussing those at this time."

She sat straight up in a prone position, paralyzed by the words. That was Mason's former employee, Jeff. With the bullet hole in the head Mason had put there. Poor Jeff. He'd worked on the wrong side of the law, but no one deserved to be murdered in cold blood. Jeff had been nice to her, even showing Angel a picture of his pet beagle.

The televised report rattled her nerves. Mason wasn't stupid. Jeff's body hadn't ended up in a Dumpster by mistake. What was Mason up to? Her hands trembled when she lifted the remote to click up the volume.

The news anchor finished with, "The authorities are running fingerprints found on the man's possessions. His employer, Mason Lorde, has issued a statement of the company's sympathy over the loss of a respected employee. Mr. Lorde went on to say he will aid the police in any way and alluded to a female employee who may be a suspect in the case. They are not releasing her name at this time."

Angel's mouth fell open. *...running fingerprints found on the man's possessions.* She'd touched the photo of Jeff's dog.

Mason intended to hang Jeff's murder on her.

Zane shuffled through the front door with Trish and a pizza. His sister's glum face and quiet countenance a result of his own discontent.

He'd decided to bring her home rather than spend two hours on the road delivering her to the house she shared with Heidi. Worry about Angel slipping away drove that decision.

Women would put him in an early grave.

"Sorry to screw up your evening," Trish whispered. The anguish in her upturned face told him he'd hit a nerve with his black mood.

The last thing he wanted to do was hurt his sister, especially in her present condition. He shouldn't take his aggravation out on her. But keeping her out of trouble and unharmed became tougher each week. Every trip he made undercover he risked not being around to save her.

He owed her better than that.

He was angry all right, with everybody, including himself.

Angel walked tentatively into the living room from the bathroom hallway. Jazz music playing low seeped into the room from the milk carton–size Bose speakers positioned above his oak entertainment cabinet.

His red T-shirt waved into view. Angel must have dug it out of the clean laundry and showered again.

He inhaled the scent of soap and shampoo. Oh, man. Drained from dealing with Trish, his brain teetered between the rigid discipline responsibility demanded and his desire to strip Angel bare in the shower.

"I've apologized to Zane, so I'll apologize to you. Sorry," Trish said.

Angel shot him a questioning look.

He fought the urge to tape his sister's mouth shut. Zane loved his sister, but he'd like one night of peace and quiet. One night he wasn't reminded of all the bad things that had happened to Trish.

"I asked him to take me home, but he nixed that," Trish said. "I'll bunk somewhere out of the way."

"You can have the foldout. Angel's in the bedroom. I'll find another spot," Zane said.

Trish gave him a strange look. She was clearly surprised that he and Angel were not sleeping together.

"Absolutely not," Angel stated. "I hardly use up a third of that king-size bed. Trish can sleep in there, too."

"You sure?" Trish said, her confused gaze flicking between the two of them.

Zane gave Trish a don't-go-there look he'd given her plenty of times in the past.

Trish shrugged. "I'm going to change and hit the sack then." Trish gave them each another look then hugged her brother and said, "Love ya. Sorry. I promise not to be pain in your side again."

His throat tightened. She was good as gold, and he'd crawl through broken glass for her. Trish hadn't really done anything wrong, hadn't slipped in months. She was slowly building the business. He hugged her. "Love you, too. Don't mind me."

"You need a vacation," Trish whispered. "With someone like Angel. Do a world of good for what ails you."

He squeezed her. "Good night."

Trish turned to Angel and gave her a hug. Zane wanted to chuckle at the surprise on Angel's face. Her face softened into one of pleasure. Again, he wondered about the woman who never left his thoughts. Where did she come from? Who were her family?

Who wanted to kill her?

When Trish tripped down the hall and closed the bedroom door, Zane turned to Angel. "I called Heidi back and told her I would just bring Trish here for the night."

"I'm glad you did."

That didn't sound good. Was Angel worried he'd make a move on her again? After the one he made earlier she probably had every right to be. What had he been thinking?

Thinking? His brain went numb the minute he was near her. Having Trish here would ensure he behaved. Dammit.

Zane stretched the stiff muscles of his neck. "Want something to drink? Water maybe? Sit outside for a few minutes?"

"Sounds good. I'm going to run and get my things off the bed. I'll be back in just a minute."

Zane trudged to the kitchen, the weight of the world hung across his shoulders. He carried a cold bottle of water to the patio. A beer normally tasted good on a hot evening, but respect for Trish's personal battle changed his mind.

Unwilling to turn the outside lights on, he navigated by the glow from the lamps inside. He sat in the comfort of dark, hidden from the world for a short while. A soft breeze dispelled some of the humidity. Weather in south Florida reminded him of visiting the coast in Galveston.

He'd loved Texas, but couldn't stay there with the memories. Besides, he'd needed a new home for Trish and a place to work where he wasn't known by half the city. Being a third-generation son of the reputed dynasty of the Jackson Oil

Refinery had its pros and cons. Zane couldn't buy a cup of coffee without some reporter considering it news if he drank it alone or not.

Everyone had expected him to sign on as a company man once he left the navy. He'd surprised his relatives and the city when he turned his back on Texas for Florida. At the time, moving Trish to Ft. Lauderdale and working with Ben, who had already settled there, seemed a good plan.

Worrying about Trish and juggling his career were starting to wear him down.

Infiltrating High Vision's operations had become an arduous process, slow and tedious. When his task force hadn't been able to get someone on the inside of their shipping operation, he'd suggested creating Black Jack Airlines charter service. So far, High Vision hadn't shipped anything questionable, which he attributed to caution and security.

The waiting sponged up every drop of patience he possessed. Maybe that's why he couldn't keep his hands off Angel—too much untapped energy.

Liar. The truth was staring him in the face, whether he wanted to cop to it or not. He couldn't let her go. Just realizing what that meant scared him to his toes.

For his own self respect, he'd walked away from his parents and joined the navy. For his sister, he'd turned his back on a career as an officer.

What did he think he was going to do now, change everything? He'd been living in the moment, ignoring the future. Even if Angel wasn't in some serious trouble up to her neck, he had anything but a normal home life.

He should just bring in the authorities. They'd deal with the jerk who was after her. Then he could walk away. She'd made it real clear she had no plans to stick around. He didn't know her whole name, where she came from or how she'd spent her life.

He didn't even know what she ate besides pizza.

What he did know was how his insides flip-flopped when she walked into a room. He'd dated some knockout women, but none of them had elicited the feelings Angel drummed up. Feelings he didn't care to define just yet.

A soft shuffling brought Zane from his mental meandering. The cherry-red shirt glowed in the dim light. Wisps of Angel's damp hair floated softly about her shoulders as she settled in a chair across from him. He understood her need for distance from him, but ached with the desire to hold her.

"What's Trish's story?" she asked.

Zane leaned forward in his chair with his hands on the patio table. For too many years to count, he'd defended Trish against his parents' criticisms and nasty comments from relatives. Time and guilt had developed a knee-jerk response to anything regarding Trish. But Angel hadn't accused or passed judgment. She sounded sincerely interested.

"It's my fault that Trish is getting a late start on life," Zane said.

"Why do you think it's your fault?" she asked quietly.

"I deserted her along with everyone else when I went into the navy. I could see my parents felt burdened with an unwanted child, but I was too caught up in what I wanted to do to notice the damage being done to Trish.

"When our parents were killed, I found out they'd left everything to me, the golden boy. Trish knows I'll take care of her and share everything I have, but that didn't change how unimportant it made her feel." He hung his head, recalling the agony and guilt for the way his parents had dealt Trish a final blow.

"I'll never forget her face at the reading of the will." Unwanted memories flooded back. Zane paused to consider the damage a piece of paper could inflict then continued.

"Trish was young and didn't understand the cold logic our parents had used. They left everything to me, once I turn forty, which won't be for a couple years. Nothing to Trish, not even a fare-thee-well." He'd read the papers over and over again, sure they hadn't done that to a child.

Angel took one of his hands in her two slender ones. Her compassionate touch drew away his pain.

Zane glanced up to see the sadness in his soul reflected in Angel's face. "I tried to tell Trish they would have changed the will once she was an adult and that their intention had been for me to watch out for her. That didn't erase the hurt. It wasn't about the money. Trish just needed to hear her name mentioned, to know she counted."

"I'm so sorry for both of you," Angel whispered. Her eyes glittered with tears. "But you can't blame yourself," Angel soothed. "Your parents deserted her, not you. She idolizes you. And I see the strength adversity has given her. She's much tougher than you think."

"That may be, but after hearing the will, Trish took a downturn. Gradually the drinking got worse. She tried AA in Houston, but didn't stick with it. She's doing great, but I feel like I'm blowing it being gone all the time. Soon, though, I hope to rearrange my work soon so I can be here for her."

"You're a good brother. Trish is very lucky. I wish I'd had a sibling."

Intentional or not, Angel was giving him a tiny piece to the puzzle of her background. She was an only child. Her mother died when she was twelve. Her father?

Zane swallowed at the sadness in her voice.

Neither spoke for a while. The ocean's surf stirred against the shore in the distance, filling the silence. Zane felt Angel's fingers stroke over his hand. When was the last time anyone had comforted him? A vague memory of being held as a small child came to mind, but nothing since then.

Her depth of caring for others humbled him.

After a bit, she moved her hands away and stood. "Think I'll turn in. We can talk tomorrow. Don't worry about Trish. I'll watch over her tonight." She'd stepped back to the glass doors.

He was up and around the table before she reached the opening.

"Angel."

"What?" She spun around.

"I was worried about you today. I can't handle you being out on the streets alone."

"I'm sorry. I had no choice."

"You do." Zane forced his hands to stay away from her, his thoughts to stay on topic.

"I wish I did." She lifted a hand to his cheek, moved toward him as if she'd forgotten how he'd taken advantage of her earlier.

"Why won't you let me do something for you?" he pleaded.

"I will."

His heart raced. "What? I'll do it."

"This." Her hands knifed up between them, around his neck. She touched her lips to his, softly.

He threaded his fingers through her hair, cupped her head, the kiss full of compassion, not carnal desire.

Oh, man, he craved the feel of her next to him. Her fingers splayed across his chest. Desire licked at every spot she touched. He loved her lips, soft, full on the bottom, hungry.

She grazed his lips with her teeth and ran her tongue across his mouth. One delicate hand slid down his neck, sending chills up his spine. If they didn't stop soon, he'd take her right there on the patio.

Zane ended the kiss, slowly, brushing his lips across her cheek and forehead.

"Honey." He cleared his tight throat and tried again. "We'll figure this out. I know you don't understand how, but I *can* help you. We'll work through this tomorrow. Okay?"

She nodded into his chest when he hugged her tight.

He let her ease away from him, reluctantly, watching her until she disappeared down the hallway.

Zane settled back into his chair and listened to a seagull

call in the distance. Wheels in his brain churned with the new information. Angel had only been a child when her mother had died. She was cagey about her father. What had life thrown at her since then? He had to know. Every minute with her tied him in one more knot.

Tomorrow he'd convince her to tell him her full name or he'd find a way to research his data, even if he had to go outside the agency.

He had to know the identity of this woman before he let it go any farther between them.

Be serious. It had already gone too far. He was in deep.

"C.K., no sign of her yet. Got another six men on the street," Joe said.

"Keep a tail on the pilot," C.K. ordered. "Leave a man on the front of the apartment entrance. I'll cover the back."

C.K. snapped the phone shut. He had a feeling about the apartment. His second sense was usually right.

She'd show up there. When she did, he'd make sure Mason's Angel didn't float away.

Chapter 13

Zane was sure he'd only just fallen asleep, when his cell phone woke him. He checked the digital clock on the VCR: four-ten. Unfortunately that was a.m.

He flipped the phone open. "Zane."

"Sammy, here. Sorry to roust you so early on a Saturday, but a *special* shipment is coming in at the docks in Jacksonville. Central office wants you to check it out, be in the area to deliver if High Vision calls on short notice. They've been known to pull that and get whoever is handy so no one has time to plan."

Zane stretched his stiff neck. This was the one they'd been waiting to hear about. "What time is it due through customs?"

"Right around nine this morning. Think your man can help?" Sammy referred to the informant Zane had met the night he'd flown in with Angel. The guy hadn't given him anything concrete in Charleston, but he might have a tip regarding this shipment. With the information market, you never knew unless you asked.

"I don't know. Let me get up there and see what's shaking. Have a car dropped at the airport. I don't have time to call for one."

"You got it. Anything else?"

Solve his personal dilemma with Angel and Trish? "No. Call you later." He twisted right and left, trying to unkink his aching back. The sofa bed needed a new mattress, one that would hold his bulk.

By the time he'd made up the bed and dashed through a shower, the coffee had finished perking. He sipped a cup of the hot brew and glanced around the spotless kitchen. He couldn't take credit for a cleaning that good.

An uneasy feeling settled over him at the thought of leaving Angel alone. He knew she'd take care of Trish until Heidi arrived, but would he come home to find her gone again?

He'd been absentmindedly studying the room, when his eyes passed near the door, then stopped.

Yellow running shoes were parked to the right of the entrance.

Oh, yeah. He knew what to do.

Next to his laundry, he unlocked the utility room and snapped the light on. Hidden under piles of boxes and junk he used for camouflage was a locked toolbox. Inside were tools for specific jobs and transmitters of all sizes he used for listening as well as tracking. After he found a transmitter the size of a shirt button, Zane put everything back in place. He took the sneakers and his Swiss Army Knife outside.

He opened the driver's door on his truck to work under the dome light where he had enough time to hide what he was doing if someone walked up. Rumbling in the distance was a precursor of the weather he'd have to fly through, creating another mental note to swing by the marina and check on the boat.

Too much stretch would leave slack in the ropes and his boat would be damaged along each side.

Pulling the laces very loose, he opened the shoe wide. He cut a slit at the base of the tongue. With tweezers he worked the transmitter inside the padded covering, deep enough that Angel would never feel it.

The next time she performed a Houdini vanishing act, he had a magic wand to make her reappear.

Pleased with himself, he almost whistled going back in the door until he met Angel on the other side.

"What are you doing with my shoes?"

Busted. "I noticed some dirt on them and you're so neat I knew you wouldn't want to track through the apartment."

She inspected the shoes.

He'd drawn the laces back as close to where she'd left them as he could. The bottoms were spotless when she turned them over, just the way he'd found them.

She cut her eyes up at him. "Are you sure? I could swear I cleaned them last night."

"You probably couldn't see well in the dark. Not a big deal. I didn't mind doing it."

"I suppose I should thank you." Her appreciation was more dubious than sincere.

"Don't worry about it. Look, I've got to make a run. I hate to ask you to do anything else after last night, but I'd rather let Trish sleep some more."

"I don't mind. When will you be back?" she asked, a slight catch in her voice.

Was it his imagination or would she miss him?

"I'm not sure, maybe tonight, but it could be tomorrow. I'll call later and let you know. Will you be here?"

He watched her face as she juggled possible answers.

"I'll try to be."

"What does that mean?" he demanded, instantly irritated. "Why would you leave? At least stay where you're safe until I get back."

"Don't worry about me, Zane. You have plenty of other things to think about." She shifted the shoes to her other hand.

He loved the way she said his name. He wanted to hear it

again and again. Hear it in her early-morning voice, husky with sleep. Yeah, she'd moan his name as he made love to her.

God, he was losing it. She *had better be* here when he returned.

He smiled inwardly. At least he had a backup plan.

It was time to go, but not before he did one last thing.

Zane gathered her into his arms and kissed her as if he'd never get another chance, because that's exactly what worried him.

The shoes hit the floor.

She tasted like toothpaste and Angel. Her fingers drove through his hair, dragging him closer to her as if she, too, expected it to be their last.

Ecstasy and misery flowed through him. He loved her scent, the feel of her lips, her smooth skin. But the question of her being there when he returned haunted the recesses of his mind.

Duty called. It was close to five-thirty. He had to go. If he stayed any longer there wouldn't be time to swing by the boat and adjust the new bowlines. One good squall would sink the boat at the dock if the ropes were too loose.

Thunder rumbled outside, assuring him the ropes would be tested soon.

Zane hugged her close and pressed his lips to her forehead. "I left my cell-phone number on the counter. I'll be back as soon as I can and we'll figure out your problem together."

"But, Zane…"

"Shh. We'll talk when I get back. Just promise me you won't take any chances."

She dropped her head to his chest.

"Promise me, Angel. Please." He'd figured out that she'd rather be silent than lie and believed she'd stick to a commitment.

"Okay, I promise," she whispered.

He lifted her chin, gave her one last kiss, then left.

Angel carried a mug of coffee out to the patio to watch the sun rise. She inhaled the salt air, enjoying the special peace found only during early-morning hours. Deep red and dusty lavender clouds tinged the edge of the horizon. Wasn't there an old weather saying? "Red skies at morning, sailors take warning."

She hoped Zane would also take no chances.

He'd done nothing *but* take a chance since meeting her. Angel raked a hand through her hair. She shouldn't have agreed to stay put. Zane just didn't understand how deep her trouble ran. His offer to help was sweet and noble considering the type of men chasing after her, but he thought it was just a relationship gone sour.

When Zane returned, he'd ask more questions. The last thing she wanted to do was tell him anything that would involve him in this mess. His first move would be to bring in the police. He'd said it too many times for her to believe she would convince him otherwise.

She'd stayed too long already.

If she didn't have to hang around for Trish she'd be making a straight line to the boat. There were all sorts of storage areas she hadn't dug through.

Then what was she going to do?

It was simple.

Find the coins and leave, or risk the life of the man she was falling for.

Wind lifted whitecaps over the waves where the canal to the Gulf Winds Marina met the bay. Zane hurried down the dock to secure the boat so he could get to the airfield and try to lift off ahead of the building storm.

Just another headache he didn't need this morning.

Like worrying about what Trish might say. She had no reason to discuss him or their family…or their last name.

He should have covered that somehow, but hadn't been thinking clearly this morning. Not thinking clearly when it came to Angel was becoming routine. Just have to hurry back and hope for a break, that Trish would be in a big hurry to go home.

Zane leaped aboard. Starting on the bow and working his way to the stern, he made quick work of tightening the ropes that had slackened overnight. The boat was old, but he might as well preserve what was there. He climbed down into the cabin.

Under the front bunk he lifted the lid to access a lower compartment and dragged out the package of new side curtains he'd had made. After replacing the lid and cushion, he tore the brown paper packaging away then carried the four curtain sections onto the deck to sort them. Zane picked one up, figured out it was for the starboard side then tossed it aside.

Thunk!

What the devil was that? He lifted the section back up. The bottom-hemmed pocket bulged. He squeezed two fingers into the pocket, felt something hard surrounded by plastic. Zane moved over to the cockpit where he kept a pair of needle-nose pliers on the dash. He pinched a corner of the plastic between the metal fingers and wiggled it out far enough to see a coin.

What was a gold coin doing there?

He carefully snaked out the rest of the long plastic sleeve and laid it on the captain's chair.

Eight gold coins ranging in dates from 1922 through 1933 were embellished with a maiden in a long gown running with a torch on the front. The flip side had an eagle.

He knew nothing about coin collecting, but it didn't take an expert to realize he held something extremely rare.

How had they gotten into his canvas curtains?

Zane retraced the package's path in his mind. He'd picked them up in Raleigh from the custom shop, carried them around until he' loaded the package into the Titan. They were with him all the way until he'd unloaded them when he landed.

The package hadn't been out of his sight.

Charleston. Angel had ridden to Charleston with him.

His skin chilled at his next thought. Had she stolen these? Was that why someone was chasing her? This must have been what she'd been searching for in the storage room *and* when he'd found her going through the cabin of the boat.

Disappointment sickened him. He'd believed he could help her out of whatever she'd gotten into, but if she'd broken the law he faced his greatest challenge—arresting the woman he was falling head over heels for.

Was it his lot in life to pick women with black secrets?

Angel said she'd taken something from the guy chasing her, but it didn't belong to him.

These coins belonged to someone.

If confronted with the coins, would Angel admit the truth? Or refuse to share her secrets until she absolutely had to give them up?

Thunder rolled overhead. Clouds thickened and the wind swirled through the marina. The day would only get worse.

Zane left all the individually wrapped twenty-dollar gold pieces on the seat and went in search of three plastic Ziploc bags from a drawer under the sink. Using his knife, he slit the side of one sleeve. With the tweezers, he lifted the package over one open Ziploc and shook it carefully until the coin dropped into the bag.

He held the empty plastic sleeve up to the light. She hadn't wiped these clean. Zane cut the one section from the long sleeve and dropped it into the other Ziploc, then placed the remaining coins in the last bag.

In the cabin he pulled the cushions out of the way and rooted around for a good spot to hide the coins. A safe-deposit box in the bank would be the best place, but since this was Labor Day weekend the banks were closed until Tuesday.

The least likely area to be disturbed by an intruder was

under the anchor rope stored in the very front compartment deep inside the nose of the bow.

He lifted several layers of rope and slipped the bag filled with rare coins between the loops.

Zane quickly snapped the side curtains into place and closed up the boat. He kept large brown envelopes in his truck under the back seat just for handling evidence.

He'd drop the coin and plastic sleeve along with the cup Angel had touched at Ben's office after he returned from Jacksonville. Ben hadn't called with news of a baby yet, so he wouldn't be in the lab today. There was no way Zane could let anyone else in on this until he knew where the coins came from.

She might have a reasonable explanation.

He might believe pigs could fly.

The balmy tropical heat didn't bother C.K., even dressed in his triple-X black T-shirt with long sleeves. Rolling thunder overhead promised some damp relief.

He lifted the infrared glasses to study the girl on Zane Black's patio. She'd just come outside to lounge with a mug of what he assumed to be coffee.

Having been there all night, he knew exactly when she'd stepped outside. His cell phone vibrated against his hip. He flipped the tiny phone open.

"Speak." He kept his voice low.

"We followed the pilot to the marina. He messed with the ropes on the boat and put some covering around the cabin. Couldn't see much from where we were, but no girl. He just pulled out and turned in the direction of Sunshine Airfield."

Was Angel's boyfriend called away on a Saturday morning to fly? That'd be too good to be true. The rest of the operation would turn into child's play with the pilot out of the way.

"If he flies out, find out where he's going. I want to know when he lands."

"Got it."

C.K. folded the phone close and lifted his field glasses.

Angel had moved to stand at the rail. A southern breeze blowing in ahead of the squall whipped long strands of hair around her face.

He sharpened the focus. The red shirt plastered against her body by the brisk wind outlined her plump breasts and narrow waist.

Mason had said not to damage his merchandise, but he hadn't dictated any parameters.

C.K. released the glasses, letting them flop against his chest. He leaned back into his cubbyhole.

He'd spend his time contemplating the potential pleasures his line of work offered.

Angel had showered and dressed in her running shorts and top when Trish tottered out of the bedroom to the kitchen.

"Morning, Trish. Want some coffee?"

"Is the pope Catholic?"

Angel smiled and poured her a mug. "Cream or sugar?"

"No, the blacker the better."

Trish swigged a drink. "Sugar, this is much better than Zane's. By the way, where is he?"

"He had a job to fly or something. He didn't really tell me much."

Trish half smiled and nodded. "Mystery man. You aren't mad at me for last night, are you?"

"No." The counter didn't have a dust molecule left after Angel had cleaned earlier, but she grabbed a rag to wipe anyhow. "Trish, your brother and I are, um, friends." Friends? Why did that sound so lame? "He's letting me stay here for a few days. That's all."

"Oh, sure." Trish smiled and lowered her attention to the cup of coffee.

Angel wondered if Zane's sister could read the inky brew like a fortune teller read tea leaves, could tell that Angel had just lied to herself? She wanted to be more than friends with Zane.

Being the truth didn't make it possible.

"I've got to get my act together," Trish said to her mug. "I'm getting in the way of Zane's life."

What do you say to that? Angel wiped more. Zane would be able to perform surgery on that counter if she didn't stop cleaning it.

"Angel, have you ever had something you wanted real bad just out of your reach?"

Angel paused her hand and stared at the counter.

For five years she had trained, studied and competed to earn the coveted athletic scholarship to Stanford only to have it snatched away. The first two weeks in jail she'd almost folded under the weight of her loss and what lay ahead of her, but deep inside, the drive to stick it out had burned. Once she'd been released, Angel had intended to prove she was better than the stranger described in a stack of court documents.

She'd trained to compete in the Tamarind, to regain a grain of respect in the athletic community. Mason stole that from her.

Now she fought to save her life and clear her name.

She couldn't comprehend not fighting to win.

Yeah, she'd wanted a few things really bad that were beyond her reach. Including Zane.

"Yes, I had something very important I worked very hard for many years to earn taken away from me." Angel knew they were talking about two different things, but the dynamics were the same. In some ways, they both wanted the same thing—a life. Trish's enemy—the bottle—was just as evil as the one threatening to destroy Angel—Mason.

"If you want it bad enough, you'll get it," Angel said, trying for support in her voice, not judgment.

Trish stared at her with soulful brown eyes then nodded slowly. "Yeah. I think I know what you're saying." She smiled. "Thanks."

Angel returned to her cleaning, attacking the sink next. She glanced at the clock on the microwave. Ten minutes until seven.

Once Trish got her act together and left, Angel was headed to the marina.

Salty air whipped through the lush landscaped terrace, slapping palm leaves and rattling the bushes. Still tucked away from sight, C.K's phone vibrated at seven-fifteen.

"Speak."

"The pilot's in Jacksonville. I got a call from a local source. He hasn't filed an exit flight for departure yet."

C.K. grinned. Life was good.

"Go to the meet point," C.K. ordered. "I'll be there in a couple hours." He closed his phone and slipped it into the pocket on the side of his black cargo pants.

He flexed his chest, loosening muscles tightened by hours spent pressing weights. After an automatic check of his 9mm Glock, he stuffed the weapon into the back waistband of his pants and moved forward toward the only patio with the glass doors open.

Chapter 14

Squatting next to the kitchen counter, Angel tied her shoes as Trish dialed Heidi for the third time. Trish held the phone to her ear for thirty seconds before she hung up, reached for her coffee mug and plopped onto a bar stool. "Heidi probably went to breakfast with someone. She loves to go to Saturday brunch."

Angel smiled politely. She couldn't leave until Trish had departed, or Zane's sister would ask where she was going, maybe want to join her.

Zane was right about one thing. Trish did not like to be alone.

Each sibling thought they had the other figured out. Although Zane's description of his sister as a social butterfly was fairly apt, she wasn't sure why Trish painted her brother as mysterious.

Finished with her shoes, Angel stood up and leaned a hip against the counter. "What did you mean when you called Zane a mystery man?"

Trish shot a conspiratorial eyebrow up. "He doesn't like me to talk about him. Says it's inappropriate."

"Why is it inappropriate?" Angel prompted casually.

Trish raised her shoulders in a shrug. "Beats me. He just says his work isn't up for discussion. His exact words. He comes and goes on a wild schedule."

Angel frowned at Trish's roundabout answer. "Yes, but a charter pilot probably has to work at odd times. He told me that's the nature of his particular business."

"This month it is. Next month, who knows?"

Intrigued, Angel asked, "What do you mean?"

Trish studied her mug as though debating on how much to share. She raised her head, smiled wryly.

"Zane must think something of you or you wouldn't be here, so I'll tell you what I think," Trish said. "He isn't always a pilot." Both of her dark sculpted eyebrows waggled as if she had a secret. "Sometimes he goes off to do some *side work*, but he won't tell me what it is, just that he's helping someone with a problem. He takes off with hardly more than a goodbye, telling me to use his cell phone if I need him, then shows up anywhere from a couple days to a week later."

Just like Zane had this morning.

Angel knew very little about Zane Black. What if his *side work* was an illegal activity? Was that what he'd meant when he assured her he could help?

He'd flown out of the airport that first night fully aware she'd stowed away with armed men chasing her. He hadn't been overly concerned about any of those incidents.

Would she always choose men to become involved with who led secret lives? Had she stepped right back into the fire?

Angel sifted through everything she knew about Zane and could put her finger on a couple of odd coincidences, but nothing of significance. She'd detected a dangerous side of him—attribute that to a man his size mixed with a dose of protective nature. He watched over his sister, worked hard at *whatever* he did and had shown Angel unprecedented kindness.

How could she fault a man who opened his home to a woman he knew absolutely nothing about? His elusive schedule might be little more than not wanting to trust Trish with sensitive business information.

"Maybe all of that is in the past, Trish. He's working pretty hard to build up Black Jack Airlines. Look at today. He's flying on a holiday weekend," Angel pointed out.

Trish shrugged again. "I don't know. You have to be around for a while to see it the way I do, but it doesn't matter. He's the best man to ever come out of the Jackson bloodline."

"Jackson bloodline?" Angel cocked her head, confused. "Who's that?"

"Us." Trish slowly lowered her mug and stared. "Haven't you two exchanged last names?"

"Are you saying Zane's last name is not Black?" Angel countered.

"Okay, I see what happened." Trish visibly relaxed, then continued, "You misunderstood. The name of his company is Black Jack."

Angel hadn't misunderstood.

Zane had introduced himself as Zane Black. She remained silent, wanting Trish to expound.

"I suppose Jack is short for Jackson or maybe he named the business Black Jack because he's always been good at cards. Our last name is Jackson." She took a sip from her mug and grinned. Zane's grin. "It wouldn't be a big deal if you called him Zane Black. He's too nice to embarrass you about something like that."

Too nice or too sly. Which was the apt description?

Angel kept her reaction hidden from Trish, but it was difficult. Zane had misled her from the beginning.

Why would he use an alias? Her heart started beating double time. She began to understand why Trish interpreted her brother's activities as mysterious.

Angel didn't want to know anything more. Curiosity would serve no purpose but to waste precious minutes, and right now it was time to go.

The minute she pushed Trish out the door, she was gone, too.

A whine from the laundry room announced the spin cycle on the washing machine. Trish had changed to fresh clothes from the ones stored in Zane's closet, opting to wash the smelly ones from the night before while she waited on Heidi.

Snagging the receiver from the wall phone, his sister switched topics as she dialed.

"Heidi spends Saturday afternoons communing with the sun, but the weather's going to be crummy so she'll probably be home soon. I wish she hadn't forgotten—again—to leave the answering machine on. Love her to death, but she's so absentminded about that. I'd take the bus, but I left my pass in her car."

Trish was right. The wind had picked up this morning and the sky was pretty dark when Angel walked in from the patio.

She considered offering Trish money from her limited funds just to get her out sooner. Bus fare was a tiny amount until you had no idea where any future money would come from.

Besides, if she waited, she could hitch a ride with Heidi when she picked up Trish, use the excuse of sightseeing to be dropped near the marina. Maybe she'd get lucky and make it to the boat before she got drenched.

Then she could search through the cabin alone.

"What are your plans for today?" Angel asked. "Think Heidi could drop me off somewhere? Thought I'd do some sightseeing."

Trish gave up on the phone and was digging through the refrigerator. "Sure, but do you want to go out in this weather?"

"Maybe it won't be so—"

Thunder boomed outside.

"Wow. Better close the glass doors before the rain soaks the carpet." Angel jumped from her chair and ran toward the patio.

She stepped into the living room in time to see a black-clothed figure climb over the patio rail just beyond the opening. Paralyzed on the spot, panic welled up inside her. Air clogged in her constricted throat.

When both feet hit the tiled surface, the massive intruder lifted cold, steel-gray eyes to hers. A face more evil than Mason's stared at her from less than twenty feet away for only a second.

He moved forward quicker than she'd imagined possible for anyone that huge.

Triggered into action, Angel streaked for the hallway, thinking she wouldn't get the locked front door open fast enough. He flew around the sofa hard on her heels. A concrete arm nailed Angel across the back, knocking her to the floor. She felt the blow to her ribs and rolled in pain.

"Sugar, that's some storm brew—"

Trish's words morphed into a scream.

The attacker snatched Angel by the hair. White-hot pain daggered her skull. Tears spilled from her eyes. She pushed up to her knees and yelled, "Run, Trish!"

He let go of her hair.

Trish screamed again.

Angel shot up and lurched around.

Trish stood rigid as a statue, her face deathly white, mouth and eyes stretched wide open in horror as the giant advanced on her.

In one long stride, Angel leaped up and landed on his back, flinging her hands around to gouge his face.

"Run, Trish, go, go, go—"

A snarled yell spewed from the beast.

Vise-grip fingers locked on Angel's forearms then snatched her over his head. Her back smashed against the floor between him and Trish, knocking the air from her lungs.

She wheezed for a breath of oxygen.

The front door banged open in the distance.

Through watery vision, Angel watched her attacker's polished bald head snap up at the sound. He raised a leg to step over her. She shoved her foot up into his groin with everything she had and was rewarded with a scream.

He fell to one knee.

She flipped over and scrambled to her feet. The door stood open. Thank God.

She almost made it.

He yanked her by the hair. Her head snapped back, stars flashed in her vision. Could she hold him off long enough for Trish to get away?

She felt herself being swung around like a rag doll on the end of a line just before a steel fist connected with her jaw.

Help.

Trish?

Zane?

Pain faded away. She sank into a black void.

Zane paced the terminal at the shipping docks in Jacksonville. Something was wrong.

High Vision's shipment was hung up in customs, but not because the officials thought contraband was involved.

A paper glitch. Computers were down and nothing would get processed before Tuesday. Probably the damn storm.

He'd made it out of Ft. Lauderdale ahead of the incoming squall ripping off the ocean only to land in a wicked thunderstorm. As soon as the narrow band of rain had moved off the coast, the sun blazed out from behind the clouds, bringing the humidity up with a vengeance.

The rental car he'd requested had been at the airport on his arrival. He'd tracked down his local information source only to be told a different version of what he'd expected to arrive at the docks. Nothing in the High Vision containers on board the ship could be construed as suspect. His contact ran an on-line check on the transfer status then informed Zane the shipment wouldn't be released for two days.

He didn't care when it got processed. The damn shipment amounted to nothing more than custom-built equipment for the new lab High Vision was constructing in Montana. Black wrought-iron fencing alone filled one container.

The shipment would be checked thoroughly by customs as well as the task force working undercover on site in Montana as part of the construction crew. So why had he been sent on a wild-goose chase? Either the agency's intelligence had a major breakdown or someone was feeding them false information on purpose.

That would point to a mole within his group.

Zane dialed his apartment again while he waited on Sammy's call to confirm what he'd figured out—that his entire trip had been an exercise in futility.

His home phone rang six, seven, eight times.

It was barely after eight in the morning. He slapped the phone shut. Where the hell were Trish and Angel? He hoped she hadn't gone for a run. She'd promised to be careful.

Then he recalled her searching through the cabin of the boat. Had she gone to hunt for the coins?

Dockhands moved along the pier, paying him no attention. Sweat streamed down his back. The ball cap he'd thought to grab offered little shade from the scorching sun. When his phone rang, he flipped it open.

"About damn time."

"Whoa, Zane. I know you're working a holiday, but I'm doing the best I can."

"Sorry, Sammy. I don't care a rat's ass about working a holiday. You know that. Just a little frustrated right now."

"Me, too. For what it's worth, everyone is jumping out their butts."

"They should be. Where the hell did the information come from?" Zane demanded.

"Don't have that this minute, but you can bet it'll be traced before the day's out. Got a bad apple somewhere. If that's the case and they're on to us, all this work is going down the drain."

Great, Zane thought disgustedly. "How much longer until I'm cleared to leave?"

"I should know any minute, but I don't think it'll do you much good."

"Why?" *Now what?*

"We've got a hell of a front blowing through. Sounds like a tropical storm building close to Miami. I don't think even you can fly back in this mess. Hang on a minute."

Another call beeped through during the silence. Relief swept over Zane at his home number on the caller ID. Maybe Trish was still asleep and Angel had been in the shower. He stretched his neck to relax his tense shoulder muscles while he waited on Sammy.

"Zane, you're cleared to leave. Soon as they track this down, you'll get called for a meeting. Going to be a huge pow-wow over this fiasco."

"I'm gone. Later," he said and clicked over to the other call. "Zane, here."

"It's Heidi. I'm at your apartment. We've got a problem."

"Why? What's wrong?" Palpitations hammered in his chest.

"When I got here, your front door was wide open and nobody was here."

"Nobody?" he shouted.

"No. I forgot to leave the answering machine on. I don't know where Trish is, but she didn't have any money for a bus." Heidi's normally high-pitched voice reached the squeaky stage when she was very upset.

"Listen to me, Heidi. I'll be back in a couple hours. Leave the apartment."

"Do you want me to call the police?"

"No." He didn't want anyone there until he'd had a chance to check it out himself. Without sufficient information, the police would actually get in his way.

"Zane, I don't want to leave in case Trish comes back. I'm worried about her."

"I am, too, but since I don't know what happened, I don't want you in the apartment. It might not be safe. If you want to wait, stay in your car. Leave immediately if anyone strange shows up. Got it?"

"Okay. I'll wait outside until you get here."

His worst nightmare had come to life.

Air. Angel needed air to fill her lungs. Her chest wouldn't expand for a simple breath of air. She was going to suffocate.

She could hear rumbling, thunder. Her clothes hung heavy on her body, soaked. She opened one eye. Black pavement shone under a veil of water. Raindrops beat down across her back, splattering against the ground. Water ran around her neck, across her throbbing face and into her eyes. Hair streamed down past her face, slapping her outstretched arms as she bounced. Her legs were held together at the knees.

Someone carried her facedown on his shoulder.

Had to be a man. Even in jail she'd never met a woman this big.

She pushed against the rock-hard back to allow her chest expansion for oxygen.

"Be still." The rough order left no room for argument.

"I...can't...breathe." She squeezed the words past her sore jaw.

He shoved her higher on his shoulder as if she were nothing more than a child. She pushed against him once again and pulled in a deep breath. Her head throbbed, nausea threatened.

It all started coming back to her. The black-clothed figure

crawling onto the patio, being attacked in the apartment, Trish…did she get away?

Please, God, don't let Trish be hurt. It would kill Zane.

The thought of Zane brought tears to her eyes. She was beyond miserable physically, but the emotional torture of never seeing him again set in. That's what she got for letting her guard down, becoming comfortable.

The bouncing stopped.

She heard the jangle of keys, then a car door opening. He slid her down in front of him, picked her up and pitched her onto the back seat of a big sport utility, bumping her head against the far-door panel. She tried to push herself up.

Either he moved with amazing speed or she was sluggish from the battering. Frigid gray eyes hovered over her. His noxious cologne and sweaty masculine odor accosted her. An obsidian gun handle protruded from the waist of his pants.

With his left hand, he reached over the seat into the rear cargo area.

She breathed shallow pants, anxious at what he'd do next.

His arm moved as though he worked to open something, his attention focused on the task. When his gaze sliced to her again, a nasty smile spread across his face. Goose bumps pebbled along her arm.

Supported by his knees, her crazed captor slid his right hand across the front of her shirt.

She sunk backward deep into the seat, trying to move away from his touch. He squeezed one breast as if to gauge her cup size then moved his hand under her neck. She shivered in revulsion.

He misunderstood her reaction.

"Good. I like my women more agreeable than you were earlier."

His coarse voice drove terror through her. Her mind shifted from fear of Mason to a new threat. Maybe this man had no connection to Mason. There were hundreds of big sport-utility vehicles in the country. Maybe he was just a sexual deviant who saw an opportunity with the patio door open.

Her fear redoubled at the possibility this could be worse than being caught by Mason. The giant had her pinned to the seat. Muscles bulged in his left arm as he raised his hand from the cargo area behind the seat.

Waves of panic shot through her. Angel swallowed and opened her mouth to scream for help, but he slapped a damp cloth over her face. She flinched at the acrid smell, then passed out.

Chapter 15

Zane slammed on brakes in front of his apartment. His sweaty palms hadn't dried since he lifted off from Jacksonville, but he couldn't attribute it to the vicious weather he'd confronted. Flying into a tropical depression didn't compare with the sick fear something had happened to both Angel and his sister.

Heidi's ancient, lime-green Volkswagen bug sat in the lot. Empty.

Damn. Couldn't at least one woman he knew follow directions?

Rain soaked his shirt by the time he raced around the corner and flung open his unlocked front door.

Heidi jumped up from the sofa, her spiked hair wilder than normal. "Am I ever glad to see you," she declared.

"You shouldn't have waited in here, Heidi. It wasn't safe."

"But, Zane—"

"I don't even know what happened to them. You could have been hurt," he blazed on.

"But, Zane, you don't understand—"

"Yes, I do."

"No you don't, sugar."

Zane spun to his left. A pale Trish emerged from the bathroom, tears streaming down her face.

She ran to him. Thank God she was safe. Zane clutched her shaking frame.

"Oh my God," she sobbed against his chest, oblivious to his wet clothes.

"Are you okay? Are you hurt?" he asked, his voice strained.

"I'm okay." She hiccuped between sobs. "It's Angel."

"What happened?" He hadn't meant to snap, but worry for Angel overshadowed his ability to remain civil.

"I'm so sorry," Trish wailed. "I couldn't help her. I tried, but I just stood there until she told me to run." Another sob escaped her.

He clenched his teeth to keep from shouting. The more anxious Trish became, the less coherent she'd be and he needed all the information he could get right now.

"It's okay. Just calm down and tell me what happened," Zane coaxed.

She sniffled and cleared her throat.

"I was in the kitchen and heard thunder. When I walked in here to close the doors to the patio, Ang…Angel was on the floor over there." She pointed down the hall.

"Go on," Zane urged.

"This huge man was standing over her. I swear he could be one of those guys who wrestle on television. He'd knocked her down. When he heard me and turned around, I just froze. I'm so sorry."

Zane felt as if his nerves were being dragged through a field of razor blades while he waited on Trish to tell him everything. Was Angel lying hurt in a hospital somewhere? He took a deep breath to keep from shouting and pushed his sister for more.

"Okay, take it easy, but tell me what happened to her."

Trish raised pained eyes to him. "Angel jumped on his back and screamed at me to run." Her voice dropped to a whisper. "So I did. I ran away, scared out of my mind. I hid behind some bushes by the next building. I was crying, trying to figure out what to do."

Trish sniffled, then said, "Finally, I *had* to come back to see if Angel was okay. Thought maybe I could get his tag number. You always told me to get a person's tag number."

Patience was paying off, but at the cost of his sanity. Chinese water torture would be easier than waiting on Trish to finish. If he could just make it through the strain of another agonizing minute, his sister might tell him where Angel had gone.

"When I got back here, I found Heidi." Tears spilled out of her swollen eyes.

"Angel's gone. He took her."

Pain drove Angel from the dark fog. Her first remnants of consciousness surfaced. A chill shook the length of her body. Where was she?

She blinked to clear the cobwebs from her brain. A dank and oily odor invaded her senses. With another blink, her vision began to clear.

Way up, maybe twenty feet, from where she was lying on her back, flashes of light backlit a row of dingy windows near the top of a rusting metal wall. Cold seeped through her bones. Wet clothes clung to her clammy skin.

When she slid her elbows back to push up, her head spun. A sharp pain stabbed her side. She swallowed hard to settle her roiling stomach. Barefoot pygmies had tromped through her mouth, leaving a dusty trail.

Very slowly, to control the dizziness, Angel shifted her head around, surveying the room. A tall overhead garage door stood on one end of the fifty-foot-long room. Wire hung loose from a panel next to the door as if someone had ripped the control box from the wall. Her eyes trailed down to a large silver padlock threaded through a shiny new hasp at the bottom of the door.

No exit there.

She scanned the next wall, opposite the windows. This one was a short interior wall, but still close to fifteen feet. It must separate the room she was in from another area. A pigeon landed on the top ledge of the wall. Several holes large enough to drop a chair through yawned across the ragged metal roof. Water pooled on the floor from past rain showers. At least it wasn't raining now.

Dreading the dizziness movement caused, Angel turned farther to check out the last barrier of her accommodations.

An oil-stained floor covered the distance between her and a standard office door. She surmised the building had been a truck garage long ago.

Other than a five-gallon plastic bucket next to an office-type door, the room was void of any furnishings.

She should go check the door, but common sense, being the funny animal it is, came to her aid. Sometimes common sense told her to do something she'd really rather not. Other times, like now, it convinced her to sit still, since she felt like the devil and that door was very likely locked. And, even if it wasn't, there was a good chance someone guarded the other side.

Sliding back down to a prone position, she tried to use mind over matter to will her body to stop hurting, but two days' sleep and an ice pack would do more good.

She massaged her forehead as she recalled her abduction. Blurry images of her running through the apartment and being knocked to her knees were the first thing she remembered. Most details were vague, but not the chilling gray eyes belonging to a behemoth of a man.

What had he done? She took a quick mental inventory of her body. Of all the pain coursing through her, none indicated she'd been sexually attacked.

An attacker with restraint? Morals? Her mind rambled

back to the apartment and Trish stepping into the room. She'd yelled at Trish to run.

The fact that Trish was not here with her should indicate she'd gotten away. Or, had the man left Angel alone because he'd attacked Trish?

Her stomach flopped again. Had Trish been hurt or worse? Guilt pushed through her physical misery. She'd brought this danger into Zane's home. What a way to repay his generosity.

If Zane returned to find Trish hurt he'd never regret anything more in his life than the night Angel had stowed away on his airplane.

She tested her ribs with a slow breath. Pain, but tolerable, so she rolled over and crawled to a sitting position. She slapped a hand over her mouth in a feeble attempt to avoid tossing up the coffee she'd drunk…when?

Her head pounded in complaint over the thirty-inch change in altitude. Little by little, stars chasing around in front of her eyes disappeared. Her watch was missing along with one of her shoes. She rubbed her wrist out of reflex, wondering how long she'd been there.

Ignoring the ache in her side, she struggled to a standing position. The room listed to one side, then righted.

Careful not to make a noise, she tiptoed across the room. She pressed her ear against the scarred door. Muffled voices came through as though they were spoken in a bucket.

She recognized the first one as belonging to the man who'd caught her.

"—me back a double burger, two fries and a big Coke. Make that two double burgers. I worked up an appetite dragging that bitch here."

"How long we staying, C.K.?" came from a second nasal voice.

"Until M.L. gets here. Says he'll deal with her himself."

So her attacker was called C.K. What could that stand for?

"What about the storm? How's he going to get here if the airport shuts down?" the whiny one asked.

"He'll get here. May take a little longer, but he's coming. Don't doubt it. The man wants her bad," C.K. said.

Angel couldn't come up with anyone she'd met whose initials were C.K., but M.L. had to be Mason Lorde.

Through the door, she heard high-pitched laughter fade with footsteps. C.K. must have stayed to guard her.

She knew exactly what Mason meant by "dealing with her himself." He'd physically punish her until she gave him the location of the coins. After that, it was anybody's guess how he'd finish her off.

Angel glanced down at the five-gallon bucket half filled with sand. A roll of paper towels sat beside it. Was this her litter box?

How could she tell Mason where the coins were if she didn't know? The only person who knew was Zane, but she refused to inflict any more pain on him or Trish.

Angel steeled herself for what was to come.

Zane closed the door behind Heidi and Trish, once more thankful for Heidi's friendship with his sister. Trish had been so distraught over Angel, he almost couldn't get her to leave.

When Trish calmed down, she'd lowered her voice to where only Zane could hear her say, "I know you do more than fly airplanes, something special. Knowing you, it has to be for a good reason, so I'm guessing you're some kind of cop."

He'd been shocked.

Before he could recover with a believable lie, Trish ventured, "I don't want to know what you do, but can you find Angel? I'll help."

His sister had always appeared unconcerned about the world around her, but in that one instant Zane realized he'd severely underestimated her resilience. That Trish had returned to the apartment filled him with dread for her safety and admiration for her bravery.

Angel had tried to point out Trish's strength to him.

At that point, he owed his sister more than his usual fabrications.

"I can find her," he assured Trish. "When I do and things settle down, we're going to talk, but not right now. You can help best by going with Heidi and staying home until you hear from me."

She'd nodded, went up on her toes and kissed his cheek. "I love you, and Angel means a lot to me. Be careful," she whispered.

Angel meant a lot to him, too. More than he cared to think about. But she was in a mess that got deeper by the minute. Now that he had the coins, he knew what someone wanted from her. If the coins didn't belong to the guy chasing her, he could only assume they had to be stolen. Coins like those didn't float around without security.

Who was the thief and who was the rightful owner?

While he processed the information, Zane unlocked his storage room and flung the pile of camouflage junk out of the way to reach his special tool chest. From a bottom drawer in the chest, he removed the Palm Pilot for tracking the transmitter hidden in Angel's shoe.

Zane booted up the small computer and ran through the configurations to zero in on her location. He locked the storage room then noticed her jeans and white shirt folded on top of the dryer. She should be easy to spot in her yellow running clothes.

Zooming in three times, he had a solid location—an industrial area in an old section south of Miami. He could make the trip in thirty, depending on traffic.

One last check through the rest of the apartment revealed nothing amiss—except for one missing tall female body.

He'd drop the gold coins and notes at Ben's office on his way south, but finding Angel just took precedence over learning her identity.

* * *

Mason carried a single bag to the flight he'd chartered. He planned to return home within a day, with or without Angel. If she told him where the coins were right away, she'd be in shape to make the trip back. If not, well, he might give her to C.K. when he'd taken what he wanted.

His cell phone rang. "Mason."

"C.K. here. You going to be able to fly into Miami?"

"With enough money, there's always someone willing to work. I've got a plane chartered to leave soon. I'll be there tonight. Don't let her out of your sight," Mason warned.

"She can't get out. You want her fed?"

"No. She'll be more pliable if she's hungry. I should be there by ten o'clock. Have someone waiting for me," Mason ordered then gave C.K. the information on his charter.

"Got it. I'll have a man in a Lorde Industries jacket waiting for you." C.K. hung up and checked his watch. Just past seven.

He had time to pay his guest a visit.

Zane zigzagged his way south on I–95 from Ft. Lauderdale to the target point indicated by the Palm Pilot. He'd assumed Angel was in a fixed location until the transmitter began to move. Too fast to be Angel on foot, even with *her* running ability. She was being transported in a vehicle.

Constant glances at the Palm Pilot confirmed the vehicle was headed for the interstate.

When the blip on his Palm Pilot reached I–95, it turned north.

Cutting through traffic and flooring his accelerator every chance he got, Zane tried to close the ten-mile gap without pricking the attention of the highway patrol. He didn't have the time to show his identification and answer questions.

When the vehicle he tracked turned off of I–95 to I–195 east, he had a good idea where it was headed.

Miami International Airport.

* * *

Angel sat at the farthest point from the office door. She'd been over every inch of the room. Unless she grew wings, there was no way out.

She was sick of water. Her skin felt like a prune. The storm sent rain pouring through gaping holes in the ceiling. If the floor hadn't been sloped to a center drain, she'd have been without the one dry corner in a room dark as a cave.

Where was Mason? Had the storm held him up or kept his men from delivering her to him? No, the bull on the other side of the door had said Mason was coming here, to deal with her.

Her hands trembled. She prayed for strength not to give up Zane's name—no matter what Mason did.

Light glowed from under the office door. No one had been in the room since she'd awakened to see if she was still there. They might have a peephole, but it wouldn't make any difference. They knew, as well as she did, there was no way out.

As if her wandering thoughts had been heard, the door to the other room opened.

C.K. loomed in the opening.

"You're up." He started forward. "Good. Thought you planned to sleep all day." His sinister voice reverberated through the vacant room.

"Cat got your tongue?" he taunted, ambling toward her, a black silhouette against the bright room behind him.

She sunk down in the corner, considered trying to run past him, but experience had taught her better. He'd been amazingly fast for his massive build. She'd just hurt herself worse. Better to save all her strength to endure Mason.

He squatted in front of her. "I've been trying to think of how to repay you for the kick in the nuts."

She flinched at the memory. No man took that move well. What would he do in retaliation?

With a flick of his hand, he ripped her pale yellow shirt down the front, leaving her dressed in the jog bra and shorts.

She braced for his next move, but instead of tearing more clothes he wrapped his hand around the back of her neck, wrenched her forward.

Bile rose in her throat when she realized he wanted to kiss her. She forced her hands not to claw at him, yet. Not until he wanted more. It would take every ounce of strength she had to fight him off if he tried to rape her, and she didn't honestly believe she'd win.

He closed his mouth over hers. Her stomach revolted at the combined odor of hamburger and sour breath. When he ended the kiss, he rocked back on his heels, let his rough palm trail over her damp hair.

Her sharp breaths echoed her fear. His touch moved down her chest to the jog bra, she trembled in terror. He wrapped short thick fingers around her right breast and squeezed. She jerked in reaction, disgusted.

He released her breast. "I know M.L. better than most. When he's finished, you'll get a chance to make it up to me. If you give him whatever you took, I'll make sure he doesn't kill you."

Agile as a gymnast, he rose to his feet and turned. Backlighting from the office cast a glow over half of his face, offering her a vision of Satan.

When he closed the door behind him, Angel let out a pent-up breath.

Who would have thought there was a fate worse than facing Mason?

Chapter 16

Early evening settled over the city under a blanket of ominous clouds. Zane wheeled his truck into the covered parking garage at Miami International Airport minutes behind the vehicle he'd been tracking. He parked in the first open space, planning to track the transmitter on foot now that it appeared to be stationary.

Carrying the Palm Pilot concealed in a magazine, he followed the signal until it indicated he'd reached the target. In the far outer region of the crowded garage sat a black Land Rover still dripping from the rain.

Zane waited until he was reasonably sure no one remained in the vehicle then strolled forward casually, scouting the area with each step. With a building sense of dread, he sidled around the far side of the SUV and glanced inside.

No bodies lay in the open.

That was a plus. A soft-drink can was lodged in the drink holder between the front seats. When he moved toward the rear to check the cargo area, a flash of yellow in the back seat caused him to do a double take.

Angel's running shoe sat on the floor.

He'd been tracking her shoe, not her. His heart sank.

So where was she? After a quick perusal of the empty rear cargo, he made a mental note of the tag number and the gold triangle logo on the side.

Zane returned to his truck where he punched the Palm Pilot back to the original fixed position. When he reached the destination marked on the computer, Angel had better be there.

If not…what?

Zane threw the truck into gear and jockeyed his way out of the thick airport traffic. He couldn't waste energy playing what-ifs.

He would find her. The alternative was too hard to comprehend.

Dodging in and out of showers, through congested roadways, transformed the drive between the airport and I–95 from arduous to excruciating. At the exit for an industrial district, he turned south to Kendall, an older area just below Miami. When he entered a commercial zone four miles west of the interstate, Zane slowed to cruise through industrial parks inundated with mammoth buildings.

Tractor-trailer rigs were backed up to loading docks on several properties, but little activity stirred at eight-thirty on a holiday-weekend night. He circled and crossed over railroad tracks, then hung an immediate left down an access road. Dilapidated buildings with real-estate signs offering the properties for sale or lease were scattered from one street to the next.

His truck crawled along the dark corridor. The original signal had come from somewhere close to this area. He squinted to see between sheets of rain and poor lighting, ready to dismiss the area, until a cat ran across the street in front of him.

Zane slammed on the brakes, visually following the feline's path as it scampered to his right.

A bright glow flickered from a tall street lamp and reflected off something shiny at the end of the vacant alley. He flipped open his console and dug out a set of infrared night-vision binoculars.

A Land Rover came into focus.

Not a vacant alley after all.

Could Angel be there?

Anxious to locate a second access to the building other than the alley, he weaved his truck through the bleak commercial area. An offshoot railroad track from the main line ran through a clearing in the trees. It appeared to run alongside the building.

He backed the truck off of the shoulder next to the track.

Zane shoved his weapon under the waistband at his back, then slipped on a poncho and leather gloves. Lightning clattered overhead. He reached in the back seat for the roll of anchor rope and wound about fifty feet into a loop, hanging it over his shoulder.

Following the glow of his flashlight, he jogged down the track then flipped the beam off as he neared the sport utility. He switched his phone to vibrate.

On close inspection, the Land Rover carried an identical gold triangle logo as the one from the airport. Bingo. He picked his way around the tall metal structure, stumbling through a minefield of piled buckets, weeds and scattered boards. Pouring rain, popping against every hard object in its way, camouflaged any unintentional noise.

Most tall warehouses had a ladder for accessing the roof, but so far this one had proved him wrong. He felt his way back toward the front.

When his hand plowed through a web of thick vines and caught on a metal wrung, he breathed a sigh of relief. Vines wrapped the ladder and covered the wall for as high as he could reach. With no idea if the access was rusted to pieces or still strong, he tentatively placed his weight on each step. Once he stood on the roof, shafts of light shone upward through small holes in the ceiling.

The illuminated room was near the front quarter of the structure.

Lightning flashed and exposed holes in the roof funneling water into the building. He switched on his small flashlight to hunt the center beam at the pitch of the roof rather than risk crashing through a weak area. Once there, he navigated to the light source.

He knelt down and crawled close enough to peer into a bright opening.

One of the biggest men Zane had ever seen sat reclined in a chair with his tree-trunk legs propped on a crate. His meaty fingers tapped a rhythm to hard-rock music vibrating out of a boom box. What had Trish said?

Angel's attacker could be a professional wrestler.

If Angel was here, he'd have to get her by not tangling with this guy, or be forced to use his weapon. And bullets might only slow him down. Seeing into the opening was like peering through a peephole. He had to squint and move around until he could detect the room's layout.

There were two doorways in the small room. One exited the building and the other accessed another room.

Zane shone his light over the roof to what should be the next room. Water streamed into the pitch-black hole through two ragged openings in the tin roof.

He crawled to the edge of one hole as wide as his over-stuffed chair and waited for the next lightning strike to finger across the sky. When that happened, it brightened the dark night to daylight for several seconds.

In those few seconds of momentary brilliance, a dash of yellow glowed one corner.

Angel was there.

C.K.'s phone vibrated against his hip. He turned down the music, but still had to click up the receiver volume to hear over the downpour pounding the metal roof.

"Speak."

"Plane just landed," Joe said. "Let you know when M.L. gets through the terminal and we're on the way. Shouldn't be more than thirty minutes."

"I'll be here." C.K. flipped the phone shut. He cranked the music up and leaned back with a smile.

His leggy captive should be primed for Mason after today. Mason wanted her pliable. Last time he saw her, she was close to being putty.

Angel shivered hard. She tucked herself into a tighter ball on the damp floor. Rain clattered down on the building. The racket echoed through the room, sounding as though a thousand nails showered against the metallic surface. Something furry bumped her hand.

She went from exhausted to terrified in under three seconds. A rat? She wobbled to her feet, ready to flee if the animal jumped on her.

Lightning exploded outside. A flash of light charged through the wide hole in the ceiling...outlining a figure in the center of the room.

Was the giant sneaking up on her? Mason would be next.

She couldn't take any more. Fear snapped her control.

Angel ran wide, but in the direction of the door, praying he'd left it unlocked when he came into the room.

Halfway across the room, she was snatched off her feet.

"Noo..." died in her throat when a hand clamped over her mouth. Strain and fear had taken a toll. She made one puny attempt to struggle against the rock-hard body, knew she couldn't defeat his strength, but wrenched hard.

Nothing budged, no flex. The man was built of granite.

She crumbled emotionally. Tears gushed down the sides of her face. Her knees gave way.

Before she could fall to the ground, the hand covering her

mouth slid away and two strong arms wrapped around her chest to support her.

"Shh. It's me, Zane."

That was the last straw. Her mind had snapped if she actually thought Zane would materialize out of thin air.

Unable to stop, she cried in broken sobs smothered by the deafening rain. She felt herself shifted around until she cried against a broad chest. Long fingers on one hand supported her around the waist as another began stroking up and down her back.

Her phantom kissed her forehead and whispered next to her ear. "Shh, baby, it's okay. I'm going to get you out of here."

This couldn't be the animal.

Zane was so very warm, even if he were a hallucination. She wanted to climb inside his heat. A shudder racked her body and he tucked her closer.

"Honey, don't cry. I swear I'll get you out of here."

A hand cupped her chin, lifting it. Warm lips she recognized kissed her gently. He was no hallucination.

Nothing had ever felt as real as Zane.

Finally, she quieted and ran a hand over Zane's face. "It is you," she said, her voice full of awe.

"Are you hurt, honey?"

The concern in his voice soothed her.

"I'm okay now that you're here." She remembered the giant nearby. "Trish! Is she okay?"

"She's fine, home with Heidi. You were right. She's tougher than I realized."

"Oh, thank God. We have to get out. How did you get in here?"

His hot breath flowed over her ear when he said, "We're going out through the roof. Are you ready?"

The roof?

If he said so, she would do it. She nodded then realized he couldn't see her and said, "I'm ready."

Zane's arms fell away. Her body moaned over the loss. He whispered, "I'm pulling a poncho over your head, don't panic." When he had the poncho on her, he took her hand and led her to the wall with the windows.

"Do you know how to climb a rope and walk your feet up the wall?" he asked quietly.

She'd done that plenty of times in weekend training classes. "Yes."

"You go first, I'll be right behind you. When you get on the roof, don't move until I'm up there."

"Okay," she whispered and grabbed the rope to start up. At the sharp pain in her side, she sucked in air and hesitated.

"What's wrong?" he asked.

Angel gritted her teeth. She could do this. "Nothing. Let's go."

Hand over hand, she moved painfully slow, but made it to the roof while rain pelted her face. She struggled over the edge.

Zane popped up right behind her. Water ran over the top of her shoeless foot from the flood rushing across the corrugated roof. He handed her the flashlight then pulled the rope up in loops and slung it over his arm. With his hands on her shoulders, he bent down close to her ear.

"Hold my belt and walk in my tracks as close as you can." Before letting go he brushed her lips with his. "Hang in there just a little longer and we'll be out of here."

Reaching zombie state, she nodded, but he must have caught her movement. He gave her a little squeeze then hooked her hand through his belt and took the flashlight. She slipped twice on the slick metal as they scooted across the roof and down the ladder.

Zane towed Angel through the thick weeds. When they neared the entrance to the building, headlights from the alley shot crossways in front of them. He hauled her up between him and the building. They would be able to see who arrived without being spotted.

Another sport utility swung around the first one to park.

He felt her stiffen when a statuesque male followed by a driver stepped from the vehicle. Under the dim streetlight, the tall man's blond hair glowed.

Zane spoke very low. "Do you know him?"

She hesitated, then nodded under his chin.

The two men moved out of view then a door banged shut.

Zane dragged her quickly through the thicket. At the Land Rover, he made her squat next to one of the vehicles, telling her not to move. With a knife from his boot, he slashed the tires then shoved the knife back in place and grabbed her hand.

They rushed along the tracks in a jog. Zane hoped for a couple more minutes to get Angel to the truck. They'd made it a third of the way there when shouts erupted behind them.

High-powered searchlights beamed frantically, scouring the ground outside the building.

Zane jerked Angel to a stop. "Take the flashlight. Go to where the tracks meet the street. My truck is there. Stay out of sight when you get there. I'll be right behind you."

"No. I—"

"Do as I say," Zane ordered, whipping out the Glock.

A beam of light shone down the tracks, picking them up.

"Now!" Zane shoved the light in her hands. She stumbled away.

A zing sounded on the tracks just short of where he stood. He fired two shots high then sprinted down the tracks behind Angel and the bobbing flashlight.

Shots rang out in the distance, landing all around him. He tripped once, caught his balance and fired back, this time lower.

One high beam disappeared.

At the truck, he threw the rope in the back. Angel dived in on the passenger side. He jumped behind the wheel, cranked the engine and spun a stream of loose gravel behind the truck, tearing onto the dark road with the headlights off. A shot pinged off the metal body.

He shoved Angel's head to her knees.

"Stay down." He wove through turns and side streets until he felt sure he'd lost them then headed for the I–95, turned north to Ft. Lauderdale.

Then where? This group knew about his apartment. They probably had the airplane under surveillance.

While keeping his eyes on the road and rearview mirror, he removed his hand from Angel's back then used his arm to lift her to a sitting position. Maybe he should drive for a while and leave the area.

One look at Angel changed his mind. She hadn't taken the poncho off and still shivered violently, even with the heater blowing. He reached over and ran the back of his hand across her cheek. She turned a deathly white face to him, her eyes glazed with shock.

Zane had to find a secure location soon. No one appeared to be following them, but he couldn't be sure. They might have planted a transmitter on his truck at some point.

Mason walked out of the warehouse as two more Land Rovers rolled up. He stepped past the two incapacitated vehicles sporting flat tires.

At the door to his ride, he stopped to give C.K. his parameters. "You have twenty-four hours to find her."

Weapon still in hand, C.K. said, "I'll find her. I always have a backup plan."

Mason smiled. "Good, so do I. Let's hope yours works, because I don't think you'll enjoy mine."

Chapter 17

Traffic thinned along Sunrise Boulevard. The digital clock on the dash glowed bright in the dark, read ten-fifteen.

Zane crossed the bridge and peeled off north on Bayview Drive to a small upscale community east of downtown Ft. Lauderdale. The rain had slacked to a drizzle. He zipped into an expansive parking lot for a high-rise apartment complex.

"There's a hotel a block from here. We're going to check in for the night. I know you're tired, but we're close," Zane said.

Angel nodded mutely, giving him reason to believe she'd hit her physical and emotional limit.

His overnight bag was still in the truck, forgotten upon returning home from Jacksonville. He tossed his weapon and cell phone inside before grabbing it.

Zane circled the truck to Angel's side and helped her down. Her icy hand barely clung to his as she shuffled along beside him.

They stepped into the lobby of the Shasta, Ft. Lauderdale's

newest five-star hotel, dripping teaspoon puddles on the cream marble streaked with rays of pink and gold.

As he approached the front desk, Zane kept his arm around Angel, who still wore the black poncho.

An impeccably dressed middle-aged man, wearing a charcoal gray suit and crisp white linen shirt, stared at them in momentary shock. After a moment, he closed his severe mouth, affecting the perfect hotel manager demeanor of polite indifference.

"Can I help you?" the manager asked with a hint of doubt in his voice.

As the son of a powerful man who'd amassed a fortune in the oil business, Zane knew exactly how to handle this guy. He read Robert Sommers on the man's name badge.

"I certainly hope someone can, Robert," Zane said, biting out each word in an annoyed tone. "First the damn flight lands three hours late, then they manage to lose our Louis Vuitton luggage. Next the rental car breaks down, leaves us stranded. So much for a vacation."

Robert's face shifted into his concerned-manager expression from Hotel 101. "I'm so sorry, sir. What can I do for you?"

"Just don't tell me our reservation has been lost. If that happens, I'm calling my sister who freelances travel articles for newspapers like the *New York Times,* so she can warn the world against this disaster zone."

That got Robert's full attention.

The Shasta hadn't been open long. A simple problem with a recent high-profile guest had been blown out of proportion in the local news. Everyone had heard about the embarrassing event.

Robert punched up his computer screen. "Can I have your last name, sir?"

"Mr. and Mrs. Zane Black."

At his words, Angel cocked her head toward him.

He winked at her, assumed she was surprised by the Mr. and Mrs. before his name.

Robert clicked keys furiously, frowned, squinted, clicked more keys, narrowed his eyes at the computer and glanced up. "Is that spelled b-l-a-c-k?"

"Yes."

More clicking and deep sighs followed. Robert relented and offered a professional, but completely artificial, smile when he said, "I have your room, Mr. Black."

Several elderly couples strolled through the grand lobby, casting appalled looks toward the desk as Zane handed over his credit card. Robert made quick work of processing the card before handing over two room key cards.

Zane took them and said, "Please call when the luggage arrives. In the meantime, we'll need some toiletries. I happen to have mine in a carry-on, but my wife's things were in the big suitcase."

Stepping into an office behind the desk, Robert returned with a bag full of items. "Please take these, compliments of the Shasta. We'd like to do whatever we can to make this a pleasurable stay for you."

Zane nodded his appreciation, thanked him then guided Angel to the elevator. If Robert had any concerns about her single bare foot, he didn't voice them.

She trembled while they rode silently on the elevator, worrying Zane as much as her catatonic state. He had an endless list of questions, but those could wait until she'd gotten a hot shower and some sleep.

He opened the door to a luxurious room with a single king-size bed. The dainty sofa in the corner didn't appear to hold a foldout bed or be long enough for his frame. Returning to the lobby to request a room change was out of the question. He'd sleep on the floor.

Zane slipped the poncho over Angel's head. He tossed it in the corner of the enormous bathroom filled with shell-white marble streaked with mauve veins. He took one look at her and clenched his fists. A dark bruise shaded her jaw. Red welts colored her ribs. Tomorrow she'd tell him who had done this and why. Then he'd deal with them. Tonight he had to take care of Angel.

Tap, tap, tap.

Squinting into the door peephole, he saw Robert, their accommodating manager, standing on the other side.

Zane eased Angel into the bathroom then answered the door.

"Mr. Black, I'm sorry to bother you," Robert began. "I noticed your wife had the misfortune of losing a shoe and thought we could be of assistance. If she doesn't care for these, or if they don't fit, tell her to feel free to exchange them for another pair in our gift shop on the mezzanine level, our compliments."

Robert held a beautiful basket with fruit, chocolates and a pair of dazzling jeweled sneakers fitting for a New Year's Eve party. The whole bizarre situation would have been hilarious if it weren't so serious.

"Thank you, Robert. I appreciate your concern." Zane took the basket, offered him a tip, which Robert graciously refused.

Zane bolted the door.

Angel emerged from the bathroom and stared at the basket. Strange probably didn't begin to describe her thoughts.

Tipping her chin up with two fingers, Zane asked softly, "How does a hot shower sound? There're two robes in the bathroom." He brushed his hand across her forehead, pushing a long wet strand of hair away from her vacant eyes.

Without a word, Angel took the bag of toiletries Zane had carried up and shuffled into the bathroom, shutting the door. He placed the basket on the dresser, then called room service to order pizza and bottled water, offering a heavy tip to deliver it quick. A taste for pizza was the only thing he knew for sure about the woman he'd rescued. Next he called Ben, got his voice mail and left the tag number to the Land Rover. Ben had a buddy in motor vehicles who would trace it for him.

The sound of rushing water ended as the shower cut off and

a few minutes later the door breezed open. There was his Angel, showered and wearing a white terry-cloth robe that hit her about midthigh, then those awesome legs.

His Angel. Warmth spread through him. Could she ever be his?

He'd never know until this was done. She'd admitted having something that belonged to the person chasing her, said what she had didn't belong to him. Maybe she was trying to return them. Maybe she had a good reason for what she'd done.

Deep in his heart he believed she had a good reason for what she'd done. Logic and duty pricked at that belief, but didn't change it.

The scent of her shampooed hair sparked a riot of lust. He'd missed her from the moment he left the apartment this morning. Missed her touch, her voice, the feel of her lips.

Swallowing to help his dry mouth, he couldn't stop his rampant thoughts from envisioning her long legs wrapped around him. He imagined the robe sliding off her shoulders to pool at her feet…until he lifted his eyes to her ashen face.

She'd never appeared vulnerable before. The sparkle was gone from her amber eyes. Her slender body shook under the bulky robe.

Another *tap, tap, tap*

"That should be your pizza. Stay back while I get it." Zane opened the door just wide enough to accept the tray and hand over enough cash to make any waiter happy with the balance, after paying the bill. He locked the door and carried the tray to a table near the glass doors to the balcony, then turned to Angel. "Why don't you eat while I grab a quick shower?"

She stared at him for a heartbeat through weary, luminous eyes. "Okay, thanks."

Zane crossed the room, gave her a quick peck on the forehead and reminded her, "Don't answer the door to anyone." He waited for her nod of understanding, then grabbed his shaving kit and a pair of shorts on his way to the bathroom.

* * *

Angel closed her mouth to keep from drooling over the smell of pizza. Her stomach growled with impatience. She shuffled to the table and lifted the silver cover. Pizza should be in a box, not on a china dish, but she wasn't complaining. Three pieces was all she could hold.

Cold leeched through Angel from one end to another. She watched as Zane disappeared into the bathroom then curled into a ball under the soft covers. Her battered body sunk into the deep mattress.

Dear God, how was she going to keep Mason's men away from Zane? Would Zane tell her where the package with the coins had gone if she explained? Or call in the police?

The situation was way out of hand. What was she going to do? Her exhausted mind refused to aid her in planning. Tomorrow she'd think everything through, not tonight. She quivered from a chill. Would she ever be warm again?

A single lamp on the dresser glowed when Zane stepped out of the bathroom. Her dark savior's hair glistened from the shower. He was dressed only in a pair of black shorts. His sculpted muscles rippled along his back and shoulders as he toweled his hair.

He tossed the towel in the corner and walked to the closet. His six-pack abdomen flexed when he stretched up to pull a pillow and blanket down then dropped them on the floor between the bed and the door.

After all he'd been through, Zane was going to sleep on the floor.

She didn't want him on the floor or the couch or anywhere that didn't include her. She wanted him close to her, forever.

Angel squeezed her eyes to stem the tears.

She couldn't have forever, maybe one night, because forever only happened in fairy tales. And one night with the man she was falling for would have to last her a lifetime, because no other man would ever be able to replace him.

Zane wouldn't want to hear what she felt for him, not after what she'd put him through. She'd hold those feelings deep inside, close to her heart.

He switched off the lamp. Soft light outside the drawn heavy drapes threw hazy shadows across the room. He stepped over to the bed. She knew he only meant to check on her, but she grabbed his hand before he could turn away.

"Zane, stay with me."

He stood still, as if he was unsure, then said, "Honey, I'm right here. I'm not going anywhere." He gave her fingers a squeeze and tried to let go.

She pulled the covers back and tugged down on his hand. "Please. I don't want to sleep alone."

Had she not shivered at that moment, she thought he might have refused. When her hand twitched from the movement of her shaking, he slid down next to her. The bed gave with his weight.

Not sure what to do next, she lay perfectly still on her side, facing him. Rapid breathing betrayed her nervousness. She shook again and he lifted her into his arms. She melted into his heat, her mouth teasing his neck. She kissed him there and inched her hand up the curved muscles covering his chest.

He shuddered against her.

His hard reaction to her explorations prodded her abdomen. Any leftover exhaustion evaporated as her body went on full alert.

"Honey, if you don't go to sleep soon this isn't going to work. I'm not a saint," he muttered.

His fingers kneaded gently along her shoulders. He kissed the top of her head and breathed out a ragged sigh.

She moved her hand down his chest, sliding her nails lightly up and down across the contour of his abs. He sucked in a sharp breath. His hand stopped massaging her shoulders.

"Angel." Her name sounded forced through clenched teeth. "Go. To. Sleep," he said, each word spoken as a severe warning.

She'd never felt so safe in her life. Being alone with Zane brought out a side of her she'd been afraid to expose to any man before.

One more touch should convince him she wasn't the least bit sleepy. Her hand drifted lower to the rim of his shorts. She slid a finger under the elastic waistband and ran a sensuous trail south.

She was flipped over on her back and covered with his body before she could blink. He had her arms pinned above her head, but his weight rested on his elbows.

"Look," Zane warned her in a tight voice, "I'm not made of stone. You're about ten seconds from pushing me past the point of no return."

"Then take me with you. I want you, Zane."

Zane couldn't believe his ears. What blood hadn't squeezed into his aching arousal found its way there now. He was harder than the foundation under their hotel.

He couldn't take advantage of her. She'd been in shock for hours. She'd regret the decision tomorrow and he'd feel lower than pond scum.

But, yeah, he wanted her.

Digging deep, he edged past his raging libido and uttered the words that would surely qualify him for sainthood.

"Honey, you don't know what you're saying. It's the stress you've been through. We can't do this."

"I *do* know what I'm saying. I may not live through this."

"Don't say that," he ordered. Nothing was going to happen to her. He wouldn't allow it.

More than wanting her right now, he needed her.

"Whether we want to face it or not," she whispered, "I may not survive. I've only been with one person, a boy in high school, and that wasn't very special. I want a special night with you. Don't you want me?"

His head drooped.

Hell, he'd never wanted to be a saint.

"Baby," he whispered, "I've wanted you so bad, I can't think." He released her hands, rubbing the palms with his thumbs.

"Then love me tonight," she pleaded.

Neither moved for a long second, then he lowered his head to gently kiss her forehead and cheeks.

He paused and expelled an exasperated deep breath.

"You may not think you're going to live, but I intend to make damn sure you do." Zane wanted to assure her everything would be okay, but he wouldn't lie to her. He could tell her she wouldn't face the world alone, but she'd been determined since the start to keep him away from her problem. She'd just have to get used to seeing him, because he wasn't leaving her side.

She moved her hands away from his loosened grasp, ran her fingers over his ribs, then up to lightly caress his chest. With her index finger, she teased each of his pebbled nipples.

"Just touch me," she breathed against his neck.

That broke the thin hold he had on his control. With a swipe, he raised both of her hands above her head again to end the erotic torture before she set off a physical chain reaction that he couldn't stop.

He lowered his lips to hers. The tender kiss held everything he wanted to promise her, all the words he didn't know how to say. His tongue probed inside her mouth in search of the taste he loved. His sweet and saucy Angel. Her lips molded to his, her hunger every bit as strong as his.

With one hand he untied her robe. His heart beat a rhythm in time with the pulsing in his groin. The robe fell away from shoulder to thigh.

Oh yeah, he never wanted to be a saint if it meant missing out on something this fantastic. He kissed along her neck and shoulders, nuzzling against what terry cloth remained in his way.

He gently cupped her breast and used one finger to draw

lazy circles around the nipple. She twisted up against him, her abdomen rubbing his erection.

A throaty whimper escaped her.

Lingering on one breast with his finger, he lowered his head to the other luscious mound and mimicked the movement with his tongue, then barely grazed the tense nipple with his teeth.

Angel lifted off the bed, the whimper stretching into pained plea.

She'd said special.

He wanted to give her the moon.

Her passion drove waves of heat spiraling through him. It would take everything he had to keep from erupting the minute he entered her. Blood pounded in his ears from the need to be inside her.

Angel's fingers raked through his hair, raising the nerves along his scalp. The feather touch danced along his neck to his shoulders, changing to an anguished grip when he removed both finger and tongue from her breast.

His lips covered hers, his tongue probing carefully past her swollen lips. Her velvet tongue stroked over his, driving him wild.

No matter how much she gave, he wanted more. He kissed her again and again, hot, hungry, needy.

With one free hand, he caressed her breast, palming the erect nipple. A purred "mmm" escaped her. She wasn't large, just a perfect handful. But then, he had big hands.

He stroked a path down through the curls shielding the heat between her thighs. With a finger, he entered the sensitive furnace and lit a fire.

She arched up, drew in a labored breath and uttered a long moan.

With his thumb, he teased the pressure point to her furnace.

"Oh, Zane…uhmmm."

He needed to slow down, find his control.

She wouldn't let him.

Her teeth scraped along his neck. She wrapped her fingers around his head, pulled him to her mouth, her warm breath poured across his cheek.

"You feel so good," he murmured. Nothing beyond this minute was real.

Every move, each response from her sent ripples of excitement across his skin.

Oh, man, for once fantasy couldn't compare with reality.

His thumb and finger pushed her closer to the boiling point.

She arched forward pressing against his arousal. "Oh, Zane…oh, I, uh…" She cried unintelligible pleas, each more passion-filled than the next.

Every move between their bodies threatened to send him over the edge, but he didn't want to go farther until she let him know she was ready.

It'd better be soon.

"Baby, just tell me what you want." The strained words croaked out of his dry throat.

She panted twice. "You have to ask?"

He'd have smiled at the frustration in her husky voice if he hadn't been equally desperate.

"Hold that thought." He snagged a condom, the only one he had, from his travel bag. With swiftness he'd only imagined in the past, his shorts were gone and sheath over his erection, he settled between her thighs. He cupped her soft bottom, lifted her up and slowly entered her. She fit him like a second skin. She surrounded him, hot and tight. Nothing he'd ever experienced before came close to being inside Angel.

Slow and gentle, he had to take it easy with her.

But she wrapped the endless legs of his dreams around his back and shoved up, driving him deep into her.

He'd live outside the realm of sainthood forever to feel this ecstasy for the rest of his life.

The harder he pushed, the tighter she dug into his shoulders, urging him on. He'd been barely hanging on to his control, but one more clench from her would snap it. Zane reached between them to stroke her fire into a one long blast.

Her body strained under him.

She shrieked her orgasm to the heavens. Frantic fingers locked on his shoulders as wave after wave coursed through her.

Microseconds behind her, his world splintered. His body separated from his mind.

Zane's last conscious thought was, *What the hell had just happened to him?*

Chapter 18

Angel awoke with her face against Zane's warm chest, wrapped in his arms, smelling his wonderful musky scent. After years of accepting every miserable injustice life had dished out as status quo, she'd altered her future.

Whether she lived or died, she'd carry this one night in her heart as she faced her fate.

Over Zane's shoulder, puffy purple clouds dusted with tangerine tufts floated past the separation in the drapes. Maybe the tropical depression had moved away.

Thinking he was still asleep, she tried to ease away. His arm locked her in place.

"Where do you think you're going?"

She smiled at the humor in his voice. "I was going to look out the window to see if the storm was passing."

"I'm not letting you go that far away. Every time you get farther than an arm's length from me, you disappear," he teased.

"Not fair," she answered, indignant over the remark. "I didn't leave your apartment by choice."

When his hold almost cut her breath off, she figured that hadn't been a good selection of topics to bring up. She smoothed her hand across the patch of dark hair centering his chest to soothe him and felt his embrace loosen.

"I'm getting a shower," she announced.

He made a move with his left hand, stroking along the inside of her thigh in an obvious attempt to deter her from moving. When his finger teased the fragile folds between her legs, Angel clutched his shoulders and conceded an immediate defeat.

Zane had a sure way to keep her within arm's reach. Or at least fingertip's reach. One of his incredibly talented fingers dipped inside her as his mouth closed over one breast.

She lifted completely off of his chest. His erection thumped against her stomach.

When he pushed two fingers inside on a steady rhythm and teased her damp folds with his thumb, she trembled from the rapidly building heat pooling in her loins.

Angel lifted away from his hands, shifted forward until she felt the tip of his arousal.

"Angel, no!"

She impaled herself on him.

"Yes." Air sucked from her lungs in a gasp of pleasure.

"No more, uh, condoms," squeezed from clenched teeth.

"I'm safe," she blurted out.

"Me, too, but..." He panted twice, held her still, his voice full of regret, need. "Don't want to get you pregnant."

Always worried about her. How could she not fall for this man?

"The Pill works as well." She shifted up then down, not willing to let him back away.

Raw desire pulsed between them. Zane grasped her hips,

lifting her almost off his member then pulling her down as he drove up inside her.

She bent low. He rose to meet her, rolled, and she was under him. He kissed her, sweet, loving. His mouth made love to her as his body began to move again, each stroke hot and slick.

His fingers massaged one breast, toyed with the nipple, slid down her abdomen. He slowed the pace.

Slow wasn't anywhere in her mind. She picked it up, hip to hip, skin to skin.

He growled and took over, giving her everything she wanted.

Two times, three times, then an orgasm spidered into every nerve of her body.

One pulse behind her climax, Zane exploded inside her. She collapsed on him, laboring for air. He hugged her tight, his heart pounding beneath her.

"You're unbelievable," he murmured.

She glowed under the compliment. Her breathing had steadied when his hand swept down her spine then smoothed across her bottom.

"What are you doing?" she asked suspiciously.

"What do you want me to do?" He studied her face with sincere eyes, grazed each cheek with his fingers.

"Answering that would be dangerous."

His hand slid farther down and under to toy with her again. Got to love a man with long arms and great hands.

She was close to giving in when his cell phone interrupted. "You better get that. It could be Trish." Angel rolled off of his chest.

Zane grumbled something that sounded like a vile curse as he reached over to the nightstand for the phone. "One day that phone is going out the window." He flipped it open.

"Zane," he snapped

Angel blew him an air kiss and slipped away to the bathroom as he said, "A boy? Congratulations, Ben."

* * *

Zane smiled over Ben's good news.

Angel dashed out of the room and the shower roared on as Ben told him he'd run by the lab today.

"I left you something else to check out when you get there," Zane said.

"What? Toe prints?" Ben joked.

"Very funny. There's a gold coin in your drop box marked Classified. I took a chance leaving it, but getting into your office is almost as tough as penetrating Fort Knox. Run a check to see if anything fitting that description has come up missing."

"Oh, man," Ben moaned. "Don't tell me this has to do with your vanishing girl."

"Okay, I won't. Just let me know when you find out anything. I really appreciate this, Ben."

"I know, but this doesn't sound like you. I hope you've got a good handle on her. Nothing is worth screwing up with the agency. You may hear back from me pretty soon. I'm heading in when we hang up."

"Thanks."

Zane dropped the phone on the stand. He was still reeling. Last night had gone beyond his fantasies, but that wasn't the problem.

Someone dangerous searched for Angel or the gold coins, or both. She'd been carrying coins that looked as if they belonged in a collection somewhere then stashed them in his boat curtains. She worked fervently to keep her identity hidden, but from whom? Nothing indicated she knew he worked with the DEA task force.

Disaster was stamped across her future in bold print. Everything he'd discovered pointed to criminal activities.

So, what was his problem?

There was no way he could let her go.

He couldn't imagine life without her. She couldn't be a

criminal. Maybe the events surrounding her were tainted, but in his heart he didn't accept that she was breaking the law.

Angel stepped out of the bathroom smiling, dressed in her jog bra and shorts. "I washed them out last night so I'd have clean clothes."

He grinned back at her until he saw the purple and black bruise on her rib cage. "If someone puts another bruise on you they may not live to their next birthday."

Embarrassment in her eyes, she covered it with her hand. "It's not so bad."

"Speaking of that, it's time to talk about what's going on," Zane started, his arms crossed over his chest.

"Don't you want to get a shower first? Can't we talk over breakfast?"

No. He wanted answers, but she probably had eaten little in the last twenty-four hours.

He sighed. "Okay, I'll take a shower and we'll order room service." Zane climbed out of bed and walked over to her. "Don't go anywhere. Promise me."

"I promise," she said. "Go shower. I'll be here when you come out."

Zane cupped the back of her head and kissed her forehead. "Last night was terrific. We have something very special and it's not just for one night. Understand?"

Tears pooled in her eyes. She turned her face up to him. "*You're* terrific and last night *was* wonderful, but I have to take it one day at a time."

His stomach twisted. She still didn't believe she would live through her ordeal. He planned to make a believer out of her.

"We'll talk. Don't order room service until I get out of the bathroom and don't answer the door to anyone. I want whoever comes in here to see me first."

She nodded.

C.K. dialed Mason's cell number.

"Lorde."

"We found the truck. They didn't go back to his apartment or out to the airplane," C.K. said.

"Do you know where they are?" Mason asked calmly.

"Not yet. We've got a transmitter on the truck and followed it to an apartment complex, but they were gone by the time my men arrived. Could be anywhere. Hard to pry in this tight little area, but soon, very soon," C.K. promised.

"And she never said a word about the coins?"

"No," C.K. answered. "I've got two men following the truck and his apartment's covered."

"Don't take him out until we have her in hand, but I want that pilot when this is done," Mason warned.

"You got it."

Angel slipped her feet into the garish sneakers the night manager had given her and snagged another apple from the basket. She munched on it as she opened the sliding glass door to the small balcony and stepped out into the balmy morning air. The clouds were dissipating, leaving a crystal-blue sky in their place.

What was she going to tell Zane? He deserved the truth after everything he'd done for her. She thought back on last night's events. The fact that he'd found her was amazing. Then he'd rescued her, no simple task there. Zane handled a gun proficiently. A lot of guys can handle a gun, but he'd been in his element.

She finished the apple, feeling much improved with the simple nourishment.

"Angel!" Zane called sharply from behind her.

"I'm right here. Don't panic," she joked, then spun around and stopped short at the sight of him next to the bathroom door. He was naked from the khaki pants up.

She ran her tongue over her dry lips.

His gaze darkened.

Her breathing stuttered. How could she want him again

so soon? If she let him touch her now, they'd never get out of here.

"Where are we?" she asked, hoping to divert his attention. She dropped the apple core in a wastebasket.

A smile kicked up on one side of his mouth. "Changing the subject?"

"There was no subject," she clarified.

"Yes, there was. It just wasn't being spoken."

She suppressed a smile, refusing to concede that her mind had traveled along the same path as his. "In that case, yes, I'm changing the subject. Where are we?"

He strolled over to her as he spoke. "This is part of greater Ft. Lauderdale. It's a small upscale community. The canal down below is the main channel for large yachts, so this is home to the local rich and shameless."

"What makes this canal so good for big boats?" Angel asked, wanting to confirm her guess.

"The smaller canals are shallower. The channel in this one is fifty feet deep."

She followed him over to the thick rail. They were three floors up. A green chain-link fence sprouted from the seawall running alongside the canal. She assumed that was to deter anyone from walking along the top of the seawall since only about two feet of landscape separated it from the hotel.

"Before we order breakfast, I want you to tell me what's going on," Zane said, his tone no longer teasing.

She shifted around and leaned back against the concrete railing. A balmy wind lifted tendrils of hair across her face for the heartbeat it took to form her answer. "I got involved with the wrong group of people, but it wasn't my fault," she started.

"I need a few more details than that. What do you have that they want?"

His tone didn't change. She couldn't read him, his face had

blanked into an inscrutable mask. How much could she say without going too far?

"I have some…items that someone else stole."

"So you stole it from him?" His eyebrow lifted slightly.

"No. I don't consider taking these items from him stealing," she stated.

"Why?"

"Because I intend to return them to the rightful owners," she said and watched his face relax until she added, "Eventually."

His mouth compressed into a stern line.

"What do you mean by *eventually*, Angel?"

"I need them for just a little while. Considering no one knew who had them and I'm going to return them, the owners should be considerate enough to let me borrow them," she reasoned.

He opened his mouth, shut it, then asked incredulously, "Just what do you have in mind?"

"I can't tell you everything."

"Oh, yes you can. Someone is trying to kill you. Starting right now, I want the whole truth," he demanded.

"No."

Anger banked across his dark gaze. "Angel, I hate that word. Say anything you want, but don't use that damn word again," he ordered.

"Fine!" she snapped, arms crossed. "I'm not telling you anything else. How's that?" She slapped a hand on each hip and leaned forward. "And, by the way, how did you find me last night?"

"Don't change the subject. We're talking about what you have that belongs to someone else."

"It's no big deal," she dismissed.

"No big deal?" he shouted. "Stolen gold coins are no big deal?"

They both stared at each other in silence.

"You have them," she accused. "Where are they?"

A muscle in his clenched jaw flexed. He obviously hadn't intended to share that little tidbit of information.

"They're safe," he said.

"Where? I need those coins," she stressed.

"For what? If you're innocent, why don't you just turn them over to the police?"

Her shoulders fell. Hearing Zane say *if* she was innocent hurt more than she'd ever let him know.

She stomped her foot. "Okay, here's the deal. Once I can confirm my alibi for when they were taken, I plan to use them to prove that my employer stole the coins."

But before she could elaborate further, Zane's cell phone rang.

They stared at each other for a nanosecond before Zane stepped over to the nightstand and snatched up the phone. "Zane, here."

"Hey, bud, this is Ben. Man, have you got a hot one."

Zane didn't think he was going to like the news, from the level of Ben's excitement.

"What have you got?"

The sound of papers rustling came across the lines and then Ben's voice. "Her name is Angelina Farentino. She's got a record."

A lead ball landed in the pit of Zane's stomach.

"Go on."

"She works for Mason Lorde, or she did work for him. Left under questionable circumstances is all I could find out without saying too much. He's listed as one of the top twenty wealthiest men in the country." More papers shuffled and Ben mumbled to himself before he continued.

"Lorde Industries is one of the largest import-export businesses on the East Coast, but he also deals in rare art and collectibles."

Oh, yeah, the hits just keep on coming. Zane never took

his eyes off Angel. Watching her and listening to the rundown was tearing his insides apart.

"What's on her record?" He knew by the way Angel straightened away from the railing she'd caught that comment.

"She did a year in a New York county jail at eighteen for transporting drugs. Her father went down for the charge of dealing and she was busted as the mule."

Drugs. Of all the things she could have done, drugs fell way down on Zane's forgive list. He worked day in and day out trying to keep drugs off the streets.

He was sure it couldn't get any worse until Ben remembered one more thing.

"Zane, buddy, you listening?"

"I'm here."

"Don't get too close to her. She's hot. The feds are in serious pursuit of her, too. Hang on." Ben's phone rattled against something solid, as if he'd laid it down.

Zane stared at Angel. The color had drained from her face on that one question about her record.

Ben was back on the line. "Her fingerprint turned up on a photograph in the pocket of the guy with the bullet hole in his forehead they found in the Dumpster near Raleigh. Turns out he was one of Mason Lorde's employees. Worked for him for the last ten years."

Zane didn't think he could take any more, but Ben hadn't mentioned the coin.

"Did you run the coin?"

"Yeah. Those are Saint-Gauden's Double Eagle gold coins. They aren't easy to come by, so I'm betting the coin came from that heist in Boston last month. I'm not sure yet, because a set of eight were stolen. Anyone paying seven figures wouldn't want the set broken up."

The other seven coins hidden on his boat confirmed Angel had been transporting stolen property.

"Thanks, Ben. I'll get back with you. Got to go right now."

Zane closed the phone. He was at a loss for words. Did he start with "Why did you do it?" or go straight to "You're under arrest."

Angel moved inside the glass doors. "Who are *you*, Zane?"

There was no point in continuing the pretense. He'd have to blow his cover to take her in.

"Zane Jackson. I work with a special task force under the DEA."

"You lied to me!" Didn't it fit? A man. A lie. Hand in hand, just as she'd always believed. Until Zane. She'd been so sure he was different.

"I've been undercover. I had no choice," Zane said. "You lied as well."

"No I didn't. I told you I had something that belonged to someone else." Could she have been an even bigger fool? He was with the law, to boot. She'd been disappointed a lot in her life, most of her life, but this was worse than all of it together. She'd come to believe Zane, to believe *in* Zane.

"Omission of information is the same as lying. Time to come clean."

Sure, when it came to her. "You know who I am and what my background is, or at least you think you know. What else do you want?"

"I don't know anything anymore," he said, despair wrapping his words. "So, maybe the question is, just *who* are you?"

Her chin lifted. "I'm not a thief and I never dealt drugs. No matter what that person just told you, I'm not lying to you. The gold coins were stolen from a gallery in Boston by someone working for Mason Lorde."

But *she* was an employee of Mason Lorde's, he reasoned. Or she had been until she stole the coins from the prominent head of Lorde Industries seen on the covers of a half-dozen business magazines.

"I worked for Mason," she continued. "In his warehouse as a *legitimate* employee, and found a couple stolen paintings, small ones hidden inside the lining of a shipping crate. They had been all over the news the week before. I recognized one of them and thought someone in the company was the thief, so I brought the paintings to Mason's attention."

"Why didn't you go to the police?" Zane asked.

She held up her finger for him to wait. "He'd given me a position in his organization in spite of my record. At least that's what I thought. What I didn't know was he'd hired me *because* I had a record. Silly me, I thought I'd gotten a break, no more cleaning outhouses and working at the dump. Decent companies don't hire people with a record. I finally had a real job." Her voice shook. A tear leaked down her cheek.

Zane started to move.

She halted him again with a raised finger.

"So, when Mason realized I wasn't going to cooperate he locked me away in his private compound near the airport where I met you. Mason had a second…more personal interest in me. The night I stowed away on your airplane was my second attempt at escaping. The first—" Her voice broke, but she swallowed and continued.

"The first time I only made it to the house garage. While the man who guarded me, Jeff, took an extra-long smoke break, I slipped through the house and made it outside before another guard caught me."

She sniffled and whispered, "Mason shot Jeff for his lapse in duty. I have to live with that."

Fire flashed in her eyes when she glared at him. "But I didn't commit any of the other sins. I've had to live with what was forced on me."

Muscles tightened across Zane's chest like a vise grip. Did he go with black-and-white evidence or what his gut told him? Would one of the most prominent men in the country steal art? How could she convince anyone she was forced to mule drugs? Had her father made her do it at gunpoint?

"Angel." His throat constricted. "Turn yourself in and I'll help you any way I can."

The disappointment in her face rocked him to the core.

"You don't believe me." Her pained laugh was full of hurt and anger. "Oh, God, how could I have been such a fool," she raged. "I can see it written on your face. *You*, the one person I trust to know the real me, believes I'm guilty of everything."

He took that one to the midsection. Zane made another step forward.

"Stop. Don't touch me. Don't come near me," she warned.

"Angel, please. Don't make this any worse."

Behind him the cell phone rang again.

Neither moved.

The insistent chirping pierced the vacuum between them. Zane finally twisted around for the phone, but Angel's movement in his peripheral vision spun him back around.

She'd climbed up on the railing, facing out to nothing.

"Angel, nooooo," he yelled, running to the balcony.

She'd leaped off the edge before he reached the glass doors.

He slammed into the railing and stared in horror as she fell to the canal. Blood rushed through his head, he couldn't hear past the roaring in his ears, couldn't think.

Her slender frame disappeared into the water.

A lifetime dragged by until she popped up, yards out from where she'd entered the canal clean as a knife.

Zane clutched his chest. His heart pounded against his breastbone as if it wanted out. His breathing slowed as he watched her stroke across the canal.

Angel climbed out on the other side, kneeled on the grass, her body heaving.

She stared up at him and shook her head.

He understood. Angel still contended he was wrong. When she stood up and jogged away, Zane wondered if he might be.

All the bones in his body had turned to rubber. He staggered back into the room trying to absorb what had happened.

Then it dawned on him where she was headed.

The boat.

He snatched up his bag and phone, running to the door.

Mason was out there. The beast who'd kidnapped her was out there. And the feds had a bead on her.

He had to get to Angel first.

Chapter 19

Zane hopped into his truck, gunned the engine and slid a corner leaving the apartment complex where he'd parked the night before. An old couple, literally on a Sunday drive, in a powder-blue mid-1980s land yacht, slowed him. Unable to pass, he ground his teeth.

Making the turn onto Sunrise Boulevard, he drove toward the bridge he had to cross to reach the beach highway. He whipped through traffic, heedless of getting pulled over.

Cars slowed to a stop just as he started up the bridge incline. Sirens screamed in the distance.

Ah, hell, a wreck.

"Dammit," he swore in disbelief.

This would take forever.

On the seat beside his leg, the cell phone began chirping. He cast a furious glance at the evil messenger then snapped it open.

"What?"

"Whoa, bud. Just thought I'd give you, as Paul Harvey says, *the rest of the story*," Ben answered.

"You've told me enough to hang her. What else is there?"

"I've actually got something good to tell you," Ben offered.

"Oh?" He'd kill for some good news about Angel.

"Okay. She was a high-school champion track star and long-distance runner, Olympic material. Fifteen or twenty top universities offered her a scholarship, but Stanford won out, then reneged after she was arrested."

"I'd figured something along those lines," Zane interjected.

"She spent the summers working as a bicycle courier in New York," Ben continued. "Her mother died of alcoholism. Nothing to indicate that she knew her father dealt drugs or ever worked with him before that one time. Her arrest was the only instance when she'd ever been involved in anything illegal. Word is she got railroaded by the district attorney and detective, some questionable circumstances, something about the whole case was predicated on one fingerprint."

No wonder she meticulously wiped her prints away.

Red taillights glared at Zane all the way up to the span of the bridge. Throwing himself from the pinnacle of the steel structure was a consideration, but too good for what he deserved. He'd never listened to Angel's side once he got Ben's first report, just assumed the worst.

She must hate him.

"One more thing." Ben interrupted Zane's self-abasement.

Zane cut him off. "I don't know which I really dislike more right now, your voice or this damn phone that brings it to me."

"Hey, bud, you've got to hear one more thing. That coin is a *1933* Saint Gauden's Double Eagle gold piece. There's a whole history on it that I'll spare you right now, but suffice it to say it's not legal for *anyone* to own it. That single coin is worth over a million dollars and it *is* from the Boston heist."

Ben added, "She doesn't sound sophisticated enough to be

the original thief. Whoever she took it from is probably very unhappy. Add that to the FBI and she has some major players gunning for her."

Sweat broke out on Zane's forehead. Everything was so convoluted at this point that he couldn't call anyone to help him. Traffic had completely stopped.

Angel was running solo until he found her.

The tropical depression had disintegrated by midmorning, leaving scattered clouds to shield Ft. Lauderdale from becoming a sauna. Angel climbed out of the parts delivery truck from which she'd hitched a ride and thanked the young guy for the lift. He'd been kind enough to drop her close to the marina.

She watched her back, weaving behind the cover of thick shrubs to reach the far end of the marina. To enter through the front gates didn't seem at all prudent with everybody and their brother after her. At the property line, she skirted the outside of the fence until she located a rusted opening in the ragged box wire.

Not much of a deterrent.

A few boats traveled from the direction of the bay down the wide canal toward the marina. More cars and trucks filled the lot than on the day she'd stopped by with Zane, but not many. People were still out celebrating the holiday.

Meandering over to the closest dock, she slipped into the bathtub-temperature saltwater and found it refreshing compared to the humidity she'd endured since diving off the balcony.

Training for triathlons meant swimming miles of rough currents, but little diving practice. Zane's frantic scream had trailed behind her until she'd hit the water, jarring her teeth.

She'd calculated the jump. Still, luck had smiled on her. She could have just as easily broken her neck. The dive had been her last resort. From the look on Zane's face after he'd heard her record, she'd been reasonably sure he'd turn her over to the police.

Her choices seemed destined to always fall between bad and unbelievably worse.

Zane worked undercover for drug enforcement. He had to be sickened once he heard she'd been convicted of transporting drugs, especially after spending the night making love.

That he immediately assumed the worst of her had hurt. She tried not to fault him, but when would *one* person give her a break? She was upset with him for deceiving her. However, she hadn't told him who she was either. In Zane's shoes, wouldn't she have reacted the same way?

Maybe, maybe not. She'd never been in love until now, but cared enough for Zane to give *him* the benefit of the doubt. Something he hadn't given her.

She'd prove her innocence to him somehow before she left.

First, she had to drive Mason away.

A few marina inhabitants reclined lazily on the rear decks of their boats backed up to the dock walkway. They were clueless a woman stroked silently through the water beyond their bows.

Angel made the turn at the end of the dock so she could swim past each row until reaching the one for Zane's boat. She dived underwater, paddling hard, and surfaced at the next one, then continued the same process.

When she reached his boat, she floated to the rear and climbed up a short metal ladder. With a fast check of the parking lot and dock, she scurried down into the cabin to search for the coins.

She dug through cabinets and felt along cubbyholes, then ran out to see if anyone approached. Mason had men everywhere. If they'd found her at Zane's apartment, she had no doubt they knew about the boat. Why hadn't they searched it?

Mason must believe she had the coins stashed somewhere that no one knew about.

Nothing had been disturbed. The only alteration was the elusive canvas curtain now surrounding the cockpit.

Where would Zane hide the coins?

Shoving aside the cushions covering the bed in the cabin, she methodically went through each of the compartments and stopped again to scan outside for anyone within proximity. She continued hunting through life-jacket bags and tackle boxes, almost forgetting to keep watch.

The next time Angel stuck her head out of the cabin, a black Land Rover swung inside the marina and parked across the lot near the entrance. She squinted to see if they were just going to observe or come to the boat.

Oh, God, the monster who'd abducted her. C.K. climbed out of the sport utility.

She ducked into the cabin and yanked drawers open until she found the keys then jumped up on deck. Her heart climbed into her throat when another Land Rover drove up to the first one.

Mason appeared.

Her hand quaked. She stabbed the first key at the ignition, hitting all around the hole with her shaking hand until it went in. She got the second key in place and realized she had to untie ropes then flip on the battery and pump the do-ma-hickey down in the deck to prime something.

Mason was talking to C.K., who pointed toward the boat a couple times then started striding her way.

She tucked down close to the deck, crab-walking across the weathered teak. At each cleat above her head, she reached up and unwound the ropes, jerking them loose and letting them fall to the water. Thank goodness they were all looped in simple S formations.

Down on the deck, she twisted a pitted chrome catch to open a section of the floor covering the engines. When it flipped up, she pushed it aside, shoved her hand in until she found the rubber balls and squeezed hard several times.

She stayed hunched over and scuttled through the curtains to the cockpit, jumped up and pulled the control handles to the middle the way Zane had.

When she glanced over her shoulder to check on C.K., he was nearing the beginning of the dock to Zane's boat.

Angel swiveled both keys at once. The motors turned over and over, but neither cranked. She glanced back up the dock.

The demon of her future nightmares hesitated then jutted his head forward and started running as if he'd just realized she was on the boat.

Somewhere behind him another man shouted something she couldn't make out.

Twisting the keys again, she begged the churning motors to start. One caught. She kept turning the other one. It caught. She pulled hard on the gears, throwing the boat in reverse, ramming the dock.

Bad idea, bad idea.

She reached over and shoved the gears ahead.

The boat lurched to one side, slamming into the walkway next to her, bouncing hard enough to toss her sideways. Motors whined in protest when the boat hung up on the right side of the slip.

She clawed her way up and watched in horror as the monster closed in to fifteen feet away.

Zane spun into the parking lot past two black sport utilities with gold triangle logos. He'd skidded to a stop near his dock just as he caught sight of the giant who had kidnapped Angel stepping onto the wooden planks.

Zane jumped from the truck, pursuing the kidnapper like a madman.

The hulking beast of a man hesitated briefly then started running.

Angel had to be on the boat.

"Halt! You're under arrest!" Zane bellowed as he charged ahead with his weapon drawn.

The giant didn't slow his pace.

A loud *bam* sounded, the dock shuddered.

Zane's gaze rocketed past the hulking body to the stern of his boat. It had hit the dock, rattling the pilings. "Stop or I'll shoot," he yelled at the kidnapper.

Never missing a step, the charging perp threw his arm behind him and fired wildly at Zane.

A shot ricocheted off a boat and splintered a wooden rafter.

Angel lunged for the controls, throwing a look over her shoulder.

C.K. dived forward from the dock, angled for the deck of the boat.

Angel wrenched hard on the wheel. The boat bounced left. Released from being hung up, the heavy cabin cruiser lunged forward under full power.

A gunshot and gargled shout carried over the motor rumble, but she couldn't let go of the wheel to look. She fought to get the boat to open water. Zane's ark plowed around the small waterway between the two rows of docks like an out-of-control, windup toy. Every turn she made was oversteered, curving the boat around in a hard left, then a hard right.

She missed a sleek yacht sticking out from the next dock over, but bounced a piling on a slip at the end. Comprehension struck as she exited the marina. Angel tugged the handles on her right back halfway to neutral. The bow lowered in the water when the motors chugged down to an idle.

With the boat under control, she jerked around to see what had happened to her pursuer, but by now a row of boats blocked her view.

"Halt!" Zane shouted again and forged ahead.

Heavy soles pounded the wooden dock behind him. A squeeze play was coming with him in the middle.

Another shot blasted at him from up ahead. It skipped against the piling next to his foot. The crazy bastard dived toward his boat, toward Angel.

Zane leveled his gun and fired at the bulky target stretched out in midair.

When he reached the slip, blood spread across the water. He'd aimed for a beefy shoulder. Had he missed and hit a vital organ?

The man's bald head bobbed along facedown on the surface. He thrashed one hand against the water.

Zane shoved his weapon in his waistband and picked up a rope to throw. "Hold on!" he shouted, intending to keep the enormous mass from drowning.

The giant's shiny head rolled back, baring a heinous smile on his face. He raised his good arm from under water to point his weapon at Zane.

With both hands full of rope and no time to react, Zane flinched in anticipation of a bullet bound for his chest, but it wasn't to be.

A shot fired close by centered the kidnapper's forehead. He sunk like a lead pipe.

Zane jerked around to see who had fired the gun.

Two winded men in dark gray suits stumbled to a stop, both with guns drawn.

"Who in the hell are you?" Zane demanded.

"FBI. Was that Angel Farentino in the boat?"

Angel. Zane spun away without answering. His hands shook as he ran to the end of the dock. Mason had almost gotten her.

He heard one of the two FBI agents close behind him yell, "She can't go anywhere. We've got the entrance to the bay blocked. In another fifteen minutes, we'll have her."

Zane's mind raced. He couldn't let them take her. She'd trusted him and he'd turned his back on her. She'd pleaded her innocence. He had to get to her first and tell her he believed her. Then he'd find a way to get her out of this mess.

He reached the end of the dock, barely able to see his boat motoring slowly down the far side of the empty canal.

Drawing in a breath to yell her name, he hoped against the odds of being heard.

The cabin cruiser exploded into a fireball.

Zane's screams echoed across the calm water.

Chapter 20

Information flew around Zane's head, some of it finding a way into his mind.

Some of it passing with the end of the day.

No one had been near the boat when it blew. Angel had been driving down the undeveloped side of the canal, so the casualties were low.

Just one dead Angel and an emotionally destroyed pilot.

Zane numbly went through the motions as if caught in the netherworld of the walking dead. He vaguely recalled thinking he was functioning as a professional.

FBI agents, emergency personnel and the public must have thought otherwise. They approached him cautiously, as though he were a rabid wolf to be avoided.

Howling like a wounded animal at the end of the dock might be the reason.

He didn't care.

His cell phone chirped one time too many. It sunk faster

than C.K. He now knew the street name of the man who had been after Angel.

That was good to know. He supposed.

The FBI agents tried to fill him in on details, like why they'd sought Angel. They knew she was not involved with Mason because they'd had her under surveillance for a while. They'd assumed when she disappeared that Mason had probably been the reason. One of their agents had actually seen her by accident the night Zane had taken her into De Nikki's to eat.

She'd been too sharp and spotted the agent's surprise when he saw her.

So that's why she ran—that time.

Somehow, Mason had slipped away from the marina when all the action started, but the FBI still felt they could nail him.

It would have made their life easier if Angel had lived.

His, too.

The FBI uncovered enough information to prove she hadn't intentionally delivered drugs. She'd been set up.

Hmm, that's also good to know, Zane mused.

Someone asked Zane if he wanted a doctor. "No," he answered. He wasn't injured—physically.

Everyone wanted to know what had happened to the coins. Zane lost interest and wandered away. He didn't care about coins.

He wanted Angel.

Twilight cloaked the marina by the time the divers confirmed no body had been found. Everyone dispersed. One of the FBI agents mentioned he'd be in touch in a day or two, when Zane was feeling better.

A day or two? Was that all it would take to stop the gut-wrenching pain?

Fog drifted in off the water. Tears trickled down each side of his nose as he strolled aimlessly along the deserted seawall away from the marina, away from the world.

He didn't want to leave.

He wanted Angel.

As if he'd conjured up her ghost, Angel floated along the seawall toward him, surrounded by a heavy mist. She wore the jog bra and shorts from earlier. He'd always wondered if ghosts really looked the same as when they died.

Her dark coppery hair glowed. She looked every bit an angel.

His angel was talking. Cool. If he were going completely mad, then he wanted to hear her voice, too.

"I'm sorry," Angel said. She floated closer and closer. "I had to get Mason to leave. I didn't mean to hurt you."

His throat constricted. He forced the words out he had to say.

"It was my fault. I should have believed you. I'm the one who's sorry." Seeing her was killing him. He wanted to touch her, but you can't touch a vision. Can you?

She kept coming nearer.

He could see her legs and feet moving. Good. She didn't have to float if she didn't want to.

"Zane, I destroyed your boat."

"I don't care. I wish you'd come back to me." Strips of his heart peeled away, one raw section at a time.

"I did come back to you," she said fervently, almost close enough for him to grab. The mist swirled between them and he blinked quickly not to lose her.

"But I want you alive," he cried out. "I love you and I should have protected you."

"I am alive," she whispered right in front of him. "You did protect me, and I've never loved you more than I do at this moment." She reached up and touched his face.

Dear God, she was alive. He hadn't gone off the deep end. Zane hovered between reality and fantasy for a split second then wrapped her up in his arms. He kissed her everywhere. Joy like he'd never felt in his life filled him. He couldn't stop touching her.

"You're really alive," he croaked out in a raspy voice. "I don't understand, but I don't care."

"I'm so sorry." She cried against his throat.

"No, honey, I'm the one who's sorry. You tried to tell me the truth. If I'd told you the truth about who I was, you might have trusted me. If I'd listened with my heart, I'd have heard you. I knew there was no way you could be a criminal."

He was afraid his knees would buckle, afraid she'd disappear, afraid this wasn't real, but none of that mattered.

Angel was back.

Their lips met. His kiss begged her forgiveness, promised her the world and thanked God for a miracle called Angel.

She pushed back a tiny bit, but Zane wouldn't relinquish his hold. He was never going to let her go.

"How can you be here?" he asked in wonder.

"I had to make Mason go away. He wouldn't as long as I was alive," she explained. "While the boat was going slow, I dug out some rags and tied them together. Then I stuffed them down the gas tank and found matches in the drawers."

She kissed him, a gentle wisp across his chin. "You said gas fumes were combustible, worse than fuel. So I lit the end of the rags and slipped overboard on the far side of the boat. I'm sorry I blew it up."

"Honey, I'll let you blow up a hundred boats if you promise to stay with me forever."

"I know I can prove my innocence. Just give me some time."

He hadn't thought he'd ever laugh again, but a chuckle bubbled up. "You aren't guilty of anything, just like you said. Nobody wants to arrest you."

"I don't understand."

"The FBI had you under surveillance. They knew you weren't part of Mason's operation and were hunting you to use as a witness against Mason. They also have information to clear your name from the drug-transporting conviction."

Zane caressed her soft cheek. "Honey, I hate what your father did to you, and no one can give you that year back. If you'll let me, I'm willing to spend the rest of my life making you happy. I'll tell the FBI *I* hid the coins on the boat and they're gone. They'll just have to deal with it."

She graced him with a blazing smile. "The coins aren't gone."

"Yes they are, baby. I stuck them under the anchor rope."

"I know. When I pulled the anchor rope out to tie the wheel, I found them. The coins are lying about fifty feet behind me on the seawall."

Epilogue

Zane placed the Titan on autopilot and leaned back.

"How dressy is the party? I don't know how anyone can get excited about Christmas in Florida," Angel wondered aloud while she poured Zane a cup of coffee.

"The longer you live here, the more normal it seems. You'll see all kind of styles tomorrow night." He took a sip and said, "Everything you wear looks terrific on...or off."

She rolled her eyes at him and switched topics. "I can't wait for Trish to get back."

"She probably misses you and Heidi just as much. I'm amazed at the change in her. I never realized she had the makings of a business dynamo."

"Her shop is really doing well," Angel said. "I hope she takes some time off after this buying trip. She's been on the road a lot."

"I don't think you're going to slow her down anytime soon." Zane leaned across to tuck Angel's sweater together in front. "Don't get chilled. I can push the heat up if you're cold."

"I'm fine, stop fussing over me." She smiled then sighed. "I'll be *real* fine when the trial is done."

"Honey, get used to being doted on." He grinned back at her, thinking he'd never get tired of having her near to pamper. "And the trial is going to be a cakewalk. The FBI has enough to put Lorde away for years."

Reaching over, he brushed a strand of hair behind her ear, an excuse to touch her. "You're their star witness, but Lorde's organization imploded once his people realized he was busted. Everyone's rolling over and cutting deals."

"How is the High Vision case coming?"

Angel could change mental gears faster than he flipped switches in the cockpit.

"It's still in limbo, but we're getting some new blood. Got a young hotshot coming down from Atlanta. He'll be part of a specialized task force we're creating," Zane explained.

"Will you have to train him?" she asked in a pensive voice.

"Don't worry. From what I hear, it's not a matter of training him so much as keeping an eye on him. He's something of a wild card. Now that I'm coordinating field operations, I just have to make sure everyone's on the same page."

He made a minor adjustment to the controls then returned the airplane to autopilot. "What are you going to do with the money from the museum?" he asked.

He'd never forget the surprise on her face when she heard about the six-figure reward offered for the return of the coins. In an effort to make up for the wrongs she'd suffered, the FBI made sure Angel received every penny.

"I'd like to go back to school," she began. "But I also want to help other women. I don't have an exact plan, but Trish and I have kicked around some ideas."

Reference to school made him reflect on her scholarship and lost running opportunities. "Are you disappointed you couldn't compete in the Tamarind Triathlon?"

"No, but *you* should feel guilty. It's all your fault," she declared, a teasing sparkle in her eyes.

"Nay, nay." He shook his finger tauntingly at her. "I'll take fifty percent of the responsibility, Mrs. Jackson. Good thing I made an honest woman of you when I did." He cocked an accusatory eyebrow at her.

"I did *not* lie. I just said the Pill was equally effective. I never said I was *taking* the Pill." Angel patted her middle, just beginning to thicken, and smiled wryly at him. "And *you* said you married me right after the explosion so you could keep me legally locked away."

Zane rolled his eyes, laughing, "You'll be able to compete in two years. Junior and I will be at the finish line to cheer you on as you win."

"Junior? You better prepare yourself for the possibility of a girl."

Zane envisioned holding a little angel in another five months. She'd have dark coppery hair and border on perfection if at least half of her genes came from her mother.

"Honey, nothing would make me happier. I'm partial to angels."

* * * * *

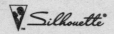

INTIMATE MOMENTS™

presents the first book in an exciting
new miniseries

FOREVER IN A DAY

A few hours can change your life.

Midnight Hero
(Silhouette Intimate Moments, #1359)

DIANA DUNCAN

New Year's Eve: Beautiful Bailey Chambers breaks up
with SWAT team leader Conall O'Rourke on the very
day he'd planned to propose. She's already lost her
father to his high-stakes job, and she won't lose Con,
too. But when they get caught up in a bank robbery
in progress, Bailey is forced to experience her worst
fears—and witness her lover placing himself in grave
danger as he plots to save the hostages. For Con,
surviving the hours of terror is easy. Winning Bailey's
heart is the true test of his strength. Can he get them
out of this with their lives—and love—intact?

*Don't miss this exciting story—
only from Silhouette Books.*

Available at your favorite retail outlet.

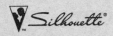

If you enjoyed what you just read,
then we've got an offer you can't resist!

Take 2 bestselling love stories FREE!

Plus get a FREE surprise gift!

Clip this page and mail it to Silhouette Reader Service™

IN U.S.A.	**IN CANADA**
3010 Walden Ave.	P.O. Box 609
P.O. Box 1867	Fort Erie, Ontario
Buffalo, N.Y. 14240-1867	L2A 5X3

YES! Please send me 2 free Silhouette Intimate Moments® novels and my free surprise gift. After receiving them, if I don't wish to receive anymore, I can return the shipping statement marked cancel. If I don't cancel, I will receive 6 brand-new novels every month, before they're available in stores! In the U.S.A., bill me at the bargain price of $4.24 plus 25¢ shipping and handling per book and applicable sales tax, if any*. In Canada, bill me at the bargain price of $4.99 plus 25¢ shipping and handling per book and applicable taxes**. That's the complete price and a savings of at least 10% off the cover prices—what a great deal! I understand that accepting the 2 free books and gift places me under no obligation ever to buy any books. I can always return a shipment and cancel at any time. Even if I never buy another book from Silhouette, the 2 free books and gift are mine to keep forever.

245 SDN DZ9A
345 SDN DZ9C

Name	(PLEASE PRINT)	
Address	Apt.#	
City	State/Prov.	Zip/Postal Code

Not valid to current Silhouette Intimate Moments® subscribers.

Want to try two free books from another series?
Call 1-800-873-8635 or visit www.morefreebooks.com.

* Terms and prices subject to change without notice. Sales tax applicable in N.Y.
** Canadian residents will be charged applicable provincial taxes and GST.
All orders subject to approval. Offer limited to one per household].
® are registered trademarks owned and used by the trademark owner and or its licensee.

COMING NEXT MONTH

SIMCNM0305